Taking a Stand

"You're barely able ta stand, partner," Westbrook said. "Drop the hogleg, an I'll let ya live."

"Mister, you'll never touch that woman while there is breath in my body," Joshua said. "You gonna start the ball or are you gonna talk me to death?"

He saw the ears on Westbrook's magnificent paint horse shoot forward, alert to something coming down the stagecoach road behind him. He figured the gang had come back and was slowly moving up behind him.

Joshua made a decision. He fired, fanned the hammer back, and fired again, and saw a large stain of crimson in the center of Long Leg's chest as he fell back, dropping his gun. Joshua immediately went to the ground, rolling to his right, toward the bloody corpse of Chancy, but on his way down he felt a bullet slam into the back of his left shoulder . . .

Titles by Don Bendell

CRIMINAL INVESTIGATION DETACHMENT

CRIMINAL INVESTIGATION DETACHMENT: BROKEN BORDERS

CRIMINAL INVESTIGATION DETACHMENT:
BAMBOO BATTLEGROUND

STRONGHEART

STRONGHEART

A Story of the Old West

Don Bendell

BERKLEY BOOKS, NEW YORK

THE BERKLEY PUBLISHING GROUP
Published by the Penguin Group
Penguin Group (USA) Inc.
375 Hudson Street, New York, New York 10014, USA
Penguin Group (Canada), 90 Eglinton Avenue East, Suite 700, Toronto, Ontario M4P 2Y3, Canada
(a division of Pearson Penguin Canada Inc.)
Penguin Books Ltd., 80 Strand, London WC2R 0RL, England
Penguin Group Ireland, 25 St. Stephen's Green, Dublin 2, Ireland (a division of Penguin Books Ltd.)
Penguin Group (Australia), 250 Camberwell Road, Camberwell, Victoria 3124, Australia
(a division of Pearson Australia Group Pty. Ltd.)
Penguin Books India Pvt. Ltd., 11 Community Centre, Panchsheel Park, New Delhi—110 017, India
Penguin Group (NZ), 67 Apollo Drive, Rosedale, North Shore 0632, New Zealand
(a division of Pearson New Zealand Ltd.)
Penguin Books (South Africa) (Pty.) Ltd., 24 Sturdee Avenue, Rosebank, Johannesburg 2196,
South Africa

Penguin Books Ltd., Registered Offices: 80 Strand, London WC2R 0RL, England

This is a work of fiction. Names, characters, places, and incidents either are the product of the author's imagination or are used fictitiously, and any resemblance to actual persons, living or dead, business establishments, events, or locales is entirely coincidental. The publisher does not have any control over and does not assume any responsibility for author or third-party websites or their content.

STRONGHEART

A Berkley Book / published by arrangement with the author

PRINTING HISTORY
Berkley edition / September 2010

Copyright © 2010 by Don Bendell Inc.
Cover illustration by Bill Angresano.
Cover design by Diana Kolsky.

ISBN: 978-0-425-23108-1

BERKLEY®
Berkley Books are published by The Berkley Publishing Group,
a division of Penguin Group (USA) Inc.,
375 Hudson Street, New York, New York 10014.
BERKLEY® is a registered trademark of Penguin Group (USA) Inc.
The "B" design is a trademark of Penguin Group (USA) Inc.

PRINTED IN THE UNITED STATES OF AMERICA

10 9 8 7 6 5 4 3 2 1

DEDICATION

I have six children and love all of them equally and dearly, but this particular book is about heroes, and one of my children is one of my biggest heroes, so I dedicated this book to her. My oldest daughter was born July 16, 1970, and I came up with her name, Jennifer Brooke Bendell, although now it is Brooke Bendell Stark.

As a child, she was very athletic, loved dancing, all kinds, was very artistic, was an outstanding student, and got headaches anytime she rode in a car. A type-A personality, she was and is a perfectionist. Her mother and I divorced when she was nine years old, and sadly we spent many years apart. Brooke became the substitute mom to her younger sister and brother because her mother worked so hard.

The two biggest things about her that always impressed me the most were her sense of adventure and her love for God. She still possesses both.

After graduating from North Carolina State University with a degree in textile design, Brooke ended up as a Christian missionary serving in Central and South America, converting Muslims into Christians in India and Africa. In Africa, she got very ill and almost died. She had already almost died as a girl, when her appendix burst.

Brooke married a wonderful youth minister and missionary himself, Burwell Stark, and they had two daughters. The first, Lindy, is a joy. Avery was in Brooke's womb and at nine months when Brooke had a driver hit her head-on. Protectively clutching her swollen belly, Brooke slammed her face on the steering wheel. Also, she crushed her heel, and Brooke had been a dancing instructor for years. They had to pry her out of the car with the Jaws of Life and airlift her by Flight for Life to Duke University Medical Center, where Avery was delivered by cesarean section, blind and brain-damaged. Brooke was in ICU for days, and after many prayers, blood transfusions, and several surgeries, she pulled through. Avery was an angel and was given very special care by Burwell, Brooke, and Lindy for four years, but sadly she died one day during a seizure. She just did not come out of it.

After that, Brooke lost another daughter at birth.

Then, after dealing with her younger sister, my other daughter, coming down with multiple sclerosis unexpectedly, Brooke mysteriously came down with MS, too, just when she and Burwell were preparing to leave again for the mission field in Africa.

She turned to God, as she has done so often in her life, and now, despite her setbacks, she has her own business near Raleigh, North Carolina, decorating homes and painting modern murals for homes and businesses. She has even rehabbed so she can now do some dancing. To her, MS is an inconvenience but not a reason to slow down.

The life God gives each of us is a gift to us, but what we do with our lives is the gift we give back to God. Brooke has certainly been preparing a wonderful gift for her Creator. She is truly a survivor, and I cannot put into words the respect, admiration, pride, and love I have for her. Since it is entitled *Strongheart*, I dedicate this book to you, Brooke.

Love, Dad

"I would give no thought of what the world might say of me, if I could only transmit to posterity the reputation of an honest man."

Sam Houston

FOREWORD

Previously, I wrote ten westerns, the *Colt Family* series, for NAL, a subsidiary of Berkley's parent company, Penguin Group (USA). Lately I have been writing military thrillers because the western market was down for some time, but I am still a real cowboy with a real horse and live in southern Colorado. On my wife's birthday, March 20, 2009, my editor and friend, Tom Colgan, informed me that westerns are starting to make a comeback and asked me to switch to writing them again. *Strongheart* is my first new western for Berkley Books, and I am happy to be back in the saddle again. I hope you will escape with me back to a time when a man's word was his bond, women were ladies and men were men, and you survived only if you were hardy. These were the people who made America.

Like one of my writing heroes, the late Louis L'Amour, I ride my horse, Eagle, on just about every piece of ground I write about. In that way you get a better feel, a vision of the country, the smell of the sagebrush and the feel the sun's heat baking a rocky canyon, while hearing the click of a horse's hooves on rocks. I hope you like Joshua Strongheart as much as I do and come with me on an escape from computers, television, news stories, traffic, and our fast-paced society, to a time when our country was simpler, tougher, and more natural. Let's take a journey back to the Old West, to the real America.

Don Bendell

1

Warrior

The warrior moved so slowly through the dense forest, he was barely noticeable. Up close, though, he was a marvelous specimen. He could look down and see the top of the head of almost any fellow Lakota Sioux he had ever been with. In fact, he had to look down at most people.

Most items that he grabbed ahold of would move. They had no choice if he wanted to move them. His long black hair was braided this day, and beneath the red and black war paint, which obscured most of his face, his cheekbones were high, his jaw firm and strong, his lips thin, and his eyes special. Deep, dark brown, they looked very intelligent and, at the same time, like he was always ready to smile.

They scoured the ground in front of him, sweeping left to right, right to left in ten-foot arcs, and every few seconds he would look to both sides and up in the trees. About once a minute, he would slowly turn his head and look behind to also watch his back trail.

At the top of each bicep and the base of each bulging deltoid, he wore a tight leather band that made the cantaloupe-sized biceps look even larger.

The bow looked tiny in his left hand as he knelt down to

look closely at a track, which, like the others, looked like
an upside-down letter V. As he examined the crispness of
its edges, a slight movement caught his eye. A grain of sand
had fallen from the edge of the V and down into the track.
This deer was less than a minute ahead of him. There was
also a small pile of round pellets. He picked up one piece of
manure in his fingers and examined it closely. It was round
like a tiny brown marble, but on one side there was a small
groove. Although most people could not tell the difference
between a buck and a doe by looking at their tracks, he
knew that the trick was to examine their scat. Bucks have a
tiny anal protrusion in their bowel tract that makes a faint
groove in each piece of feces. He knew this was a very
large, heavy deer just by the size and depth of the tracks,
but now he knew it was a buck, which is what he wanted.

The warrior turned and looked back into the deep green
morass to his rear. Finally, she was noticeable. The young
Lakota woman had been shadowing him at a distance and
was very well camouflaged herself. But even at that distance, her great beauty was obvious, the long, shiny black
hair, olive complexion, and dark eyes. He held his hands
up to the side of his head, extended fingers sticking up in
the air, the sign for buck deer or bull elk. She smiled and
remained motionless. This warrior was helping her and her
mother so much. He was tall, handsome, and, unlike so
many braves, he truly cared.

He moved forward slowly on hands and knees, his bow
in his left hand. Every few seconds now he paused and
looked. He spotted movement, as a large twelve-point buck
grazed on buck-brush and tufts of grass a short distance to
his front. It took him five minutes, but he rose to his feet
and inched forward, the bottom of his bow now almost
touching his hip. He moved with his left side forward, his
right hand on the bowstring. The nock of the arrow rested
between his index and middle finger, and his ring finger
also curled around the string. He would not look directly at
the grazing deer, as he knew that deer and most prey animals, as well as some learned and experienced warriors,

had a sixth sense, a sense of knowing when a predator was staring at them. He watched a spot a few feet behind the deer, but from the corner of his dark eye he was looking for one movement. There is a nerve in deer that causes a slight twitch in their tail, a millisecond before they raise their head up. By experience alone, this brave knew that deer had a different type of vision than humans, one which allowed them to see only the graze beneath their head when their head was down grazing. He knew from experience and his childhood teachings that the deer, no matter how close he was, could not see him as a person even when its head was up, as long as he did not move at all. Each time the warrior saw the little warning flick in the buck's tail, even if one foot was raised, he froze.

A half hour passed and now he was so close that he had to squint when he froze, so the shine off his eyeballs would not spook the deer. His bow came up slowly, inch by inch, and while the buck's head was down, he drew the arrow back.

The tail twitched, and he froze. Most men could not have held the powerful bow at full draw for very long without their arms shaking from total exertion, but this man was conditioned and very disciplined. The deer's head went down and the string slipped off his fingers, and he saw the arrow's almost instantaneous impact as it tore through the buck's left flank just behind the lower part of the left shoulder. It passed through the heart and then through the right lung, exiting the far side, as the buck leapt with the shock. He ran less than fifty feet, struggled, as the life drained from him, and lay still.

The warrior prayed to the deer's spirit and wished it well on its spirit journey. Then the young woman, who was closer to the age of a girl, came forward and watched his dexterity with the knife. He first removed the heavy musk glands on the inside of the buck's back knees. Then he carefully cleaned the razor-sharp Bowie knife, knowing the smelly gland could taint the meat. She marveled at the heavily beaded and fringed sheath on his left hip, the giant shiny blade, the elk antler handle. He removed the testes and anus and again cleaned the blade thoroughly. He then cut through the pelvic bone and slit the belly all the way up well into the chest cavity. Next, he slit the throat, reached in and cut the esophagus, and then pulled the entrails out along with the lungs and organs.

Walking to her village, she was amazed at how small the mighty buck looked across this brave's shoulders. Soon, they were at the lodge, and it was hung outside to be skinned and butchered.

Lila Wiya Waste, which meant "Beautiful Woman," was his cousin. Because her husband had been killed by the great bear, she and her mother had nobody to bring meat to their lodges. When Joshua Strongheart came to her village, he helped her to hunt for the lodge, because he was her closest relative. She accompanied him, so she could learn. Joshua told her not to just marry again but to wait on a warrior who was worthy of her. She wanted to know how to be self-sufficient, for her cousin was not around the village circle very often, just a few times per year.

The tall warrior grabbed his bag and headed to the nearby stream to bathe, clean off his war paint, and change clothes. The Lakota and their allies the Cheyenne and Arapaho were meticulous about bathing and keeping clean, and he was amused how so many racist *wasicun*, or "white men," used expressions such as "filthy redksins." The Lakota actually viewed many whites as being very dirty and unkempt.

Thirty minutes later, he returned from the stream to the circle of lodges. Lila Wiya Waste looked with a great longing at him approaching. She wished he was not her first cousin, but wished more he would look at her the way the other braves did. He now was dressed in his normal manner and looked like a totally different person, a white man with Lakota features.

His long, shiny black hair was no longer braided but hung down his back in a single ponytail, and it was covered by a black cowboy hat with a broad, very flat brim and rounded crown. A wide, fancy, colorful beaded hatband went around the base of the crown.

He wore a bonehair pipe choker around his sinewy neck, and a piece of beaded leather thong hung down a little from the front with a large grizzly bear claw attached to it.

His soft antelope-skin shirt did little to hide his bulging muscles, and the small rows of fringe that slanted in a V shape from his broad shoulders to his large pectoral muscles actually served to accentuate his muscular build and the narrow waist that looked like a flesh-covered washboard.

Levi Strauss had recently patented and started manufacturing a brand-new type of trousers made of blue denim, which whites were calling "Levi's." Joshua had bought a couple from a merchandiser. They fit tight with brass rivets and did little to hide the bulging muscles of his long legs.

Around his hips, Joshua wore his prized possessions, one a gift from his late stepfather and the other a gift from his late father. On the right hip of the engraved brown gun belt was the fancy holster, with his stepfather's Colt .45 Peacemaker in it. The gun had fancy engraving along the barrel and miniature marshal's badges, like his stepfather's own, attached to both of the mother-of-pearl grips. It was a brand-new single-action model made especially for the army in this year, 1873, and this one had been made to special order for his stepfather's friend Chris Colt, who was a nephew of the inventor Colonel Samuel Colt.

On his left hip was the long, beaded porcupine-quilled and fringed leather sheath holding the large Bowie knife with the elk antler handle and brass inlays. It had been left to him by his father.

He wore long cowboy boots with large-roweled Mexican spurs, with two little bell-shaped pieces of steel that hung down from the hubs on the outside of each and clinked on the spur rowels as they spun while he walked.

Because he had always been trained to keep his weapons clean and his knife sharp, Joshua pulled the large knife from its sheath and examined the blade. As usual, it was scalpel-sharp.

Lila Wiya Waste handed him a cup of hot coffee from a large pot he had given her months earlier. He sipped the steaming brew and thought about his childhood quest to learn about his biological father and search for blood relatives.

His biological father, Siostukala, "Claw Marks," had disappeared when Joshua was young and had been a total mystery to him for many years. His mother would not tell him anything about the man, and Joshua quit asking, because tears would well up in her eyes every time his name was mentioned. Joshua figured he must have caused her very painful memories.

Whenever family friends went off to trade with the Sioux, he traveled with them, seizing every opportunity to locate his father. Finally, at sixteen, he met his half brother, who grew up with Siostukala . His thirteen-year-old half brother, named Cate Waste, meaning "Cheerful," told him that his father had died a year earlier.

Joshua was very sad that his father had died, but he was also excited to meet a brother and several cousins. His half brother had since grown to manhood and proven himself in battle several times. At eighteen, Cate Waste's name was changed to his manhood name, Akayake Mato, meaning "Rides the Bear."

Joshua recalled the story of their shared legacy.

Claw Marks was one of the few men in the village along the banks of what was called the Greasy Grass. In three years, many Lakota, and their brothers the Cheyenne and Arapaho, would fight there against Long Hair Custer. They would call the mighty victory the Battle of the Greasy Grass, while the *wasicun* would always refer to it as the Battle of the Little Bighorn, and some would call it Custer's Last Stand.

In the small circle of lodges, Claw Marks had been recovering from a stab wound to the thigh suffered when he vanquished two Crows in a hand-to-hand fight with knives and war clubs on the banks of the Hehaka Wakpa, which meant "Elk River" but was called the Yellowstone River by the *wasicun*. Most of the men had left the tribal circle and gone out on a great hunt when a vast herd of buffalo was spotted a half day south.

A large band of Crows approached the circle of lodges and the warning went up.

Claw Marks, a war chief, had been hobbled and was walking with a makeshift crutch, but this day he tossed the crutch aside. With two older warrior volunteers, he faced the charging band, after sending the young warriors and children, including Cate Waste, down the banks of the Little Bighorn to what the warrior called the Badger Coulee. From there the remnants of the tribe could escape up the coulee, covering their tracks as they went.

He and the two gray-haired warriors knew they would die. Although he was wounded, he was younger and stronger than the other two men, so he knew it fell to him to keep the Crows at bay as long as possible, to cover the retreat of the family circle. They sang their death songs while firing shots and arrows at the charging Crows. He looked up at a pair of red-tailed hawks swirling high overhead in the cloudless, endless Montana sky, and he smiled to the warriors, saying in Lakota, "This is a good day to die." They nodded and smiled.

Leaving them, he raised his hand to bid them stay back, and ignoring the leg pain, he leapt on his pinto mount and rode toward the reassembling Crows. They had lost several warriors already and were shocked at the ability of these three determined men. They had to admire their perennial enemies.

The Crows were planning a final charge, with the idea to count as many coups as possible, touching the enemy in battle. They were encouraging each other to "Brave up!"

Thirty yards off, Claw Marks dropped off his war pony and tied a long rawhide thong to his leg. He tied the other end of the twenty-foot leather thong to a stake, which he jammed into the ground and pounded down with a nearby rock.

Claw Marks then faced the Crow, a challenging grin on

his face, and raising his rifle into the air with one hand and his war club with the other, he yelled, *"Hokahey!"*

The Crow knew he was going nowhere, but would fight to the death, taking as many of them as he could with him. They yelled back, more in admiration for his raw courage than to taunt a warrior. They agreed they would ride him down, and each warrior wanted to count coup on this mighty enemy, touching him without killing him, with a coup stick, bow, or rifle. They charged screaming and yelling, and he raised his rifle taking careful aim, and bodies started falling. The group rode down upon him, and he swung his rifle one way and the other and broke the stock over the face of the largest Crow. Then he started swinging his war club, as he felt stab wounds and strikes hitting his body all over. His scalp was a great reward for the hardest fighting of the Crows, who finally struck the fatal blow against him. Near Siostukala's body eight Crow bodies also lay on the grass by the shallow sand- and rock-bottomed Little Bighorn, and several more moaned with wounds.

The two elderly warriors wanted to help the courageous young man, but they knew they must lay back and wait, buying more time for their extended family members. They knew they, too, would make the great walk this day. Inspired by the young warrior's ferocious fighting and tremendous courage, they too held the Crows off, for another hour, giving the tribal remnants plenty of time to hide in Badger Coulee.

After they hid far down the river valley, Joshua's young half brother crept through the tall, waving buffalo grass high on a ridge that would be traveled years later by Custer and his men. He found a vantage point and actually watched the heroic death of his father. With no other warriors or tribal members around, he cried. But then he returned to the others. He was bursting with pride at the incredible courage of his father and vowed then never to tarnish such a family legacy.

Joshua felt like he could easily cry wishing he had known

his father. After his stepfather died and his mother gave him the gun and knife, only then did she reveal to him her relationship with Claw Marks. When his name was mentioned, she did not cry out of bad memory, but out of pure love-loss.

2

Forbidden Love

Abigail Harrison was the daughter of a British-born father and French-born mother. They were shopkeepers back east, where she was born in a small Ohio town, New Philadelphia, along the banks of the Tuscarawas River, in the midst of southern Ohio farming and coal-mining country. New Philadelphia, or as locals called it, "New Philly," was first settled in 1777 by German immigrants, who named it Schoenbrunn, which actually meant "beautiful spring."

But wanderlust struck the Harrisons, and having heard about the green of Oregon and mining riches in California, they headed west. They were headed to see both and then settle in one. However, the trials of the westward movement took their toll. He died first, when trying to free a mud-encased Conestoga wagon wheel. As it came free and the horses lunged forward, he slipped, and the wheel rolled over his neck, crushing his larynx and fracturing his cervical spine in two places.

He was buried not far from the tamer lower headwaters of the mighty Mississippi.

Ironically, in Montana, Abigail's grief-stricken mother fell getting off the wagon, striking the left front wagon wheel with her forehead and snapping her head back, fracturing her neck as well. She died instantly, and Abby quickly became even more of a survivor, as she was the only child.

After the loss of both parents, she was in a state of total despair and depression. Abby knelt by the hastily dug grave and just stared. She did not care about living or dying. After many attempts to motivate or move her failed, she was left alone with her family wagons by a heartless wagon master. After two days of crying, and taking nothing but little sips of water, she built a fire as her father had taught her and made a nice breakfast. She had come to the realization that she did indeed want to survive, and she would. The beautiful fifteen-year-old made herself a hearty breakfast of bacon, biscuits, eggs, and coffee.

That is when, two miles away, the big silvertip plains grizzly bear stood on his hind legs and slowly popped his teeth, sniffing the wind. On the breeze, he picked up the delicious smells, and he headed that way at almost a dead run. Bears have an incredible sense of smell, and this big bruin was no exception. He had survived thirteen winters already and was cunning, ferocious, large, and very powerful.

He came up out of a draw and again stood on his hind legs, testing the wind, his nose well over eight feet in the air when he lifted it and smelled. He picked up Abigail's scent as well and dropped to all fours, let out a ferocious growl, and made his charge. A grizzly bear can outrun a Thoroughbred racehorse on flat ground, and his flat-out charge was so unnerving that Abby stood transfixed and actually paralyzed in fear and denial. As a last resort, she raised her frying pan.

He was almost upon her when the arrow penetrated his rib cage from the right side, passed through his right lung, left lung, nicked his heart, and wedged into his left shoulder muscle. He let out a roar and stopped mid-charge, then stood again to face his new enemy: the powerful, handsome Lakota warrior Zuzeka, whose name meant "Snake" and who stood there with a large Bowie knife in his hand, his bow cast aside on the ground next to him.

Now the bear redirected his charge and dashed for the warrior, who refused to give ground. At the last second, the bear stood on its hind legs, bent slightly forward at the waist, and took a swipe at Zuzeka, raking his upper chest with four large claw marks, from the left side to the right side. Blood started streaming down the warrior's chest and rippled abdomen. He plunged the knife into the bear's chest just as it let out its death howl from the arrow. As it fell forward in a heap, its shoulder slammed the brave young man back ten feet, and he lay there unconscious.

He awakened to the smells of food and was very hungry. The startled brave sat up and looked around. It was daylight, and he finally realized that he was in the wagon of the *wasicun* woman, lying on her bed. He shook his head trying to clear his brain. Zuzeka looked around the inside of the wagon and recognized that this young woman was a good housekeeper.

She bounded up the steps and into the back of the Conestoga, and he jumped, reaching for his large knife, but the sheath was not around his waist. They looked at each other, and their eyes locked. Her chest started heaving a little in and out. His eyes entranced her. She smiled softly, and he relaxed, and she opened a box and pulled out his knife and sheath and handed them to him, as well as his bow and quiver full of arrows.

Abby said, "Do you speak any English?"

"Yes, a little maybe," he said. "What happened?"

She smiled. "You saved my life. This giant bear was charging at me. You killed it with an arrow and your knife. You are so brave. Thank you."

"Ah, I remember. Where is bear? When?" he asked.

"Three days ago," she replied. "You were wonderful. I skinned the bear and saved it and the paws for you."

"You did?" he said, then it hit him. "Three suns? I sleep three suns?"

"Yes," she said. "Your chest wounds got infected, but I have medicine, and it is getting better now."

She had to teach him how to drive her second wagon,

loaded with the many supplies that her parents had brought with them to open their new store in Oregon or California. As they traveled in the coming days, Abby and Zuzeka both spoke constantly about what would become of them, for they were two people from very different worlds. His courage to her was incredible, as he traveled alone with her to protect her, driving a white man's wagon in the area known as Montana, which was not even a territory yet, let alone a state.

After a few weeks, with the canvas off the Conestoga, and lying under the millions of stars in the night sky, they made love for the first time. And it was on one of those nights in the big sky country that Joshua Strongheart was conceived.

Abby and Zuzeka first headed toward Oregon on a route known by fur trappers and Indians, which would become the northern route of the Bozeman Trail to Oregon some years later (and more than a century later, Interstate Highway I-90), but the farther they traveled the sadder Abby became.

It was in a lush, fertile valley surrounded by high mountain ranges that Zuzeka hid the wagons in a thicket where he and his father had camped years before on their way to the Yellowstone, ninety miles to the southwest. Where they camped and hid the wagons would, years later, become the city of Bozeman, Montana. From there they traveled on horses with a packhorse. Zuzeka wanted Abby to see what life was like in the lodges of the Lakota.

She met his family, and the baby grew inside her. Abby was shocked by how family-oriented, clean, organized, hardy, and happy these people were. She was made to feel at home in the lodges of Zuzeka's tribe. When she had revealed the story of his amazing courage and his people had seen the wound on his chest, he had been given the warrior name of Siostukala, "Claw Marks."

On their way back to the valley that would become Bozeman, he planned to finally make the talk he had contemplated. They stopped in a thicket along a crystal-clear glacial creek, and she prepared them a meal, as they had not eaten for hours. He had the horses positioned so he could talk but still watch their ears and heads for signs that anybody was approaching or nearby. One horse was worth ten watchdogs, if you simply watched what the horse did with his head.

"The *wasicun* use the word 'love' and it means many things," he said. "I have thought of this and it is what I feel with you, here in my heart."

Tears welled up in Abby's eyes.

He said, "You carry our son in your belly. I know he is a son."

He thought of the honor that had just been bestowed on him when he was renamed.

"My family circle has begun a good thing. It is called the Strong Heart Society." He paused, sadly. "Maybe someday all the Lakota will have a Strong Heart Society. It is our best warriors; only a few can belong. I now belong," he said, as he proudly pointed at the fresh claw marks.

"I will make you safe," he went on, "then I must go."

"No," she protested and started crying, "I love you!"

"You hear my words, Abby. They are iron," he told her. "My world is red and yours is white. You carry our baby. It will be hard for him, for he will have two hearts. My mother was sold to a *wasicun*, a, what do you call, a *wanasa pi*, a hunter—no, a trapper. He trapped beaver, shot *tatanka*, buffalo. This is how I learn to speak the white talk. My life was very hard, but we did not live in the towns."

"*Siostukala*," she said, "I need you! Please?"

Claw Marks set his jaw and spoke. "No. I have spoken. You will name our son Strongheart, for he will grow and become a mighty warrior with two hearts. Sometimes, you will visit my people or the Cheyenne or Arapaho, our brothers. They will know of him. We will talk more."

They finished the trip to the green valley and her wagons and sat the first night by the fire. She had spent the trip there quietly thinking about his words.

She said, "You are right, but I am not going to Oregon or California. You would be killed."

He started to speak, but she raised her hand. "Please, let me finish. I love you, but I have been thinking when we rode. You are right. This world is unfair. If we want to marry, we should be allowed, but that is the way it is. I will stay here, so our son, or daughter, can grow up in this beautiful valley, and I know white men will move here, and they will buy things from my store. Maybe someday there will be a town here."

He left the fire then and walked long into the night.

The next day, Claw Marks told her he would find a place for her home and rode off. He knew of a place in the valley where the mountain men would sometimes rendezvous, and some Crows and other red men would come to it, too. The Crow and Lakota were bitter enemies, so he had to be very careful.

Two hours later, he found a bonanza. He saw two families near a stream with several other men. The warrior rode forward, his right hand up in greeting. He was met warmly. The two families had been on an early wagon train and decided they could make a wonderful life in this valley. There were also two fur buyers there, planning a mountain man rendezvous, and a man in a large tent who was an engineer, and even Claw Marks knew he was working on the planning for either a railroad or a spur for a mining operation. Another man was a farmer, and another a blacksmith and lay pastor. They were excited about having someone join them with all the supplies to start a mercantile, especially the men planning the rendezvous, who would now have a source for the many items they lacked. Little did Claw Marks know that in just over a decade, the Bozeman Trail would go through this valley. Little did he know it would become what would be called Bozeman, Montana, and Abby would then make a lot of money and own several successful businesses.

For now, they knew this place only by the name the Indians used, the "Valley of the Flowers," because it got more rain than other parts of Montana and had very fertile soil.

Abby was welcomed with open arms as a new member of this small community, but soon it became time for Claw

Marks to leave her. He removed his large knife and fancy sheath and handed them to her.

"I am a warrior," he said. "This is my store. When you know our son is a man, you give this to him. Tell him he must keep it clean, keep it sharp, and only use it with wisdom. Tell him of his father. Let him learn of my people, too."

"I will. I promise," she said.

Abby threw herself into his arms and kissed him the way she had taught him, which he always liked very much. She would never forget how safe she felt wrapped in those massive arms. She would never forget the feeling of wrapping her own arms only part of the way around him, as if she were hugging a giant, gentle bear that would always protect her.

He turned and walked to his pony, then vaulted onto its back and rode away without looking back. That day was the last time Joshua's parents ever saw each other, but she kept her word.

Joshua grew up often going to Lakota and Cheyenne villages and learning of his red half. He was very proud of his heritage.

3

Lawman

Joshua longed for a father, and he was excited as a young boy when the town marshal, Dan Cooper, of the blossoming community of Flower Valley got serious about his ma. Marshal Cooper was tall and slender, maybe six-two and 190 pounds, but that was all muscle and sinew from all his years of hard work.

The marshal had high cheekbones, a prominent nose, and honest, intelligent hazel eyes that would bore daggers through anybody. Much older than Joshua's ma, he had a little gray in his mustache, which was always well trimmed and ran full down in a point just past the corner of each thin lip. Like his hair, it was primarily dark brown.

He was not given to talking, just doing. Dan was a very harsh taskmaster on Joshua when he was growing up, but he was all man and he was bound and determined to make his stepson a man. He said the country was too unforgiving for him to go easy on the boy.

The thing Joshua remembered most about the only father that he ever knew was how good the man could fight, even though he was much smaller than some of the giant buffalo hunters and mountain men he had to arrest. Dan had actually taken a section of log weighing over two hundred pounds, shaved the bark off of it and the two thick branches that extended out for two feet, and sanded the whole thing, rounding the ends so they would resemble thick arms. Joshua would watch the man for hours on end tossing that log backwards, sideways, and various combinations thereof, working on numerous grappling moves.

Dan was also an incredible shot with pistol or rifle. He started Joshua when he was small and taught him first how to shoot a long gun. He learned to shoot with an 1860 Henry .44 repeater, and his stepdad gave it to him when he turned twelve years old.

It was a Saturday morning, and he handed Joshua the rifle with two bullets and an admonition: "Boy, you have two bullets. One is for emergency. The other is for a deer, turkey, antelope, elk, or bear. We need meat. Your ma packed you some fixings. Saddle up old Beau and get us meat. Come back when you have it."

"Yes, Sir," Joshua said and walked away from the grim-faced lawman, his shoulders back and chest puffed out.

It was scary when he had to spend that night in the woods by himself, but he thought of his ancestry and the mighty warrior who was his father. He finally tracked down a small doe, shot her, field dressed her, and returned home hoping for praise. Dan was proud of him, very proud, but would not show it. His mother was bursting with pride.

Dan said, "Good. Clean your rifle and sharpen your knife?"

"Yes, sir," came the quick reply.

"Good," the marshal said. "Give me the second bullet."

Joshua got a sheepish look. "I can't, sir."

"Why not?"

Joshua replied, "I had to use both bullets. I missed with the first shot."

"I told you the second bullet was for emergencies," Dan said. "What if you had run into a grizzly or band of Crows on your way back?" He did not wait for an answer but said, "Out to the shed, Joshua," grabbing the leather razor strop off the wall.

Before he gave Joshua his swats, he said, "If you point and cock a gun at an animal or a person, son, you shoot, and you do not miss. One bullet, one hit."

Joshua Strongheart never forgot those words, "One bullet, one hit," and subconsciously he touched his rear end every time he recalled the quote.

Dan never said words of sentiment or affection, nor did he praise Joshua, but a look of approval would make Joshua's day. And the man sure did teach the young lad how to fight with his hands and his pistol and rifle, and more importantly, with his head.

One of the incidents that impressed the young dark-skinned cowboy was an event that at first scared him for Dan. Some of these big men that came into town to blow off steam looked like they were related to the buffalo they hunted they were so large, and some were very nasty and mean.

Three behemoth mountain men were drinking heavily in the saloon and soon were slapping customers around. One of the victims came to fetch Dan, and Joshua happened to be with him. He tagged along behind.

Each of the men had murdered before but had never been caught. With Joshua following, Dan walked briskly, with long, easy strides, to the family's mercantile store. Joshua was very curious as to what would come next. Dan walked up to Abby, and she forced a kiss. Joshua grinned, knowing this man hated to show affection, but his ma would never let Dan get away with that where she was concerned. The marshal then walked over to a shelf of clothing and grabbed a pair of socks, and then to the hardware supplies along the far wall, where he grabbed a large wooden axe handle. Next, he went to a big jar of marbles and started pouring handfuls into one of the long boot socks. Joshua was still perplexed.

"Got these marbles, Abby, pair of socks, and this axe handle. Put them on our account. Gotta get back to work. See ya."

Curious, she gave a half wave as he strode out of the

store. He tied a knot into the end of the marble-filled sock while he walked, then stuffed it into the right pocket of the long tan duster he was wearing. Next, he slid the handle of the axe up his right sleeve, but it stuck out. He pulled it out and put it under his left arm, inside the long coat, squeezing it along his body with his left elbow and forearm.

Without hesitation, he stepped up onto the wooden boardwalk and into the saloon. He spotted the three giants in front of the bar, and one had lifted a woman of pleasure up in the air, taking his own pleasure at the very obvious abject fear showing on her painted face. That man looked at the others and laughed, a booming guffaw that seemed to echo from a deep cavern.

"Lookee, boys," he mused, "a teeny little lawman come to arrest us!"

He laughed at his own joke and was joined by the others. Dan never broke stride and walked straight up to him. Off-balance, the brute dropped the red-haired tart on the rough-hewn bar with a thud and tried to gather his thoughts. He did not have time. The sock filled with marbles came out of the right pocket of Dan's duster, swung around one time, and struck him with a louder thud on the left side of his jaw, breaking it and dropping him to the floor unconscious. Now Dan had one giant behind him and one in front of him, and they immediately closed in, but Dan had already untied the sock, and with his left hand he let the marbles fall to the floor behind him. That brute saw them too late and went down unceremoniously on his back with a thundering crash. In the meantime, Dan's right hand grabbed the axe handle and raised it high, taking hold with both hands and now facing the third giant. The brute's eyes opened wide as he saw the massive piece of wood coming down toward his head, and his eyes crossed looking up on contact, before rolling back as he fell to the floor unconscious.

The victim of the marbles had now regained his footing and was about to grab Dan from behind, when Dan shoved the axe handle straight backwards into the man's solar plexus and heard the wind leave him with rush. Dan spun around and swung the axe handle upward like a butt stroke with a rifle, and it caught the three-hundred-pounder under his chin, snapped his head back with the force, and he, too, went down out cold.

Dan grabbed the woman and helped her down off the bar, saying, "Lucy, isn't it about time you consider a different profession?"

She was so amazed and still frightened that she could not even speak. She just fluttered.

Dan said to the frightened, but now very relieved, bartender, "Fred, get some men and a buckboard and get these three down to the jail before they come to."

Fred said, "Yes, sir, Dan, and thank you very much."

Joshua was bursting with pride over the cool-headed way Dan had handled that crisis.

As if he was reading Joshua's mind, Dan put his hand on the young man's shoulder, spun him around, and said in a low voice, "When you are outnumbered, keep them off-balance and do the unexpected. Come on to the office with me."

They walked out the door, Joshua half-running to keep up with the stern lawman's long stride.

Joshua said, "Pa, how come you didn't just pull your gun and arrest them?"

Dan said, "They kept their knives sheathed and guns holstered. Remember what I told you. If you draw a gun, use it. Don't pull it just because you're afraid."

Joshua said, "I ain't ever seen you afraid."

"You just did, son," Dan said, giving a slight grin, which hardly anybody ever saw from him. "You see the size of those three grizzlies?"

The stories of his biological father and the example of this man who stepped in were the male influences on Joshua as he grew into young manhood. They served him well.

4

A Man Alone

A man of two worlds, Joshua was now alone in the world, and in many ways that was how he liked it. With a nice inheritance, he had a good bank account socked away in the Pioneer Western Bank—First of Denver. He figured it was enough to buy a large ranch someday.

The problem, though, was that Dan had taught him that a man had to have job to feel like a man, and a profession to be happy. And Joshua had just such a profession. He was a Pinkerton secret courier.

Actually, he was officially a Pinkerton detective, but his primary focus of late had been to hand-carry and hand-deliver critically important documents. These papers were almost always either coming from or going to the Office of the President of the United States or Congress. He had earned their trust, as he was unbending in his principles and his dedication to finishing every mission, regardless of obstacles.

Several Washington insiders now would ask specifically for Joshua Strongheart to be their courier. He always remembered these words of Dan's: "Get a job, work hard, and make yourself so invaluable they won't want you to ever retire."

Some of the management with the Pinkerton Detective Agency referred to him now as "Strong-Willed Strongheart." Allan Pinkerton himself, who had risen to national prominence a few years earlier when he personally foiled an assassination attempt on President Abe Lincoln, took notice of the young half-breed detective and kept track of his comings and goings. Quietly and privately, the Pinkertons in general were gaining a foothold in the trust of Washington's elite. Joshua Strongheart was one small part of that legacy-building.

Another one of Pinkerton's rising stars was Francois Luc DesChamps, who was born in Paris but came to the U.S. as a young boy and changed his name to Frank Champ, although everyone in his family and all his American friends started calling him "Lucky," for his middle name, when he was a slightly larger than a bean sprout. Lucky was on a train from Chicago to meet up with Joshua in Denver, to give him his new assignment. Frank was a no-nonsense manager and was totally dedicated and loyal to the Pinkerton Agency and all it stood for. He also considered Joshua Strongheart a tremendous asset for the Pinkertons.

Joshua had been riding south from Montana Territory and decided to spend the night in a town along the way, opting for Cheyenne. It had only been established in 1867, in what was then Dakota Territory, but a newspaper editor had already dubbed it the "jewel of the plains," because it had grown so rapidly. Joshua remembered crossing Crow Creek and heading to the Cheyenne Social Club to wet down some of the prairie dust he had been swallowing for several days.

He blinked his eyes and felt dizzy. His head felt like he was spinning in a circle, and his tongue seemed to have fuzz on it. A sweet-sour flavor crept from his stomach into his mouth, and Joshua sat up quickly on his bunk, making everything worse. He looked in the corner and saw a waste bucket for his use, and he ran to it, emptying whatever might have been left in his stomach into it. His head pounded as if his horse were standing on it and trotting in place. Finally, he spotted nearby a bucket with a bar of soap and a towel, and he crawled to it on hands and knees and dunked his head in and out of the bucket three times. His head cleared a little as he shook it like on old dog who had just crossed a creek.

He blinked his eyes and then rubbed his face with the towel, looking around. Joshua Strongheart was in a dark, dusty jail cell and could not, for the life of him, figure out how he got there.

The outer door opened with a loud, rusty squeak, and Joshua scrunched his shoulders up with the sound, which made his headache hurt worse. He had never seen a more beautiful woman in his life. Dark auburn, her hair hung all the way down to the small of her back, and it had a natural curl in it, the morning sun streaking through the window making it glisten like dew drops. The classy full-length shiny green dress she wore could not hide the natural curves of her body, but what entranced him were the light hazel, almost yellow eyes. She smiled looking at him and walked right up to the bars. Hesitantly, he got to his feet and walked forward.

"The deputy said I could visit with you briefly," she said through full crimson lips.

Joshua knew this beauty was speaking to him as if they were close. Her body language showed it, but he had no idea what had transpired the night before, or nights before.

He said softly, "Hi," still wondering why he was here and what had happened.

"Oh, you poor thing," she cooed. "Your eye is black, and you have a nasty cut on your cheekbone. I was certain those men were going to kill you. How can I ever thank you?"

He suddenly realized his left eye was swollen almost shut, and he winced as he touched his cheekbone.

"Well," he said, actually trying to access information, "they were awfully tough. Weren't they?"

"Them?" she said, throwing up her hands. "You almost killed all three of them."

Now Joshua was really concerned, and it was driving

him crazy trying to figure out a missing piece of his history. Had he nearly killed someone? Did he use a gun, or his knife? What started it? He made a silent promise to himself to never drink again. It seemed like every time he tried to drink, things like this just happened, even if he planned on having only a cold beer. He also knew he had made himself the same promise before, but now here he was again, wondering what he had done.

She suddenly pulled him forward, kissing him full on the lips, and the door burst open again.

A very large and sloppy-looking strawberry-headed deputy walked into the room, saying, "Time's up, ma'am."

She whispered, "Even though they were paying customers, I could not believe how you took exception to them touching me. You were such a gentleman protecting my honor."

Joshua stepped back and sat down hard on his cot.

He smiled at her feebly, saying, "Sorry. Hangover. Are they okay, ma'am?"

She headed toward the door, saying, "Don't know, sweetie. Ask him," indicating the deputy. "Thanks again."

Joshua gave the deputy a sheepish grin and said, "Did I hurt some men last night?"

"Naw," the deputy replied, and Joshua felt relief.

Then the jailer added, "More like half kilt 'em. Ya broke up Bugger Johnson's face bad, knocked out a lota the teeth he had left, broke his jaw, smashed his nose. Lessee, Big Ed Thomas, ya snapped his arm like it was firewood. He screamed like a durn banshee. Then poor ole Lucipher Rhames. Took the doc mosta the night to get him awake. He cain't remember what happened neither."

The deputy shuffled toward the door, then stopped and scratched his ample beard stubble, chuckling.

He added, "In fact, Lucipher cain't remember anya this week or last, the doc said. His face looks like the walls of Black Canyon out yonder. Phew. Ya gave them lads a whippin', Injun. You are durned shore rattler mean when you git some rotgut in ya. Guess you will be going down to the

territorial prison down ta Canon City fer a long visit. Hope
ya like eatin' hog slop."

Laughing at his own joke, he exited, leaving Joshua with
his confused thoughts.

What troubled the hungover, mixed-up young man was
that this had happened before when he drank. He could not
remember at all what happened, and he obviously turned
into a monster when he drank.

Joshua got up and paced back and forth across the cell mut-
tering to himself, "I can't trust myself. Even if I have a beer
this seems to happen. I get drunk and get whiskey mean."

He set his jaw and told himself he must have the red
man's weakness for liquor, and he would never, ever drink
again. No sooner had he made this solemn oath to himself,
than the outer door creaked open again and the strawberry-
headed jailer walked in with the keys, followed by a well-
dressed middle-aged man in a tailored business suit. Joshua
could clearly see the handles of the pair of Colt Navy .36s
the man wore under his suit coat.

It was Lucky, and Joshua moaned out loud, "Damn!"

The cell door was opened, and a startled Joshua walked
out, unsteady on his feet.

Lucky waited until Joshua had been given his weapons,
then they walked out into the blinding sunlight, with Joshua
squinting his eyes and not realizing he was moaning out loud.

"This weel never happen again," Lucky said with a
slight French accent, his face red with anger. "I had to call
een a favor with zee judge, and the three men you broke up
were happy to get a hundred dollars each for zeir injuries."

Joshua felt horrible.

He said, "I am very sorry, Lucky. I will pay Pinkerton
Agency back for the three hundred dollars."

Lucky interrupted. "Zee Pinkerton Agency deed not pay
it. Zey do not know about thees. I paid eet, and you weel
pay eet back, and your five-hundred-dollar fee for damages
I paid to zee judge. You weel pay eet back each paycheck,
one hundred dollars at a time, to me."

Joshua said, "Thank you very much, Lucky. I mean it,

I will pay back two hundred dollars out of each paycheck, and I will never get into that kind of scrape again. I will never take another drink the rest of my life."

His own words hit him suddenly, and he shivered, but he had given his word and that was that. If he dared ever break his word, he knew the ghost of Marshal Dan Cooper would come back to haunt him. The man's stern lessons had stuck, especially about keeping your word, and would remain with Joshua Strongheart all his days.

"Come on to zee café," Lucky said, cooling down a little. "You can buy us breakfast, and I weel tell you about your assignment."

There was a restaurant on the main street that had people walking in and out of the door more than any other building. That is where Lucky headed. They sat in the corner, both facing the entrance. That was a common choice among lawmen, gunfighters, and all warriors. None felt comfortable with his back to the door.

Minutes later, Lucky leaned forward over his steaming black coffee and whispered, "Thees ees your next deelevery."

Strongheart took the oilskin envelope in his left hand and stood.

He winked, saying, "Got to run out back. Be right back. Please order me a steak, potatoes, and apple pie."

Lucky knew what Joshua was going to do, as the tall cowboy-Indian headed to the outhouse behind the restaurant. Inside, he dropped his drawers, undid the leather money belt around his waist, and carefully folded the envelope so it would fit.

Having redone his trousers and gun belt, he returned to the café, figuring most of the customers would not give a second thought to him not carrying an envelope back in that he had carried out. He sat down by Lucky.

"It's safe now," Joshua said. "What's it about?"

Lucky said, "Zat ees zee most important document you have ever protected. Eet ees a personal letter from zee President."

"The President of the United States?" Joshua asked.

"*Oui!* Yes," Lucky replied. "He wrote an urgent message to Major General Jefferson Davis, who ees in Oregon, wheech you must deliver as queeckly as possible. Let us order, and I weel explain zee situation."

Over the course of lunch, Lucky explained the problem that the U.S. government was facing that had prompted the need for urgent delivery of a message to Major General Jefferson Davis, who shared the same first and last name as the more recognizable president of the Confederacy. He himself was a true character and the army really could not have picked a better leader to handle the Modoc War.

Harvesters of fish, waterfowl, seeds, bulbs, and other wild game, the Modoc were a tribe that lived in the area of northern California and southern Oregon. Their houses were very similar to the hogan of the Navajo, which looked very similar to a beehive.

They, too, dealt with the same problems as their red brothers, which included white men looking for gold and other riches in their territory and settlers populating their lands, having found the area very attractive for a variety of reasons. This began in earnest in the 1860s. The Modoc had finally given in and were moved onto the old Klamath reservation in southern Oregon. But they wouldn't stay there.

In 1870 Captain Jack led his Modoc band to California, and the government tried to get them to return to the reservation. In fact, U.S. soldiers pursued them all the way to Tule Lake. The problem for the military, though, was that that area became known as the "Stronghold," and for very good reason. Sharp, hot, rugged, volcanic lava beds and all the caves and tunnels networking through the area made it an almost impenetrable fortress. The rugged terrain gave the Modocs numerous excellent shooting positions with outstanding "fields of fire" from which to rain withering firepower on advancing troops while maintaining total protection. The small band of about 150 poorly armed Indians held out there for six months. Repeatedly beaten back, the

U.S. soldiers kept asking for reinforcements, and before long they had increased their force to one thousand men.

In spring of 1873, the turning point came, when in the course of peace talks, General E. R. S. Canby and Eleazer Thomas came in under a white flag of truce to speak with Captain Jack and his tribal leaders. The Modocs opened up and the negotiators were killed. It was the first and only time any American general was actually killed by Indians in the Indian Wars. This infuriated the U.S. government, and the efforts against the Modocs were significantly stepped up. Now there were enough men to outlast the band of warriors, as the government kept supplies coming while cutting off supply routes for the Modocs.

Retreat was blocked more often, and food and ammunition started dwindling for the red fighters. Soon, some of Captain Jack's supporters started losing heart and hope, and under promises of amnesty they started sneaking away from Captain Jack and surrendering. Then a couple of his own leaders turned on him and agreed to lead the soldiers to the chief.

In 1873, Captain Jack and his band of approximately thirty finally surrendered.

Captain Jack and his three top leaders were arrested. Major General Jefferson Davis knew that Captain Jack had become a hero among the other American Indian nations. He wanted to make an example of the man who had murdered an army general in cold blood under the white flag of truce, so he planned to simply execute all three by firing squad. He did not, however, want to get court-martialed, so he sent a message to Washington that he was planning to shoot all three.

His superiors were horrified. The government had already spent more than one half million dollars on the Modoc War, had an army general shot and killed, and Captain Jack was becoming a legend among other tribes. The last thing they wanted was for him to become a martyr.

Lucky explained to Joshua that he was to get to Oregon as quickly as he could and deliver an urgent response to

General Davis. The contents of Joshua's envelope were not to be seen by anybody but the general, and Davis knew a courier-delivered letter was on the way. The letter ordered the general to take all precautions to insure that Captain Jack and his three leaders were publicly tried in a very fair and judicious manner and then hung after being found guilty.

Joshua had to leave immediately to head toward his meeting in Poncha Springs and then on to Oregon from there.

5

The Stage

Joshua Strongheart was on a large red Concord stagecoach traveling west out of Canon City, after a quick train ride down along the Front Range. He was traveling along the Arkansas River. Later he would cross the river at Parkdale and head out Copper Gulch Stage Road, climbing from 5,300 feet elevation to 8,000 feet some twenty-seven miles southwest of Canon City. From there the stage would take Road Gulch Stage Road downhill for five miles. This would bring him out at a spot along the river where another gulch came in from the north, nestled in the mountains and the rocky corridor cut through by the wild, raging Arkansas River. He would head west from there toward Poncha Springs, make his delivery, then head west and northwest as quickly as possible on horseback to Grand Junction, where he could start using trains again. He figured to stop along the way, trade in the horse he would use, and buy another, so he could stay in the saddle at a slow gallop or fast trot a good part of the way.

The tall, handsome half-breed looked at his fellow passengers. There was a drummer with a carpetbag held close to his chest from the start of the ride, an old cowboy who'd tossed his saddle and bedroll up on the roof of the stage before he sat down, and a beautiful young woman who had long black hair, brilliant blue eyes, a proud jaw, and high cheekbones. What stood out most clearly, however, was the intelligent look in her eyes. Joshua, always alert, could detect a distant sadness there, too. He was instantly attracted to her, which happened with most men, but that attraction turned into a slight disappointment when he noticed the beautiful antique-looking wedding and engagement ring on the third finger of her left hand.

Joshua said, "On your way to meet your husband, ma'am?"

She smiled, but a tear formed in the corner of her eye.

She shook her head almost imperceptibly, saying, "No, sir. I lost him to a fire several months ago."

"I am sorry," Joshua said. "I saw the ring, or I would not have asked. Were you married long?"

"No," she replied. "Two years. We were happy though. He was a lieutenant in the U.S. Army. The cavalry. He was out on patrol and got caught in a grass fire, and he and his horse were trapped. High winds."

The cowboy doffed his hat. "Sorry, ma'am."

Joshua added, "Me, too, ma'am. Very sorry for your loss."

"Thank you both very much," she added, giving a slightly cold look to the silent drummer.

They went west of Canon City and climbed up a long, steep hill and across a small plateau. In the distance to the south they could see the top of the giant slash through the rocks that was called the Grand Canyon of the Arkansas. Over there, a rock-walled canyon encased the Arkansas River, which tumbled along in a churning, angry foam. The cliffs rose straight up from the narrow canyon floor, more than one thousand feet in most places. At the west end of the plateau, the stage road dropped down sharply to the river in a serpentine route. The driver had to hold back on the team and used his brake a lot down the steep, winding, twisting wagon road. At the bottom, a large wooden bridge crossed the river. Crossing it, the passengers looked east along the river and saw the roaring foamy flume of water charging into the high-walled canyon like a liquid avalanche crashing and plunging into a giant rocky funnel. To their right, the west, they saw the river snake its way through a broad valley, which narrowed into a similar rocky canyon that stretched for miles to the west, with numerous herds of Rocky Mountain bighorn sheep and Rocky Mountain goats inhabiting its impassable granite walls.

They turned southwest and left the river canyon behind them. The big red stage crossed a narrow, fairly flat valley as it wound its way toward another high-walled canyon, which had inspired the name of the route they were traveling on, Copper Gulch Road. The road would wind for miles, slowly climbing uphill. The coach would stop in ten miles so the passengers could take a break and the team of horses could be watered at Sunset Gulch, where there was a spring and a tank among the trees back up the very narrow gulch.

Unfortunately, Jeeter and Harlance McMahon were planning to hold up the stage at Sunset Gulch, where they were now hiding among the trees. They had tied up the stage employee who manned the watering spot at the spring, and they had him tucked back safely in the scrub oaks.

Orville Reichert's eyes darted all about the scrub oak thicket, as he lay there, gag wrapped tightly around his mouth. A silvertip grizzly had frequently watered at this spring, as well as a number of black bears and mountain lions. Orville was tied up and gagged, so he was even prey to coyotes if they chose to attack him, which he sensed would be in their predatory nature. There was one very small spring, which only had water part of the year, farther up Copper Gulch Stage Road, before it topped out at the intersection of Road Gulch Stage Road, but even in good years the spring did not produce enough water to provide for more than a few deer or bighorns. The spring at Sunset Gulch was a good one and was the main watering place for a number of miles for most of the wildlife in the area, especially larger animals. All these thoughts went through Orville's mind as he lay there petrified about getting mauled and eaten alive.

The Copper Gulch Stage Road wound up through very
steep, narrow passes like a giant rock- and piñon-encrusted
serpent, but just below Sunset Gulch it opened up a little
into an elongated bowl, surrounded by wooded rocky
ridges. It was in this bowl that Sunset Gulch poured out,
and the spring would be on the left side of the coach. Most
of the highwaymen were assembled there in the cover of
the evergreens and cottonwoods growing near the spring. It
was a great place for them to pull off a holdup because Sunset Gulch ran uphill from there one ridge over from Copper
Gulch Stage Road, paralleling it, but actually made a sharp
right turn up on top and came out onto Copper Gulch. They
could travel the rugged gulch when escaping and come out
farther up on the stage road and then turn onto Road Gulch
Road and head downhill about ten miles and come out on
the Arkansas River. Or they could stay on Copper Gulch
and come out a little north of the town of Westcliffe and
head south or east from there. They planned to hold up the
stage, move up the gulch a mile or so to a good ambush
site, quickly divide up their spoils, then continue on toward
the Arkansas River, the same direction the stagecoach was
destined. First, they would scatter the team from the coach,
so the horses would not be available for anybody from the
stage to trail them on.

Across the road, one of the outlaws, Long Legs Westbrook, was standing lookout on one of the rocky outcroppings rising high above the canyon floor, from where he
caught glimpses of the stage road far down the canyon,
winding its way up the twisting hardpack. Using a small
piece of mirror, he flashed light on the patch of trees where
Jeeter and Harlance were hiding. He then made his way
down the rocks, hopped on his beautiful gelding, and hid
it across the road, behind a large cottonwood and a pile of
collected dried logs and boulders left there from the last of
the flash floods that occasionally plagued Copper Gulch.

Jeeter and Harlance had grown up in the steep mountains of West Virginia north of Charleston and felt right

at home in these rocky canyons, which were like exaggerated versions of their home territory. The canyons out west in southern Colorado, however, were much larger, rockier, and more rugged than their homeland, but that presented the two criminals with a haven that was like Heaven to them.

Besides Westbrook, they had Ruddy Cheeks Carroll, Wilford "Slim" Dyer, Stumpy Shaw, Gorilla Moss, his son Percival, and Big Scars Cullen in their gang, each a dangerous and calculating outlaw capable of murder and other types of mayhem.

It was understood that once they divided the spoils from the holdup, any of the gang could go where they wished, and in fact, Moss and his kid had always liked traveling and seeing new country, so they planned to break off on top and head down past Westcliffe and cross over the Sangre de Cristo mountain range on Music Pass. They would come out in the San Luis Valley at the Great Sand Dunes, and they knew that when they crossed them, the wind would take care of covering all their tracks. The Great Sand Dunes were located at the base of the Sangre de Cristos and contained pure sand dunes over five hundred feet high, stretching for some miles. There was no vegetation at all, just sand, which was constantly shifting. It was an area in the western slope of the range where all the sand from the largest high mountain valley in the world accumulated. The others would stay with the McMahon brothers for a while, pulling off more holdups, and they had spoken about trying some train robberies.

When he was thirteen, Jeeter had had a problem with a neighbor boy who had stolen some muskrats and beaver out of the trap string Jeeter had run along a stream that emptied out into the Elk River, near its junction with the Kanawha River, near Charleston. Jeeter and his younger brother Harlance told their pa about the neighbor boy stealing their animals from the leg hold traps they set along the creek.

His solution was simple: "When someone takes waz your'n, ya kill 'im."

That was that. Jeeter grabbed a pick handle, and Harlance took his uncle's hickory walking stick that stood two feet above the boy's head. There were steep ridges on both sides of the heavily wooded stream, and the brothers took off into the woods, heading toward the stream. There, they slept during the night behind two side-by-side trees halfway up the hillside. Sure enough, the next morning right after daybreak, they heard Wilford Fisher walking down the bank toward the muskrat trap below them. As he approached the log where the trap was attached, the two started slowly down the hill. They made it within ten feet before Wilford heard Harlance step on a twig and spun around. The two rushed him, screaming like banshees and swinging their heavy clubs. By the third strike to his head, Wilford saw the sky swirling above him and felt himself falling faceup into the cold stream. The brothers plunged in after him and stomped on his face and body, holding him under until he was a lifeless, bloody mess. They let him go, and the body slowly disappeared down the stream, heading toward the big river, where it was found two days later caught in a pile of branches along a bank of the Kanawha. Wilford's folks knew who did it and why, but they wanted no part of Jeeter's family and surely did not want a blood feud. The family packed up a wagon and moved south, finally settling in a large valley near Wytheville, Virginia.

That was just the first of several killings for Jeeter and Harlance, and although it was winter in West Virginia, they felt the climate had become a bit too hot for them, and they should move elsewhere, far away.

The two made their way across the country the best way they knew how, by holding people up and stealing what was not theirs. Their father taught them to protect what was theirs, with killing if need be; however, they'd been taught no respect whatsoever for the property of others.

Now they lay in wait with their gang wanting to rob a

stagecoach. If people died in the process, neither of these men cared.

There was one thing about highwaymen and holdup men that was a constant throughout the West. If they robbed and stole on a consistent basis, many of them bought or stole the very best horses they could find. Many times these men were chased by posses for days. They needed a horse with speed, staying power, and endurance. Such was the case with Long Legs Westbrook. He was a scoundrel of the worst sort, but he had a horse that was the envy of everyone who met him. He'd actually purchased this one from a wealthy breeder in Texas, although most of the horses he'd had were stolen. The breeder had named the horse Gabriel, which was Spanish, meaning "God is my strength." The very first Arabian horse imported into America was an Arabian stallion brought over in 1725 by Nathan Harrison of Virginia. Gabe was a direct descendant of that stallion, and so was his father, a purebred Arabian stallion. Gabriel's dam, however, was a chestnut horse that was called an American saddle horse or American saddlebred. She had five different gaits and so did Gabriel. She was a direct descendant of Denmark, which was the foundation stallion of the breed, born in 1839 in Kentucky. Her father was a son of Denmark. Gabe's dam had a long stocking on each leg and a white blaze face. Gabriel ended up as a brilliantly marked Overo pinto with a predominately chestnut, or red, head and body, and numerous white jagged or splotchy patches covering him all over. He stood sixteen hands tall and had very muscular legs, rump, and shoulders. His head looked very Arabian, but Gabe had a very long pure white mane and tail, which he liked to toss from side to side with great pride.

Because of his Arabian blood, he had larger lungs and nostrils than most horses and one less rib on each side, so he could intake much more oxygen and go for hours while being chased by posses. His trot never bothered Long Legs Westbrook because it was so smooth, and Gabriel even did what one cowboy watching described as a "floating trot," with his legs very straight, almost as if his knees were locked, as he seemed to float along an inch or so above the ground. The horse was only five years old and had plenty of years left to sail across mountains, desert, and prairie, leaving many other horses behind lathered with sweat and with chests heaving for breath.

Little did Joshua Strongheart know what a vital part such a horse was going to play in his life, in a very short period of time.

He looked across the stage at the beautiful young widow, and he felt a longing he had not felt in some time. Joshua started fantasizing about a romance with the grieving young lady, then remembered how quickly entranced he'd been when the woman had come into the jail and he had felt she was the most beautiful woman in the world. Then he recalled his feelings when he learned how they had met and what her profession was, and he grinned at himself. Maybe it was because he knew his ma's love story with his father, and his stepfather as well, but he found he could not just be attracted to someone. It seemed like Joshua always fell in love with women. Also, remembering his father riding away because of what he knew was best for his mother and him, Joshua always had ridden away no matter how attracted to a woman he was.

The young widow was so vulnerable and seemed to be trying to act bravely while feeling such sorrow. Joshua wished there was some way he could help her. He knew, though, that she had lost her beloved husband not long before and was therefore off-limits to him.

Doffing his hat, the tall half-breed reached out his hand. "By the way, ma'am," he said, "the name is Joshua Strongheart."

She took his hand and smiled with those intense blue eyes peering into his, saying, "I am sorry. Pleased to meet you Mr. Strongheart. My name is Annabelle Ebert."

Just those eyes alone framed by the shiny black hair

made Joshua feel his heart quicken in his chest. He smiled warmly and sat back.

He looked out the window at the jagged rocks that rose above the wagon road on his right. On the left, there was a steep mountain ridgeline covered in cedars, with rock outcroppings sticking through here and there. Joshua looked ahead and saw that the narrow canyon was getting ready to open up into a larger bowl, with gulches coming in several places. The treed ridgeline on the left was suddenly right next to the stagecoach road, and the driver started slowing the team of horses.

Annabelle looked out the window and the ranch hand explained, "We're pullin' up ta Sunset Gulch, ma'am. They might change the team or water what we got. There's a place we stop about ten mile up, too, so they'll probably change teams there. We'll see."

"Thank you, sir," Annabelle replied. "I did not get your name."

"Sorry, ma'am," he said. "Folks call me Chancy."

"Just Chancy?" she replied.

He said, "Yes'm. Don't use the last name. Jest Chancy."

"Nice to meet you, sir. And you, sir," she said, looking at the drummer. "My name is Annabelle."

The drummer quietly said, "My name is Tom Smith."

Joshua interrupted. "Nice to meet you, sir."

The drummer seemed even more nervous and started looking out the window after forcing a smile. He clutched his valise even tighter to his chest, and Annabelle shot Joshua a quick, slight grin and head shake. He acknowledged with a similar grin.

The stage pulled up in front of a long watering trough and a couple ramshackle sheds.

The leathery old driver wrapped the reins around the long brake handle and hollered, "Quick break, folks! Hop on out and stretch them legs. Fresh spring water in the bucket."

Chancy opened the door and hopped out, followed by the

drummer, and then Joshua. He turned and took the hands of Annabelle as she stepped down and looked around at the small mountainous valley. A tiny, intermittent brook ran along the side of the stage road, fed by the spring there at Sunset Gulch, but it went underground right before the place where they walked into the mouth of the gulch to drink some cool fresh water. The stream reemerged some one hundred yards beyond, just bubbling up through the sand. The sun was baking off the rocks and sand, buzzards circled lazily overhead in the cloudless sky, and the passengers were as ready to wash off road dust as to get a drink of cool water.

The driver seemed to be searching around for someone and hollered out, "Reichert!"

He turned and explained, "There's a old boy heah who keeps up the spring and makes this a right comfortable rest stop for the stage folks. He oughta be heah."

As if it was a signal, Jeeter and Harlance both came riding up out of the gulch. They nodded at the passengers with phony smiles. The idea was to make an estimate of who could give them trouble. Long Legs and Scars both hiding behind rocks, armed with Spencer carbines. They were simply waiting for a signal from Jeeter. If he pointed at somebody, they were to be shot immediately with a head shot, because they were dangerous.

Joshua Strongheart grew up with a lawman, but there was something more important going on right then with him. It came from his Lakota ancestry and his time training with uncles and cousins.

If a person is staring at someone's back, some people will actually feel that person staring at them and get a chill down their spine. For that reason, good bow hunters such as American Indian hunters would never stare at a deer, elk, or other game they were stalking, but instead would frequently look directly behind it. Prey animals, some people have theorized, as well as some warriors, have another sense that is undeveloped in most people, the feeling of being watched or stalked. Some call that sense the "sense of knowing."

Some call it strong intuition, but Joshua Strongheart was not thinking of anything like that. He was only thinking that these two were not alone, and that they were trouble no matter how much they were smiling. His bad feelings were so strong that his right hand went down on the handle of his Colt. He was ready to draw, and when Strongheart pulled a gun out of his holster, something or somebody got shot.

Jeeter pointed at him, saying, "Mister, what's wrong with you?"

Two shots rang out almost simultaneously, but Long Legs's shot was a split second faster. Joshua's head snapped back and blood appeared on his forehead as he slammed against the stagecoach and fell to the ground, still and unmoving, his face now covered with blood. Jeeter and Harlance drew their guns and dismounted as the rest of the gang came riding up.

Chancy took a chance and was mowed down with a hail of withering gunfire. He didn't have a real chance at all. Annabelle wanted to scream at the top of her lungs, but she made up her mind she would show no fear. The stagecoach driver raised his hands as if he desperately needed to grab ahold of two clouds, and the drummer leaned against the coach whimpering and clutching his valise to his chest with both hands and arms.

The gang dismounted and started approaching the drummer, Annabelle, and the driver. Jeeter went over to the still form of Joshua Strongheart and unbuckled his gun belt, removed it, and wrapped it around his own waist, buckling it. He left his own gun and belt on the ground.

"How about this rig, boys?" he said. "This is fancy. I always wanted me a rig like this."

He then knelt to check Joshua's pockets and felt the money belt through the trousers with the back of his fingers. He undid the trousers and whistled when he discovered it. Harlance walked over and looked at the new find. Jeeter opened the belt and found the letter to General Davis. He opened it and quickly read it.

He said, "Nice money belt. Ah'm a gonna whar it,

Harlance. Let's save this letter. Looks important. Maybe we can git some money fer it."

"Hey, you got the durned gun and knife, Jeeter," Harlance answered. "I oughta git the money belt."

Jeeter handed him the belt, saying, "Yeah, yer right."

Harlance carefully put the letter back in the belt and proudly put it on under his trousers.

They went over to the cowering drummer and started laughing when they saw how tightly he clutched the valise. Ruddy Cheeks Carroll yanked the valise from the man's arms and opened it, and his mouth dropped open. He reached in and started laughing. Annabelle had been very curious about the contents of the valise, and the drummer started crying and whimpering as Carroll pulled out a shiny purple dress, lingerie, a pair of women's shoes that would fit the drummer, a woman's red wig, and a makeup kit.

"Stand up!" Harlance roared. "Yer one a them dandies? I don't like dandies at all."

Harlance reached over and drew Joshua's .45 out of Jeeter's holster, cocked it, and as the man screamed in a high-pitched yell, he shot him in the middle of the forehead. His head snapped back and hit the stage with a sickening sound, and he buckled to the ground like a totally limp rag doll.

Harlance snapped, "Cullen, go through his pockets!"

Jeeter walked up to Annabelle, and she stood tall and stuck out her chin defiantly. He reached up and jerked the necklace off her neck and stuck it in his pocket without looking at it. He then spotted her antique ring and grabbed her hand to remove it.

Now she spoke up, tears in her eyes. "Sir, please if you have any decency at all. My husband died not long ago, and he gave me that for our wedding. It is all I have to remember him by."

Jeeter grinned and said, "Harlance, aim at her purty little leg. If'n she don't gimme the ring right off, put a round in thet leg."

She made an angry face, pulled off the ring, and slammed it into his hand. Tears slowly rolled down her cheeks. Dyer emerged from the back of the coach carrying the strongbox. He grinned a half-toothless grin and set it down.

Jeeter turned his attention to the driver and pointed Joshua's pistol at him.

"Key to the strongbox."

The driver just nervously shook his head no.

Jeeter grinned. "Okay, I'll put a bullet in you and then shoot the lock off."

Shaking, the driver reached into his vest pocket and pulled out a large key. He handed it to Jeeter, who unlocked the strongbox. There were a number of stacks of bills inside. Jeeter started counting stacks and dividing them, then handed a stack to each man. Next, they went through the luggage and got out all the valuables they could.

Finally finished, they all mounted up except Long Legs, who walked over to Annabelle, grinning.

Jeeter hollered, "Come on, Long Legs!"

Westbrook said, "Boys, look how good she looks in thet dress. Wonder how she looks unner it."

Harlance said, "Boy, this is the West. You know we don't treat women thet way."

Moss chimed in, "I'll have no truck with such talk. I'm pulling out. Come on, boy."

He and his son galloped off up Copper Gulch Stage Road.

"Come on, Long Legs!" Jeeter said.

Long Legs was now motivated by lust.

He yelled, "Go ahaid. Ah'll catch up mebbe."

Long Legs turned back, and now the stage driver got brave. There were not that many women in the West, and even if only out of practicality, some outlaws turned rapist were even strung up or shot by their own gang members. Most men were respectful to women no matter what. The stage driver stepped in front of Annabelle.

Longs Legs laughed, drew his pistol, and said, "Mister, I was gonna tie ya up, but ef ya wanna be a hero, ah'll jest shoot ya."

The driver set his jaw and said, "That is the only way you'll git ta this young lady, son. Over my dead body."

Long Legs stepped forward two steps and cocked the pistol, "Okay, ole-timer. Ya wanna play yer cards thet way, we'll do it."

Annabelle stepped forward, saying, "Wait! I will cooperate, but you agree not to shoot anybody else."

He laughed, saying, "Sounds good to me."

"But not to me!"

Everybody turned and saw Joshua Strongheart standing over his own pool of blood, wearing Jeeter's shed holster and belt and holding the man's .44 in his right hand. It was pointed at Long Legs. Joshua's face was completely covered in dried blood, and he was swaying, but there was no mistaking the clear look in his eyes.

The bullet had sent a deep furrow down Joshua's skull, and he now had a horrible headache to go with it. As he had been taught, he pushed all that out of his mind and steeled himself to the task at hand.

He did not know, though, that Shaw and Dyer were riding back to help out Westbrook in case he got in trouble. They also thought about how beautiful the woman was and what easy prey she would be.

Joshua stared into the eyes of Long Legs, and the tall man got very nervous. Joshua could see that this man was trouble, wounded or not.

Westbrook said, "You're barely able ta stand, partner. Drop the hogleg, an I'll let ya live."

"Mister, you'll never touch that woman while there is breath in my body," Joshua said. "You gonna start the ball or are you gonna talk me to death?"

He saw the ears on Westbrook's magnificent paint horse shoot forward, alert to something coming down the stagecoach road behind him. He figured the gang had come back and was slowly moving up behind him.

Joshua made a decision. He fired, fanned the hammer back, and fired again, and saw a large stain of crimson in the center of Long Legs's chest as he fell back, dropping his gun. Joshua immediately went to the ground, rolling to his right, toward the bloody corpse of Chancy, but on his way down he felt a bullet slam into the back of his left shoulder, which spun him. He crawled forward quickly to Chancy's body, drew the cowboy's gun, and spun around, as another bullet slammed into his right thigh. He saw both Stumpy Shaw and Slim Dyer. One held a Winchester and the other a six-shooter.

Joshua knew he had to save the woman no matter how many bullets hit him. Instead of firing wildly, he forced himself to stand. He fired first at Dyer, the rifleman, and hit him in the right hip, and then a second shot hit Dyer right on the face, tearing his lower jaw off. His eyes rolled back in his head, and he fell back dead. Stumpy Shaw looked over and was terrorized by the sight of his dead riding partner, and he fired as quickly as he could, one bullet hitting Joshua in the upper left arm. Joshua pointed, aimed, fired, and the bullet hit Shaw in the right cheek, breaking the cheekbone and tearing the man's ear off. Strongheart limped forward, fanning the hammer back to a cocked position, and he squeezed a shot from the hip that hit Shaw's upper torso center mass.

Shaw thought to himself. "I'm dead," and that was his last thought, as his back slammed into the rocks.

Now Joshua turned, and barely able to walk, he started toward Long Legs.

Annabelle ran forward, tears streaming, "Oh, Mr. Strongheart. You have been shot over and over."

He grinned. "They are just little holes in me. Don't worry."

Then he fell forward into her arms in a faint. His weight took both of them to the ground. She tried to lower him as gently as she could while falling with him on top of her. He opened his eyes, and was an inch from her face. They stared briefly into each other's eyes, and he smiled.

"Annabelle," he said, feigning shock to tease her. "We just met."

He stood, and she grinned, jumped up, and helped him

rise up on wobbly legs. She immediately started tearing shreds from her petticoat and bandaging his wounds. Smiling, Joshua pushed her aside.

"Excuse me, ma'am," he said, walking toward Long Legs lying on the ground, holding his bloody chest.

He smiled weakly up at Strongheart, saying, "Mister, ya kilt me. Will ya gimme your word, you'll take good care a mah horse? Ah even got a bill a sale on him in mah saddlebags, an' Ah'll sign him over ta ya. Ah am a rotten skunk. Always was, but Ah jest cain't die, partner, knowin' he is jest gonna wander off. He was the only good thang Ah ever had in my life. You'll never find a better horse'n ole Gabriel."

Joshua said, "Mister, I give you my word. What do you want on your headstone?"

Westbrook grinned. "Jest leave me in the rocks. Coyotes got ta eat, too. At least Ah can do one good thang in mah life."

Annabelle stepped up next to Joshua, holding him up by the upper body.

She said, "Mister, you will be buried properly and read over. Any man who cares that much about his horse at least deserves that. I give you my word."

Long Legs stared up at her.

He spoke weakly as blood started coming from his mouth, "What Ah tried to do to ya? Ma'am, you are a lady ef Ah ever saw one."

He smiled at her and that is how he died. He lay there unmoving, eyes staring toward Annabelle and a smile on his lips.

Strongheart's legs gave out, and he dropped in place into a seated position. Annabelle started tearing petticoat strips again. She wrapped the first around his bicep, but the driver held his hand up and rushed to the stage, where he climbed up into his seat. He reached down and pulled out a bottle of whiskey and an oilskin bag.

Tossing them down to her, he said, "Ma'am, pour that

whiskey on his wounds first, and I got clean bandages in there from the doc down ta Pueblo."

She started doctoring Joshua, and the driver ran into the trees toward the spring. He came out of the gulch with Orville Reichert, who was rubbing his wrists and moaning and groaning but did not seem too bad.

Joshua had fainted again, and when he opened his eyes, he looked up at the beautiful face of Annabelle. She saw him awake and smiled. She was still bandaging him. He felt himself falling into a pit of blackness.

Strongheart opened his eyes and there was a fire. He looked at the faces around him. The two men were drinking coffee and the fire shined on Annabelle's face. She was cleaning blood off a cloth. He felt himself slipping into blackness again.

Joshua's mother sat on the edge of his bed and smiled at him when he opened his eyes.

"Where am I, Ma? What happened?" he said.

Smiling softly, she said, "You are in bed, Joshua. You have had a very bad experience, but the doctor said you will be fine with rest. Do you remember what happened?"

The fourteen-year-old boy looked down at his body under the goose down quilt. He was naked, and he could see four straight lines going down his right rib cage on an angle and crossing over onto his belly under his navel.

He thought for a minute and remembered that he and Dan had been out hunting for an elk or mule deer for the family coffers. They had split up and decided to work both wooded sides of a large draw. The ridges were steep, and they kept fairly abreast of each other's location by using bird whistles occasionally.

Dan was following a set of tracks from what appeared to be a large buck, which he knew probably was bedded down somewhere above the head of the draw. This was something old bucks frequently did, so they had a sweeping view

of anything approaching up the draw and strong breezes to
carry scent to them. They also could get over either ridge
in case of trouble. Dan also knew that big bucks did this
instinctively and could not actually reason such things out.

Joshua was following a narrow game trail through
the trees and went around a bend silently and slowly and
froze. There before him not twenty feet away was a large
tom mountain lion on top of a fresh deer carcass. The doe's
neck was broken and twisted in an odd way. The big cat
had just about finished eating the entrails. Strongheart
knew that was the first part of a deer that cougars ate after
making a kill. The lion looked at Joshua, laid his ears back,
and bared his fangs, hissing. A low growl began in the big
cat's chest, and then Joshua saw the big tail start swishing
back and forth. He knew from his hunts with Dan and with
Lakotas in the villages that swishing the tail back and forth
like that was what mountain lions did right before making
a charge. They normally shied away from humans, but he
had come upon this one eating a fresh kill, which the cat
would protect.

Joshua slowly raised his rifle and aimed at the lion's
forehead. It was too close to aim at his chest and take a
chance on only wounding him. A cougar like that could
cover more than twenty feet in one leap. His muscles were
tensing, and Joshua took a deep breath and let it out halfway. The cat sprang, took two big strides, and leapt at his
face. The shot rang out and the lion hit the ground after
crashing into Joshua, his left front paw scratching Joshua
where the marks were now. They bled some but were only
bad scratches and not deep cuts like his father Claw Marks
had gotten from the grizzly. The cat crashing into Joshua
was two hundred pounds of dead weight, and landing on
top of him, it knocked the wind out of Joshua, plus his head
snapped back and slapped into a log. The sky spun around
in circles as he panicked and fought to regain his breath.
Then everything went black. Dan found him with the dead
mountain lion on top of him.

He awakened in his room at home with his mother

babying him, and it became one of his warmest memories. Like most males of any age, Joshua loved getting babied by his mother when he was hurting. On top of that, he had stood in there in the face of danger and done what was needed, while maintaining a cool head. We develop poise and confidence in life from little successes, and this was a big success that was important in Joshua's personal development.

His mother bathed his head with cool water, and he closed his eyes. It was so soothing. He opened them again and looked into the deep, bright blue eyes of Annabelle Ebert. His head was in her lap, and she was rubbing his face with a cool, wet piece of petticoat.

She saw his eyes open and smiled warmly, saying, "Welcome back to the living. You had a very bad fever and were delirious. Your fever broke. How do you feel?"

"Starved," he said. "How long have I been out?"

"Since yesterday," she replied.

He shook his head and blinked his eyes, then stood up, moaning as he did so. He had never been so sore or hurt so much in his life. He had a bandage on his leg, one on his shoulder and back, and another on his upper arm. He looked at all his bandages and smiled at her.

"Did you patch me up?"

"Yes," she said. "The driver helped me. We had to take two bullets out of you, but fortunately they were easy to get to. You need to lie down though."

"I can't," he replied. "I have got to get after those men. I have to get that money belt."

She said, "Mr. Strongheart, you can always replace money."

He interrupted. "Mrs. Ebert, call me Joshua, please. I didn't have any money in that. I had a letter from the President of the United States to a general in Oregon State. I am a secret courier for the Pinkerton Agency."

"Why does that not shock me? And call me Anna or Annabelle," she said. "I know, then, nothing I say will change your mind."

"No, ma'am."

She said, "Maybe they will see the letter and turn it in somewhere."

Strongheart grinned at her.

"Okay, I guess that is silly," she said. "Just hopeful."

He said, "Even without the money belt, I have to get my holster back. No choice."

"Why no choice?" she asked.

He said, "I gave my word to my ma on her deathbed that I would always keep that gun and knife. The gun and holster were left to me by my stepdad, and the knife was left to me by my father."

"You gave your word to your mother?"

"Yes," he said, "but even if I gave it to the spring keeper here, my word is my word. A man's only as good as his word."

She smiled and looked off toward the full moon over the ridgeline.

"Something wrong, Annabelle?"

She said, "That just reminds me of someone."

She turned around, tears in her eyes, and said, "Joshua, since I can tell you are going after those men no matter how foolish, will you give me your word on something."

"Just ask," he said.

"My wedding ring. You saw it," she said. "It is the only thing I have left of my marriage. Please get it back for me, too."

"You have my word, Annabelle," he replied solemnly.

"Oh thank you," she said. "To me, that is as good as having it back."

He said modestly, "Oh, I wouldn't say that."

She interrupted, "I would."

She started breakfast for him while he checked out his new horse, Gabe. Strongheart found the bill of sale in the saddlebags and figured he would get sworn statements from Annabelle and the driver that the horse and gear were left to him. He had a good rough-out saddle, saddlebags, and the horse was trained to work with a hackamore instead of a bridle and bit.

The hackamore was a firm leather band going across the bridge of the gelding's nose, and when the rider would move the reins to the left, it would push down on the left nostril. Horses only breathe through their nose and not their mouth, but if the rider had light hands, the hackamore was very comfortable for the horse. If, however, the rider had heavy hands or short-reined the horse, then the hackamore could even cause a horse to rear or start bucking. Heavy hands are when a rider jerks on the reins or pulls hard. In the case of a hackamore, this would pull down hard on the horse's nose, and if held, it could cut all the air off, making the horse panic.

Joshua Strongheart would soon be riding the magnificent spotted horse and would learn that he could turn, stop, or motivate the horse with leg aids alone.

Leg aids are when you use your heels, calves, and knees to touch the horse or push on parts of the horse to turn it. For example, if you want a horse to turn left, you would slightly move the reins to the left while lightly squeezing your left calf against the horse's left side, or even touch it on the left side with a heel or spur. You could even make a horse turn faster if you also pushed inward on his front shoulder with your right knee. Gabriel was so well trained, even before Long Legs bought him, that he could feel the body lean of a rider or a leg aid and respond, even without the rider touching the reins.

Gabe was also trained to ground rein, which was critical for a traveler like Joshua who traveled long miles over large distances. What that meant was that Joshua would be able to dismount and leave his reins hanging down and Gabe would not move. At the breeder's where Long Legs bought him, the trainer had had pieces of lead line tied to logs buried in the ground. The lead lines had hooks on the ends of them. He would teach Gabe to follow him when his reins were up over his neck or wrapped around the saddle horn.

However, whenever he wanted Gabe to stop and stand, he would drop the reins, and secretly do it at each lead line. Without letting the horse see it, he would hook the lead line up to the bottom of the hackamore.

He would then command, "Stand," and walk away.

Gabriel quickly learned that if he moved at all, the band on his nose would pull down and make it uncomfortable. Horses are pattern animals, so they quickly learn and develop certain routines. Gabe found that if he moved when the reins were hanging down, it was no fun, so from then on, he would ground rein, or never move an inch, if the reins were dropped.

There were two other things Joshua would soon be learning about him. The first was that he always would come when called, whistled at, or even given a hand signal. The horse had learned even as a foal that he would get rubbed and nuzzled when he did that. This was going to be refreshing for Strongheart, because unlike so many horses just picked out of the remuda, or the horse herd with cattle, the kind so many cowboys were used to, Gabe would become Joshua's trail partner.

The second thing Joshua would learn was that Gabe had a mile-eating, very comfortable fast trot that he always went into. However, if Joshua wanted to eat up ground but slow things down, he would simply be able to say, "Slow trot," and Gabe would trot much more slowly. The normal walk on this long-legged athletic horse was much faster than some horses' trots anyway.

Joshua returned from packing the horse and was shocked to learn that Annabelle had fixed bacon, eggs, biscuits, and coffee for him. He was hungry enough to eat the pan also.

Joshua sat down on a log by the fire and said, "How did you manage this? This is wonderful. I have had a goat inside my belly wanting to eat everything."

Annabelle giggled. "The driver was taking a load of steaks up Copper Gulch Stage Road and was meeting a wagon from Westcliffe. The driver carries eggs and a slab of bacon with him in case of breakdowns."

"Why would somebody in Westcliffe want steaks all the way from Canon City?" he asked. "Don't they have cows in Westcliffe, and where is Westcliffe?"

Annabelle grinned. "You eat and I'll tell you about Westcliffe."

While Strongheart ate, she told him about the beautiful high mountain population center. Little did either know that in just a couple years silver and gold would be discovered in the area, and Silver Cliff would be started just east of Westcliffe, and both would become boomtowns. Copper Gulch Stage Road would become a very highly traveled road.

Annabelle explained that Westcliffe was located in a large, high mountain valley. The town was just under eight thousand feet in elevation and had the fourteen-thousand-foot Sangre de Cristo range directly to the west of it, and the mountains could be seen from one horizon to the other. On the east side of the valley was the Greenhorn mountain range, with much shorter peaks, rocky and covered with trees in most places. At the far south end on a clear day, you could see the twin Spanish Peaks near the border of New Mexico Territory. And to the far north end of the valley the Collegiate mountain range was visible. Joshua would be heading that way and would cross over that range later.

In 1806 the men of Lieutenant Zebulon Pike's big exploration project were the first white men, aside from the occasional mountain man or wanderer, to pass through and explore the Wet Mountain Valley, which was inhabited only by Ute Indians, grizzly and black bears, many large harems of elk, large herds of mule deer, and wolves, and the valley was so large, there were also large herds of antelope and buffalo. In 1870, a wagon road from the Wet Mountain Valley to Canon City opened up.

The first real group, besides the Utes, to settle in the Westcliffe area were German-born adventurers. A colony of these people from Chicago arrived in 1870, led by a Civil War veteran named General Carl Wulsten. Annabelle, fascinated by the area, had read the actual news story about it.

Leaving Chicago in February, the group was described this way in the Chicago newspaper account:

So they started from Chicago, a group of 250 people, the pioneers of civilization. A notable event in the history of Chicago transpired yesterday. It was the departure of a colony of Chicago citizens for a home in the western wilds, the first of its kind which ever left this city and the first, it's believed, ever organized in America. An immense throng of relatives and friends gathered to bid them farewell and God speed.

They were a splendid looking set of people including muscular athletic young fellows with rifles strapped to their backs and 20 fair haired, clear skinned German girls, all young, good looking and seemingly capable of taking good care of themselves and making excellent wives for those same gallant rifle bearers.

They traveled by steam locomotive and train to Fort Lyons, Colorado, far out on the prairie, then switched to Conestoga wagons, each pulled by a six-mule team. They did not actually begin the town where Westcliffe was, but fifteen miles from the eventual Westcliffe site. It was called the "Colfax Colony," because the vice president of the United States, Schuyler Colfax, had taken this enterprise on as one of his personal pet projects and arranged for federal government financing, even for cavalry troops out of Fort Lyons to escort the group of settlers to the Wet Mountain Valley.

The Colfax Colony started in March 1870, only one month after leaving Chicago. Some businesses in Denver who wanted to help this town bloom sent supplies, but the colonists were used to Chicago. They planted fruit trees and some gardens, but an unexpected early frost ruined their produce. Then, after getting some buildings put up before winter set in, they had another terrible thing happen. One of the major buildings exploded into millions of splinters when a keg full

*of dynamite was accidentally detonated. They had
already lost their supply of funding from the government just due to politics, so the town basically disappeared before it was even a year old.*

However, there were other residents and a few with
money, such as Dr. William A. Bell, who owned land
where Westcliffe was now located, Annabelle explained,
and really wanted to try to get a railroad to come into the
valley. Dr. Bell had already started another town, Manitou
Springs, not too far west of Colorado Springs, nestled in
among the northeastern foothills of Pikes Peak. General
William Palmer was one of his closest friends, and at Dr.
Bell's urging he came to Bell's ranch lands in 1870, the
same year the colony started and ended. Palmer was the
man who created the Denver & Rio Grande Railroad. He
was also the founder of Colorado Springs.

Bell started Westcliffe on his own property and named
it Clifton, but he changed the name to Westcliffe shortly
after that. Palmer wondered if this might be the area
for a southern railroad route, which eventually was going
to go farther south, then right along the Arkansas River
by Canon City and straight west to Salida and Poncha
Springs.

The railroad would eventually be started and run in and
out of Westcliffe eight years after Annabelle and Joshua's
conversation, but because of rock slides, avalanches, and
washout from occasional torrential rains and flash floods
in each of the steep canyons running away from the valley, the railroad would eventually die out. However, even at
that time, Westcliffe was gaining a reputation in the inner
circles of Denver and Colorado Springs as one of the beautiful safer tourist areas to visit in Colorado. The Utes were
friendly with the white man, and the other tribes usually
did not come into that area.

It was almost daylight, and Strongheart could see the
grayish blue skies of false dawn. He was ready to mount

up. The sky was occasionally spinning, and he knew he had to keep packing strong food into his body. To that end, Annabelle packed what she could into his saddlebags, and she handed him a cloth bag.

He said, "Thanks. What's this?"

She said, "It's hoecake."

"Hoecake?"

She laughed. "Corn dodger. The driver had some corn-meal, so I made you a bunch in the griddle. There was a jar of honey, so I stuck it in there. You can roll them up and dip them in it. I also put a bunch of coffee and his extra small coffeepot. You make sure you drink a lot of water. And try to get rest."

He grinned. "Yes, Mother."

She started laughing at herself and put her hands on his chest, looking up into his face. Joshua wondered if she could feel his heart suddenly beating much faster.

"Thank you so much. Please be careful, Joshua."

He grinned at her again and mounted up.

Annabelle was still grieving her husband, but she could not help herself. This man made her heart flutter, and her face would get red just having any thoughts about him. He was so handsome, with his dark complexion, long, shiny black hair, high cheekbones, intelligent eyes, and that almost smile most of the time, even in what she knew was excruciating pain. He was tall, and he had muscles on top of muscles. Half-Indian and half-white, he was such a man of mystery, and she just knew that in his arms she would feel more protected than with any man in the world, even her late husband. Even thinking that made her feel guilty.

Joshua winked and spun the big horse around, then trotted up the stage road. He had left written directions for her to give to whoever came along the road and could get them help. He would also summon help as soon as he ran into anybody who could get messages through. Strongheart had only ridden two miles up the road when he ran into such help. A virtual posse came riding around a sharp corner, and he pulled up.

The man in front held up his hand and said, "Howdy, Chief. You happened to see the stagecoach along the road?"

Joshua felt a brief twinge of anger, but he smiled and calmly said, "I am not a chief. The stage was held up, people were killed, and the team of horses was run off. They are waiting two miles behind me. I'm after the men who held us up. I have to go."

He kicked his new horse and saw how easily the steed could leave a crowd behind. The posse leader didn't even have time to ask the first of the many questions that popped into his mind.

Strongheart was very impressed with this flashy new horse. He was not only beautiful, he was a dream to ride. The seat was so smooth atop his back, and the gelding seemed to love trotting, which would eat up the miles. The gulch slowly climbed, with high, rock-strewn, tree-covered ridges on both sides. Every once in a while, he would pass by a pile of large boulders obviously carried there by the latest flash flood.

After several more miles, the canyon suddenly opened up and gave way to rolling small hills with piñons and stunted cedars, as well as mountain gamma grasses. Gabriel trotted up over a couple of those hills, and suddenly a high mountain valley opened up, and Strongheart looked at the snowcapped Sangre de Cristo mountain range, which ran from the left to the right, with peak after peak stretching up into the clear blue sky. The more he saw the mountains, ten miles distant, the more fascinated he became with them. These thirteen- and fourteen-thousand-footers were the most majestic Joshua had ever seen, and he had seen plenty already.

He kept riding, and within another mile, he saw where Road Gulch Road ran off to his right, crossing the high valley for a couple miles, before dropping down into the trees. The road, which kept winding its way toward the big range, fell behind him as he moved across the flat, high mountain valley. This was like prairie now, with no trees except all along the fringes of the valley. To his right, a small tree-covered ridge rose up maybe five hundred feet, a mile away. Off to his left, only a half mile away, another ridge cut halfway across the valley. It stood maybe four hundred feet above the valley floor. Near the base of the ridge to his right was a small herd of pronghorn antelope, and at the base of the ridge to his left Strongheart spotted a small herd of mule deer grazing. After two miles, the Road Gulch Stage Road started dropping down into a tree-sided gulch. This gulch dropped down to Texas Creek for the next six miles, and from there Texas Creek dropped down in a northward direction and poured into the Arkansas River. Strongheart, however, kept heading west and crossed the creek and a surrounding meadow, which held a harem of more than one hundred elk and several large herds of deer. He rode a few more miles, then the stage road veered right and started a faster descent toward a place along the Arkansas River that was called "Cotopaxi" by locals.

There were a few miners' cabins in the area and a few other buildings. Joshua decided he would find out if he could get a line on any of the gang. He had watched their tracks and seen two split off, but the rest had headed to this location.

That is when Joshua ran into a good source of information.

About five years or so earlier, George Henry Thomas had settled in the area where Strongheart now was, and he nicknamed one of the mountains Cotopaxi for an active volcano he had seen in Equador. George became known locally by the nickname Gold Tom, because of some money he made in the area doing placer mining. Gold Tom had traveled a lot in South America, and the hard rock ridges around Cototpaxi really reminded him of that place, and he shared that information with everybody. Cotopaxi would eventually become the official name for the small settlement where these gulches came together on the fast-flowing Arkansas River.

E. H. Saltiel was a bigwig, and he had been visiting

Cotopaxi a good bit and already made offers to buy Gold Tom's mine. He eventually would, but had not by the time Strongheart arrived. In fact, Gold Tom had just founded the mine earlier in that year, but already people who passed through the area knew who he was, as he was one of those salty characters that seemed to permeate the West. Unfortunately, seven years after Joshua Strongheart passed through Cotopaxi, Gold Tom would be shot and killed in a ridiculous argument over a dog.

There were only a few buildings in Cotopaxi in the early 1870s. Harry Hart and his wife, their two sons, Harry Jr. and Myer, and their two daughters, Addie and Phoebe, had moved to Cotopaxi and felt its location might be a good spot to build for the future. They built a general store and a hotel right there a stone's throw from the churning, bubbling Arkansas River and adjacent to the large wagon bridge across the river, connecting to the north bank.

The general store was run by another character, Zachariah Banta, who had a twinkle in his powder blue eyes, a head like an ostrich, and a mischievous half smile ever present on his wrinkled countenance. He would become for Joshua the source of information that might put him on the track of the killers.

"Wal," Banta said, "I reckon you don't live around here. You may wanna ask me how I reckon such?"

Joshua grinned. "How did you figure that out, sir?"

Zachariah Banta picked up a small wooden barrel of potatoes and moved them to a different part of one of the shelves.

He turned and grinned, saying, "Wal, that was purty easy to deduce. Ya see, in Cotopaxi—that's what we call this area—wal, there ain't much to see in a place so small, but what ya hear makes up fer it."

Strongheart chuckled while Banta continued on. "Now, mind ya. I personally ain't a gossip. But I am informative."

Joshua laughed aloud.

Banta continued. "So since I ain't ever seen ya before,

and I heered no gossip about ya, I reckon ya must be new ta Cotopax. Possible jest passin' through."

Strongheart said, "Actually, maybe you can help me."

Banta chuckled. "All a them bullet holes and bandages on ya, somebody sure as hell needs ta help ya."

Grinning, Joshua said, "My name is Joshua Strongheart, sir. I got shot up during a stage holdup on Copper Gulch Road."

"Hell," Banta growled. "Any folks kilt?"

"Yes, several," Joshua said.

Zachariah poured him coffee, and Joshua told him about the holdup and described the gunmen.

"Thet is the McMahon boys," the oldster said. "Jeeter and Harlance are brothers and rattlesnake mean. Sounds like ya kilt Long Legs Westbrook. Thet's his horse yer ridin.' Thet's why I was probin'."

Joshua said, "He gave Gabriel to me before he died. Made me promise to take good care of him."

"Wal, he shore did take care a Gabe. Only good thing about Long Legs," Zachariah said, "he took durned good care of thet purty painted up critter. Never bought me a horse fer color, but thet is about the best horse I ever seen, and I have seen plenty a horses thet have crunched lotsa gravel under their hooves."

"I have to catch up with those killers fast," Joshua said.

Banta said, "Alone?"

Strongheart said firmly, "Yes."

"Wal, I reckon ya better have ya a good education on how to put that hogleg inta action," the white-haired old man mused, "but studyin' ya, ya have thet look. Ya have seen the elephant, ain't ya, boy?"

Joshua grinned. He had heard that Civil War phrase from Dan. Boys in the Civil War who had that faraway look of battle fatigue in their eyes were said to have seen the elephant.

Smiling, Joshua said, "Sir, I have traveled the ridgelines a few times."

Zack said, "So are ya injun or half-breed?"

"My mother was white," Joshua replied matter-of-factly, "and my father was Lakota, a Sioux the white men call them."

"So when your mama decide ta sail on the sea a matrimony," Zack said, "she decided ta use a canoe?"

Zack and Joshua both laughed heartily at Zachariah's joke. Strongheart finally replied, "I guess so, sir."

"Don't go sirring me, son," Banta said, "makes me feel old. Call me Zack. Wal, one good thing is they split up, so ya kin tangle with 'em one or two at a time," the old man continued. "I heerd 'em talking about it."

"Do you know where they headed?"

"Wal, lessee," Zack responded, "as I recall, big old Gorilla Moss and his kid, Percival, headed south down past Westcliffe. I think Ruddy Cheeks Carroll said he was gonna ride with 'em as fur as Westcliffe. They asked me how ta get to Music Pass. Ya know where all them places are?"

"Yes," Joshua said. "We were talking about Westcliffe and the Colfax Colony on the stage."

Zack replied, "Now, mind ya, Colfax Colony sprang up southwesta Westcliffe. Music Pass is beyond that and runs ya over the Sangre de Cristos and smack into the Great Sand Dunes. Make sure ya got a good kerchief when ya travel over there."

Joshua was feeling weak in his knees from blood loss, and Zachariah took notice. The old man did not miss much.

"Were I you," Zach said, "I'd git me a bed fer the night in the hotel yonder and rest. Eat some now and eat good of the mornin'. Then ya kin proper track and kill them rascals as needed."

Joshua said, "Thanks, but I'll be all right, Zack."

Zack chuckled. "You are a man what keeps his oath if ever I seed one. I know they took yer money, son. I'll go fer ya on the hotel and the vittles. It won't do ya no good in a shoot-out to be passin' out from blood loss. Ya kin pay me back someday."

Joshua grinned and said, "I am very grateful, Zack."

The next morning, after a hearty breakfast including ham, poached eggs, coffee, and peach pie, Joshua headed off south to locate three of the holdup men. He had gotten more information the night before and had his wounds cleaned up and bandaged again. He felt much more refreshed and a little stronger, although he was sore from head to toe.

The magnificent horse climbed the long, winding road up to the center of the Wet Mountain Valley. Up above, Joshua looked at the awesome snowcapped peaks looming above him to his right, as the horse's smooth, fast trot ate up the miles.

It was still morning when he rode into the small town, and he headed for a squat building that had the simple word "Saloon" neatly painted on a long wooden sign above its door. Joshua had vowed never to drink again, and he would not, but he knew this would be the best place to get information. Saloons were in every town in the West. In fact, when new towns sprang up, the saloon was one of the first businesses, if not the first business, to open up, no matter where. The saloon was where all the men in each town met to pass and learn the latest gossip, socialize, and discuss everything from beef prices to politics. It was for exactly that reason that Strongheart entered the place of drink.

He walked up to the bar and a very tall, very slender man with a long handlebar mustache walked up to him.

Joshua said, "Can I have a glass of milk, please?"

The bartender pointed above the bar at a sign, which read "We do not serve Utes."

Joshua said, "Do you have fresh milk?"

The bartender said, "Forgot, you can't read. We don't serve Utes."

Joshua replied, "Good, because I did not order one. Now do you have milk or not?"

The bartender said, "Look, we don't serve any blanket niggers here."

Joshua's hand shot out before he even thought about it, and he meant to pull the tall skinny man forward, but he actually dragged him all the way across the bar.

Strongheart said, "You want to repeat that statement?"

The bartender said, "No."

Strongheart replied, "No what?"

"No, sir."

The warrior smiled and said, "Who is in charge?"

The bartender said, "I am."

Strongheart slapped him across both cheeks rapidly, and blood started dripping from the man's lower lip.

Joshua said, "Wrong answer. Who is in charge?"

The six foot, ten inch beanpole said, "You are, sir."

Joshua stood him up straight and let go of his neck, saying, "Good, now go get me a glass of milk and tell me the price."

"On the house, sir," the bartender said, scrambling back behind the bar.

He opened the ice chest, pulled out a container of milk, and poured it into a beer mug.

Joshua said, "Here. I don't want anything free from you, mister."

He tossed some coins on the bar and, taking his mug of milk, walked to the far corner and sat down facing the door. It was then that he noticed the man sitting at the table in the front corner of the room. He had really blond hair and very ruddy cheeks. It was Ruddy Cheeks Carroll. His head hung drunkenly, and then he suddenly recognized the face of the half-breed from the stage, and he came wide awake, hangover be damned.

Joshua was on his feet first and had his gun drawn already. He walked sideways to the bar, while still looking at Carroll. He turned his gun toward the bartender and stuck out his left hand.

Still watching Ruddy Cheeks, he said to the barkeep, "Hand me the scattergun you got."

"Yes, sir."

The man reached under the bar and pulled out the express twelve-gauge sawed-off double-barreled shotgun stored there. He set it gingerly in Strongheart's left hand. Still looking at Carroll, Joshua unloaded the shotgun and tossed the shells across the room, then set the gun on a table.

He glanced briefly at the bartender, explaining, "I don't need any buckshot in my back while I handle this problem."

He turned his full attention now to Ruddy Cheeks Carroll, saying, "Mister, where is my money belt? Where is the wedding ring of the young lady on the stage?"

The outlaw had drunk late into the night and slept on the table. He had to relieve his bladder, his stomach felt like a pair of badgers were inside it, and he had a horrible pounding headache. He wanted to be anywhere but there facing the angry big half-breed. His mind raced.

"Don't know."

Joshua said, "Wrong answer," and the gun boomed.

The man screamed as he grabbed his left earlobe, but it was not there. His hand came away covered in blood.

"Injun," Carroll said, "Jeeter McMahon has your gun and rig, your money belt. I don't know who taken that ring. I swear. All I have is my cut."

Strongheart said, "Hand it to me."

The man reached into the back of his trousers and pulled out a roll of bills. He thought he might challenge Joshua to put the gun away and fight him like a man, but one look at Strongheart's size and musculature changed his mind. He only had one last chance to save himself from a rope. He had practiced quick draw a lot and was pretty accurate. It was worth a try, he figured.

Carroll held the roll and said, "Redskin, you shore act tough with that iron in your fist."

Joshua said, "Not a problem."

He spun the pistol backwards into his holster.

He had a half grin on his face that frightened Carroll even more, but the crook was determined not to hang. Besides, he knew he could outdraw most men. His hand flashed down as practiced, but there was no gun there. He looked up and saw the barrel of Strongheart's six-shooter. His heart skipped a beat as he looked up above the gun and saw the deadly grin on Strongheart's face.

"Barkeep!" Joshua said not looking. "You have law in this town?"

"No, sir, none," the bartender replied.

Joshua held his gun on Carroll, saying, "Where do I find Jeeter McMahon?"

"Lookout Mountain. You can see it as you ride down the valley north," Ruddy Cheeks said, now very nervous hearing there was no law around and knowing Joshua would want to get going.

He was certain Joshua would plug him.

Joshua said, "When you drive down Road Gulch Stage Road, is it that rocky outcropping sticking off on the north side of the road?"

"Yes, sir," Carroll said. "They got a hideout somewhere on the backside, but I don't know where. His brother was going with him, but they talked about splitting up then."

Strongheart said, "Pick up your gun and holster it."

Carefully, very gingerly, Carroll did so.

Joshua spun his pistol back into his holster and said, "You sure you want to do this?"

Ruddy Cheeks chuckled and said, "Partner, I never found nobody yet who can beat me."

Strongheart smiled and said softly, "Yes, you have. You might beat me, but you will have to put all six shots in me, reload, and shoot some more before I'll go down."

He was simply posturing to unnerve his opponent, and it worked. His words sent a chill down the outlaw's spine, and he drew too early, clawing for his pistol in panic. It was out, cocked, and coming up, when he felt something slam into his chest and his eyes came up automatically to see the flame from Joshua's muzzle blast, as he felt the second bullet slam into his chest, tear through, and take away half of his right shoulder before it passed out his back. He tasted blood and started feeling weak, but did not understand the reason. It felt like the building had been picked up and spun around in fast circles, but he did not know why. Suddenly, his knees felt like they could not hold his legs up anymore, and he sat down in place. He tasted more blood and realized it was pouring out of his mouth, and then it dawned on him that he was dying. He panicked and wanted to scream, but nothing would come out; he was drowning in his own blood, and it made him gag. He died that way, sitting down, his back against the wall and arms hanging down at his side.

Joshua started for the door, and the bartender said, "Hey, who's gonna take care of him?"

Joshua glared at him. "You are. And if I hear of you speaking that way about any of my red brothers again, I will come back and finish what I started. Do you understand?"

"Yes, sir," the man said. "What is your name, mister?"

"Joshua Strongheart."

The tall half-breed strolled out the door and went directly to his horse, mounted up and headed back the way he had just come. Now, though, when he was just a few miles out of town, he headed right up a pine-lined gulch called Reed Gulch. He rode several miles seeing many harems of elk, flocks of wild turkeys, and herds of mule deer. There seemed to be ample graze, cover, and water in this gulch. He almost came out eventually on Copper Gulch Stage Road, well west of where he had originally turned off on Road Gulch Road. Joshua could have turned right on Copper Gulch Stage Road a few miles earlier, but he was looking for a cross-country shortcut to Lookout Mountain, and he found it right before actually arriving at the stage road. He would angle to his left front and pass to the left of the long ridge before him. He was actually on the reverse side of the tree-covered ridge he had seen in the giant flat meadow when he first turned onto Road Gulch Road, when there had been lots of deer at its base. The locals actually called it Deer Mountain.

Strongheart realized Lookout Mountain had to be called that for a reason, so people must have been able to look out easily in every direction and see anybody coming. He remembered the ridge and the terrain and figured that ridge with the deer at the base, Deer Mountain, to be something that would block his view in between Lookout Mountain and his travel. He also remembered patches of trees in the giant mountain meadow, and figured he could ride between them quickly without exposing himself to view too much. Maybe he would even make camp and travel after dark, so he would not be observed from the tall, rocky peak.

It did not take Joshua too long to reach the end of the ridge, and he was able to move through several draws, where one patch of trees led to another. Through the holes in the trees he was able to see the high, rocky sentinel sticking up into the sky. Joshua had already done a lot of traveling that day, and it was now late afternoon. He decided to camp before he got too close, where his campfire might be smelled and the light of the fire might be seen.

In this country, wise horsemen always took note of water and shelter. Strongheart recalled his ride down Road Gulch Road and remembered seeing a little side gulch running up toward Lookout Mountain. There was a lot of green, and he saw birds flying in and out of it as he traveled by. This told him there was probably a spring at the head of it. He made the road without being spotted, turned left, and headed downhill for a couple miles, until he spotted the small side gulch to the right. He headed up and within a half mile found a small spring and a little tank, where his horse could drink his fill. It was well protected by a higher ridge, trees to break up the smoke from his fire, good areas to observe anybody headed his direction, and good graze for Gabe around the spring. He would make camp early, eat well, and get plenty of sleep, allowing his wounds to heal even more. He was tired and very sore, but oddly feeling stronger at the same time.

It was false dawn when Joshua climbed into the saddle.

He reasoned that he could go up over the ridge and hope-
fully would come out at the far end of the giant mountain
meadow, which actually ran about halfway up the eastern
side of Lookout Mountain. The western, northern, and
southern sides were rocky and more straight up and down.
An hour later, Joshua found himself riding through rocks
and a small mining trail which ran from the long meadow
out onto a fingerlike ridge coming off Lookout. He was
now on the northern side of that ridge, which had the most
cover, too. Every other direction would have forced him to
abandon his horse.

Jeeter McMahon's brother, Harlance, had left the day
before. He told his brother he did not hanker to spend all
his time in some rocky hideout watching for posses, lawmen, or bounty hunters. He was going to head for southwestern Colorado Territory and spend some time near
Animas City looking for gold. His brother thought he was
crazy, but Harlance explained about what was happening
there and encouraged his brother to go with him. The area
would in less than a decade host the new gold-smelting
town of Durango.

Over whiskey-laced coffee two nights before Strongheart
arrived on the scene, Harlance told Jeeter about the area.
Southwest Colorado was not a place many white men ventured into because of the southern Utes and mountain Utes.
But, Harlance explained, the brand-new Brunot Treaty of
1873 removed the Utes from the mountains and opened up
the area for prospectors, and much placer mining was done,
and finally full-scale mining. This meant a settlement of
surrounding businesses, such as saloons, brothels, an assay
office, and normal retail businesses to support the mining,
was created. Mountain towns were springing up in the San
Juans, like Telluride, Silverton, Rico, and Ophir. Animas
City was a little north of what would become Durango, and
Animas City would eventually disappear. The railroad was
not there yet, and the area was wild, with many prospectors
and mining engineers starting to flood into it. What was
ironic was that the Cripple Creek and Victor areas not too

far from Lookout Mountain were where Colorado's richest gold strikes would be, as well as Westcliffe and nearby Silver Cliff, an area where Joshua Strongheart had ridden to and from all in a day's time.

Harlance was not that enthused about actually prospecting; he was thinking more about the remoteness of southwestern Colorado Territory and all the women and alcohol being shipped in there, as well as many possible holdup victims, miners with bags of gold dust, and, of course, those brothels.

To that end, he also talked his brother into giving him the beautiful antique wedding ring of Annabelle's, in case he met somebody "special" at one of the bawdy houses or saloons around Animas City or any of the other towns.

Now Jeeter was alone in his hideout which was in the rocks high up near the peak. There was a natural cave formed by an overhanging rock that had fallen decades earlier on three different rock outcroppings. He had shelter from rain and sun and could watch a wide area, especially to the west, since he had come that general direction from Cotopaxi. There were two drawbacks. He had to keep his horse picketed far below, on the northern side of the peak, where there was a small spring in the rocks and piñons, and some grass, and he then had quite a climb to his hideout. He also had to go all the way down to that spring to get his water, but to him it was worth it. He felt safer and more secure when he knew he could see in three directions over a wide area.

There were also numerous deer and elk all over the sandy piñon- and cedar-covered foothills surrounding him. There were plenty of mountain lions, too, so he could find lion kills as he scouted around, and he would take the carcasses from their kill sites without firing a shot. Mountain lions were very finicky eaters and would leave a deer carcass for other predators when the meat had gotten the least little bit tainted. They would also eat the intestines of a deer first, and twice Jeeter found fresh kills with both the front and hindquarters of the deer intact. In both cases, the lions were lying on nearby ledges overlooking the kill, but they would not attack a human. It was just not something cougars would normally do, unless one was starving or had come upon a small child alone. They were too shy, and they were usually nocturnal anyway.

Strongheart got Gabriel under a large rock ledge, so the sun would not be on him, and dropped the reins. The horse stood calmly in the shadows. He removed his spurs and boots and grabbed a pair of soft-soled Lakota moccasins from his saddlebags and put them on. He grabbed his Henry carbine and slowly, quietly moved into the rocks, angling himself up higher toward the peak.

A half hour later, he quietly emerged from the rocks close to the peak and saw that he was looking down into a jumble of rocks making a natural fortress. There were tracks from Jeeter and Harlance all over the soft, sandy ground. Jeeter suddenly appeared below him with something in his hand. It was some paper. He looked out over the valley then disappeared back under the overhanging rock. Joshua did not move, and seconds later, Jeeter reappeared to Strongheart's right front. He was completely naked but wearing Joshua's gun belt, holster, and weapons. Strongheart raised the rifle and settled the sights on Jeeter's spine, halfway up his back, and then he lowered his rifle. The man was going to a spot partway down the ridge from his hideout, apparently his bathroom. Joshua shook his head and quietly chuckled at the sight of the naked armed man striding away from the rocks.

Joshua quickly and silently backed up away from the edge. He moved like a cougar himself down the rocks and slipped into Jeeter's hideout. He had shelter, food, and a campfire and had made himself a nice evergreen bough bed, and there were excellent fields of fire and vision in almost every direction. He even had spaces between large rocks from which he could easily observe or shoot anybody approaching from the blind side of the mountain, along the base of the steep rock. If Joshua had tried coming that way, he would have been easily bushwhacked. Like many people and animals, though, Jeeter had failed to watch for danger from above.

Joshua poured himself a cup of coffee and found it to be strong, fresh, and very hot, just the way that he liked it. His standard request was that anybody making him coffee should grab a small rock and set it on the brewing coffee, and when it floats the coffee is ready.

Quickly looking through Jeeter's things, he found his money belt, and the letter was inside. He checked to insure that Jeeter was not at hand, then lowered his drawers, strapped the belt around his waist, and cinched his gun belt back up.

None of his wounds were hurting right now, because of adrenaline, but Strongheart still was a long ways from having all his strength back. He sat down and waited a couple minutes, and soon he heard Jeeter whistling a tune as he made his way up the path to the hideout. Naked but for the gunbelt, Jeeter strode into the cave and froze at the sight of a grinning Joshua Strongheart, bandaged all over, a pistol in one hand and a cup of coffee in the other.

With a thick accent, Jeeter finally spoke. "What you doin' heah, ya damned blanket nigger?"

Strongheart smiled, saying, "I gave my word to my mother on her deathbed I would never give away or sell my rig that you are wearing."

Jeeter shook his head, saying, "You come after me wounded up bad to get back yer gun and knife?"

Strongheart said, "And the wedding ring you took, and I got my money belt. Why did you still have the letter?"

Jeeter spat some brown tobacco juice out. "Wal, I reckoned I would sell it ta the highest bidder. If ya was a man and let me make a play, then after I kill ya, I would go do jest that."

"Well," Joshua replied, "we don't have to worry about that."

"What, letting me ta make a play? I figgered as much."

Strongheart said, "Where is the ring?"

Jeeter said, "The hell with ya. I give it ta one a mah gang, and I ain't tellin' ya nothin' else."

Strongheart said, "Well, I have already killed about half your gang, and I will hunt the rest down until I find that wedding ring. So you won't tell me where your brother or the rest are?"

"Hell, no. Why would ya spend time lookin' for a damned ole ring?"

Strongheart said, "Because I gave my word."

Jeeter chuckled, shaking his head. "Craziest thing Ah ever heerd of. Ya been shot a bunch, ridin' hard I guess, and all over a gun, a knife, and a ring."

Strongheart stopped smiling and said, "No, because of integrity. You would never understand that concept." He spun his pistol back into the holster, saying, "You asked what I meant when I said we won't have to worry about that."

Jeeter said, "Yeah."

"I was not talking about giving you a chance. I was talking about you being able to kill me." Jeeter looked into Joshua's dark, dark eyes and what he saw made his spine shiver. Suddenly, he wished he was back in his natural bathroom.

He laughed halfheartedly, saying, "At least let me put some clothes on. Ah'm naked."

Strongheart said, "That's how you came into this world, but now you are wearing a gun, my gun. That is how you are going out of it. You chose the owlhoot trail. Don't whine."

A shadow literally passed over Jeeter's face and then the rocks, and he looked up. Three buzzards circled lazily along on the updraft from the mountain, looking for food. A dread came over him. He had to kill this Indian. His hand went down for the gun, and as it touched the handle, he thought he was going to do it, but he looked up and saw the muzzle flash from Joshua's right hand. Jeeter was amazed that Joshua had been sipping coffee and not spilled a drop. At the same time, something slammed into his chest and then another, and somewhere he heard two loud booms. He was struggling to breathe.

Looking at Strongheart in a panic, he said, "How kin ya bury me in these heah rocks?"

Joshua said, "Don't have time. You wouldn't give me names or places. Remember? Besides, buzzards have to eat, too."

The thought sent Jeeter into sheer panic. He suddenly went blind, then deaf, then he could not breathe but kept trying. He was too young to die. That was his last thought.

Strongheart retrieved his rig and grabbed whatever Jeeter had of any value, returned to Gabriel, and rode down, getting Jeeter's gelding along the way. He saddled him and led him down toward Texas Creek, along a sandy gulch with an intermittent creek seeping in and out of the sand. It was known locally as Likely Gulch.

An hour later, he led the horse into the small group of buildings called Cotopaxi. Zack Banta came out, the ever-present twinkle in his eye, and this time a large corncob pipe in his mouth.

The old-timer accepted the saddle and carbine Joshua handed him, as well as a bag of money and some jewelry.

Banta said, "Wal, I reckon ole Jeeter McMahon has no need fer none a this anymore. Ah also reckon the way ya do things, young Strongheart, thet Harlance ain't gonna have much need fer this horse or his things purty soon. We'll put him in the stable behind the hotel."

"See that he gets a good owner, yourself or whoever," Joshua said.

"Yassir, reckon I kin use a good mount. My ole piebald has crunched him a buncha gravel under his hooves in these mountains," Zachariah mused, "but he likes to jest stand now a lot and remember those good ole days whilst he rests his eyes."

"You have a good mount now," Joshua said, winking.

Zack said, "Get any more 'sides Jeeter? Someone rode in here. Said they was a hell of a shootin' up to West-cliffe."

Strongheart said, "Yep. Ruddy Cheeks Carroll in West-cliffe."

"Hee, hee, ya shore don't waste no time," Zack said. "Who's next?"

"Oregon," Joshua said, "I have to courier a message there. Very important, but I will be back. I'm looking for an woman's antique wedding ring. Somebody in the gang has it."

"Wal, ya better rest up tanight and leave first light. Who ya courierin' fer?"

Strongheart said, "The U.S. Army. I work for the Pinkerton Agency."

"Yep, I knewd when I seen ya an sized ya up," Zack said, "ya wasn't some young half-breed tryin' to figger out which world ya fit in. Could see right off ya was a man ta ride the river with."

A cute befreckled teenaged girl came in and Zack said, "Hiya, missy. Now, Esther, why doncha run and tell yer ma to fix up our friend Mr. Strongheart here some vittles and a food pack fer his saddle tomorrah."

She smiled broadly and said, "Yes, sir, Mr. Banta."

The girl flashed a longing smile toward Joshua and ran to the hotel.

Joshua was feeling much stronger when he left Cotopaxi at first light and made his way westward toward Poncha Springs. He had some long hard riding ahead of him, but he would make the trip on his magnificent new mount, Gabriel, and load the big gelding when he could onto trains to make the long trek shorter. He hoped that the general had indeed gotten his orders to hold off and wait for the dispatch.

Strongheart saw some beautiful country with snowcaps in every direction when he got to Poncha Springs, and he set out west from there to take the winding road over the Continental Divide. There were plenty of pines, and he was at over eleven thousand feet when, on the rutted trail some had left, he finally got over the rough pass folks were calling Monarch.

He kept on, amazed, when he saw what was called the Black Canyon of the Gunnison, which was a very deep, beautiful sheer-cliffed gorge. He finally came to a part of the Colorado Territory where all the mountains were flat-topped mesas, and soon he headed into Utah Territory. He knew the Golden Spike had been driven in a few years earlier at Promontory Point, south of Salt Lake City. He knew once he got there, he could board a train and ride the rails most of the way to Oregon.

Strongheart was very sore and very tired when he finally got his horse settled in a car and hauled some water and hay in for him. He laid his saddle down on its horn and cantle in the corner, so the horse would not step on the saddle and break the wooden tree.

Joshua's wounds were itching now, which was a good sign. They were healing.

He was sound asleep in the nice Union Pacific Railroad car when the voice brought him out of the blackness. "Stand up Injun. No red nigger is riding in any car with me."

Strongheart opened his eyes, tilted his flat-brimmed black cowboy hat with the wide beaded headband, and looked up at a very large grizzled man, reeking of old sweat, cows, and other odors not quite so pleasant. He had a large wild beard with gray permeating its ruffled interior regions, struggling to break out into the light of day.

Joshua smiled. "Well, mister, only half of me is red. The other half is white and that part of me is trying to catch up on some much needed rest."

The bearded bully growled, "Oh, that's worse! A stinking half-bree—"

Joshua interrupted, laughing. "Mister, I walked by most of the people in this car, and you did, too. I think only one of us stinks, and they know it is not me."

There were chuckles throughout the car, and the behemoth's face got beet red. He grabbed Joshua's arm and yanked him up out of the bench seat. Joshua put his hand up in a halting gesture.

Smiling, he said, "Sir, there are ladies and children in this car. If you insist on us not riding in the car peaceably, we must go outside."

The man said, "Well, at least you know your place, Buck."

All watched in horror and a few women in curiosity as Joshua led the giant down the aisle, tipping his hat to each lady, smiling. They reached the door and Joshua grabbed the handle, held it open for the big man, and the bully stepped out onto the small platform. Joshua followed him out, raised his right foot, planted it on the monster's chest, and shoved, sending him screaming off into the prairie brush and dirt along the tracks. Joshua shook his head as he walked back in the door.

Inside, he said, "Was anybody traveling with that man?"

A small, wiry cowboy raised his hand, saying, "I was, mister."

Joshua said, "Your partner decided he did not want to ride in this car with me, so he is walking the rest of the way. Do you have a problem riding with me, or anybody else?"

Several men chuckled, and Joshua saw a beautiful blonde smiling broadly and making eyes at him. He nodded and tipped his hat.

The slim cowboy, now smiling, said, "Naw, sir. I thank you. I just had ta push a herd a cattle with him, and he rode everybody hard all day and night. Good riddance."

Joshua nodded and returned to his seat while all stared. He leaned back, pulled his hat over his eyes, and grinned to himself at his antics. Within a minute though, exhausted, he slipped off again.

A hand grasped his shoulder, and he came out of his seat like his tail was on fire; he heard his gun cocking before he even had his eyes focused, and it was pointing between the eyes of the blonde, who stared in shock, while several in the car screamed. As quickly as he'd cocked it, he uncocked and holstered the Colt.

Joshua heard a man saying to another, "Did you see that speed?"

"I'll say, pard."

Joshua said, "I am sorry, ma'am. After what happened I guess I was jumpy."

She said softly, "I should have known better. May I sit next to you?"

He let her in, and she sat down by the window.

Joshua whispered, "Ma'am, I'm afraid I . . ."

She interrupted, offering her hand. "I'm Scarlett Johnson."

He kissed the back of her hand and saw her breath catch.

"Name is Joshua, Scarlett, Joshua Strongheart."

She smiled and cooed, "I know I was being awfully forward just now, but after what happened, I just wanted you to know not everyone thinks like that man."

Joshua smiled. "I know, ma'am. There are idiots among the Lakota lodges, too."

"Lakota?"

"The Sioux," he said. Then he leaned back and added, "If you will forgive me, I have got to catch up on sleep."

"Please do," she whispered. "I just will feel much safer sitting next to you."

He smiled and pulled the hat down again.

Scarlett spent much of the next five hours glancing at Joshua Strongheart in deep slumber. She wished she could lay her head on that massive chest.

As tired as he was, Joshua thought about how pretty she was and the obvious curves that could not be hidden under her dress. Then he thought about the woman who visited him in the jail and his first reaction to her beauty. He remembered going fishing with Dan as a little boy and learning how to tease a fish with the bait until it would bite. Dan essentially forced the bait toward one fish, and Joshua watched it back away. He thought to himself now that relationships worked the same way. He grinned slightly, and the blonde saw this and wondered if he might be dreaming about her.

Unfortunately for her, when the train pulled in at the station in California, Joshua got off, doffing his hat and smiling as he went. That was all she would ever get of any kind of relationship with Joshua Strongheart. She was not the only woman who'd longed for him like that, but he usually did not even notice.

It took several days of hard riding, but eventually Joshua,

now feeling exhausted but much healthier, found himself
riding into a military stronghold in Oregon. He got plenty
of stares with his copper skin, long black hair, and black
flat-brimmed, round-capped hat with the wide beaded hatband, common headgear for Indians wearing white man's
garments. The Modocs had beaten up the army pretty well
in their labyrinth of volcanic caves and crevasses, and cost
the government much embarrassment.

Strongheart was there to see Major General Jefferson C.
Davis, who had been the commander of the Department of
Alaska for three or four years and was considered to be very
"hard-core" in his attitude and temperament. This started
in the Civil War. Davis originally enlisted as a lieutenant
in the artillery, but he proved to be tough and enthusias-
tic and was quickly promoted up through the ranks. Then,
after commanding the Indiana Twenty-second Infantry as
a colonel in 1861, he was promoted to brigadier general of
volunteers and commanded the Third Division Army of
the Southwest at the Battle of Pea Ridge.

Next, he commanded the Fourth Division Army of Mississippi at Corinth. He got very sick, actually going on
sick leave, but got out of his sickbed to rejoin his forces to
defend Cincinnati from Confederate attack.

In Louisville, Kentucky, at the Galt House, his career
almost ended when he got into an argument with a superior
officer, Major General Bull Nelson, who ended up slapping
Davis across the face with his gloves, so Jefferson Davis
yanked out his pistol and shot the general dead. He was
arrested and jailed.

Luckily, the Union Army needed general officers
with combat experience, and his good friend Major General Horatio Wright intervened on his behalf, and he was
released. He was later acquitted.

He ended up sometime later as the overall commander
of the Department of Alaska and then in 1873 found himself in Oregon in charge of the Modoc War fiasco. He
was tired of waiting for his dispatch and was about ready

to execute Captain Jack and his leaders, but he had been told the dispatch was on its way, being hand-delivered. His guards had been told to watch for a cavalry contingent arriving at any time.

Instead, they saw a lone half-breed Indian, Joshua Strongheart. Joshua continued to get stares, and one in particular came from Rowdy McAvoy. Born in Scotland, Rowdy was a brawler and a boozer, and also a sergeant, but he had been a sergeant and a private an equal number of times. He was frequently in the guardhouse for fighting and other drink-related activities. He could see by Joshua's demeanor, the way he sat his saddle, and his build, hard to disguise under his clothing, that he was indeed a warrior and not what Rowdy would consider a "dandy" in any way. He welcomed the challenge. Unlike many bullies, Rowdy usually did not see other men as bigger and stronger; he was almost always larger and more powerful than any man he faced.

Stepping out in front of Gabriel, he held his hand up. "Hold on there, laddie," he said. "We got mosta our redskins stuffed up in a cage. Where're ya thinkin' yer goin, Injun?"

Joshua got off his big pinto and stuck out his hand, which was ignored.

"Hello, Sergeant," Joshua said. "I need to speak to Major General Davis. I have a dispatch for him."

Rowdy put his hands on his hips exclaiming, "You? We have had redskins bushwhacking our officers, and ya think I am ta believe ya got a distpatch fer the general?"

Joshua said, "I have a dispatch for General Davis. Where is he?"

Rowdy chuckled and looked at the other men he was trying to show off for.

"I'll tell you what, Chief," Rowdy said with a smirk. "Ya gimme yer dispatch, an' I'll be givin' it to the general, lad."

Joshua was losing patience with this behemoth and saw

that Rowdy was trying to impress the men that were standing nearby. He started expecting trouble to come at any moment.

He said, "I can only give this to the general, Sergeant. I need to see him now, and when I do I will tell him you tried to stop me if you want to keep this up."

"Why, you uppity blanket nigger!" Rowdy roared. "Who in saint's peejamas do ya think ya are? Why, I oughta!"

With that, Rowdy, red-faced and veins bulging, stepped forward and threw a cantaloupe-sized fist at Strongheart's face. The young warrior was waiting for it. He held up one of Gabe's long leather reins with both hands straight out, about two feet apart, and quickly swung one arm up and one down, to wrap the reins around Rowdy's fist. Then Joshua simply stepped backwards, allowing Rowdy's momentum to carry him forward and crash face-first into the water trough behind the Pinkerton man. Rowdy went completely under, with water splashing out everywhere. The men who had been watching laughed heartily.

Joshua turned to them and said, "Where do I find the general?"

Two of them, still laughing, pointed at a long building at the end of the street, and he started walking that way, leading the big spotted horse. Glancing back, he saw the enraged and embarrassed giant being helped from the trough by two soldiers. One was chuckling, and Rowdy punched him full in the face, sending him sprawling.

It became obvious to Joshua that there were high anti-Indian feelings around there. Very respected men representing the U.S. government had trusted in the honor of Captain Jack, only to be gunned down while moving forward carrying a white flag of truce. That did not sit well with these soldiers at all, and Strongheart could certainly understand the anger at red men. As a man with red blood, he was angry because he took great pride in his red heritage and considered such an act cowardly and disgraceful in both the white and the red man's worlds.

It took another half hour of speaking to soldiers, with several giving him very cold stares, before he finally got into see Major General Jefferson Columbus Davis. Strongheart's eyes studied the man carefully.

He wore a double-breasted tunic and had a thick, scruffy beard and prominent mustache. His hair was parted on the right but was long and unkempt. His uniform fit and was clean, but it looked crumpled. Joshua realized Davis was a doer general, not one who sat in a chair all day and then changed trousers to make sure the pleats were well creased.

The general was appraising the tall Pinkerton agent as well. He could tell the man had been traveling hard for many miles. He read the dispatch from the War Department and the President's endorsement and smiled.

Then he simply said, "Glad I didn't hang the son of a buck yet."

Joshua chuckled.

Davis went on. "I will send a dispatch back by wire and military courier stating that I got your dispatch and will comply. No need to make you stick around for a trial. There is no doubt that Captain Jack and his owlhoots will hang, but I will keep Washington apprised until they do. The orders make sense."

Joshua said, "General, I think I will resupply at your store and head on back to Colorado Territory."

"I think it will become a state in a few years maybe. Heard some talk of it," the officer replied. "Did you have much trouble getting here with the dispatch?"

Strongheart chuckled to himself. "Nothing I couldn't handle, Sir. The Pinkertons deliver."

"Surprised they hired a redskin, no offense."

Joshua grinned. "None taken, General. They hired the white half of me. The red part tagged along."

The general chuckled and then guffawed.

He escorted Joshua to the door and warned, "I have some men with pretty strong sentiments right now. I hope you understand."

Strongheart said, "General, men being shot down and killed under a flag of truce is not something any red man of good upbringing condones. We have honor, too."

Davis stared at him and extended his hand, saying, "I believe you, Mr. Strongheart."

The general thought about having his first sergeant escort him to the store and away from the garrison, then he grinned, thinking that this man would handle whatever the general's men handed him.

Strongheart left the headquarters building and asked directions to the store. Unfortunately, Rowdy and his hangers-on were outside the place. Joshua thought he should probably just leave, but he was already headed directly toward the store when he spotted the troublemaker. He could not just turn tail.

Rowdy came forward, chest sticking out and chin jutting defiantly.

"Well, laddie," he said, "ya think ya bested me 'cause I had a slip. We're gonna change the dance."

Strongheart said, "Sergeant, you are playing the wrong tune. I am tired, just traveled halfway across the country to deliver one letter, and plan to buy my supplies and leave. So step aside kindly."

Rowdy stepped forward and tried to give Joshua a shove with both hands. Joshua's hands shot forward and up, the way Dan had taught him, with his palms forward. They went up in front of his chest in little semicircles from the inside out, and he grabbed Rowdy's fingers, while the circling movement naturally made both of Rowdy's hands turn palm up, with the fingers bent down towards the ground. Rowdy screamed in pain from the pressure on his wrists and knuckles, which all felt like they were ready to pop totally out of joint, and he stood up on his tiptoes it hurt so bad.

Joshua grinned, whispering, "You said you wanted to dance. How about a do-si-do?"

With that, he marched the crusty old brawler twenty feet to the watering trough he'd swum in before. Suddenly,

Strongheart swung him sideways, spinning on his own heels, and let go, laughing as the big sergeant crashed into the watering trough again, while all his men laughed. Joshua walked on to the store, while Major General Davis chuckled to himself, watching from his outer office window. Even the general laughed aloud as Rowdy came out of the trough cursing and yelling, slipped, and fell back into the water.

As he had hoped Strongheart bought his supplies then headed to the telegrapher to send a wire to Lucky. He wrote that he would check for any replies in Salt Lake City. He picked up medical supplies at the military store and treats for himself and his horse. On the train to Salt Lake City, he made up for more lost sleep.

6

Returning

The stars were as plentiful as the rocks all around them in the canyon north of Westcliffe, where they had ridden up the long mining trail that wound around Spread Eagle Peak. Here, they lay on a blanket by a crystal clear lake. Earlier in the day, they had eaten cutthroat trout from the glacial-fed lake where they had made love all afternoon. The moon shined brightly on the many patches of snow still clinging to the sides of avalanche chutes and the northern slopes high above the timberline all around them. The warmth of the fire bounced off the large rocks around them.

Joshua looked into the eyes of Annabelle and relished her nakedness and natural beauty in the unfiltered moonlight. He watched as the reflection of the flames from their campfire played across her voluptuous body.

She kissed him deeply and touched his face with her left hand. The antique wedding ring sparkled in the moonlight, and he looked at it.

His heart skipped a beat, and Joshua said, "Oh, Annabelle, your husband isn't even cold yet, and here I am making love to you."

Strongheart sat up suddenly, blinking his eyes, and saw

that he was on the train headed toward Salt Lake City. He was breathing heavily and his heart was pounding. Joshua felt guilty over fantasizing about the beautiful widow.

He stared out the window at the passing mountainscapes as he thought his problem out. Strongheart was very attracted to the woman, but she had recently been widowed by a man she obviously loved, and who had died nobly. She might feel herself falling in love with Joshua, but he could never trust her feelings to be total love. She might feel extreme loneliness, emptiness, and a need for comfort, and might mistake any or all of those things for love.

The handsome warrior had the practicality of his stepfather, Dan, along with the passion of his father, Claw Marks. He also remembered the example his father had set for him, even before he was born, by forsaking love because he knew it would not be right for Joshua's mother. Joshua wanted that kind of love, and sadly he knew he would probably end up riding away from Annabelle without ever fulfilling his fantasies.

In Salt Lake City, Joshua had to switch trains, and he decided to get a hotel room, a feather bed, and a good night of sleep. Earlier in the day, a man in his railcar had awakened him screaming and yelling when a hot ash from the engine came in the window and caught the sleeve of his jacket on fire. Incidents like that, plus the discomfort of sitting in a train seat with his long legs, did not make for restful sleep. Joshua decided he would get the room, take a nice hot bath, and have a large dinner, as well. At the same time, Gabriel would get a nice stall, bedding straw, fresh water, some oats, and some nice alfalfa/grass hay, as well as the company of other horses in a livery stable.

The first thing he did was send a telegraph to Lucky and tell the telegrapher where he was staying, so he could get ahold of him when the message reply came in.

Then he boarded his horse and even hired two boys to give Gabe a nice grooming, and he told the blacksmith to give the big horse new shoes. The man was large and Irishborn, with a twinkle in his eye and a giant shock of red hair and beard, and joke after joke. Strongheart saw by looking around the stable, however, that the man took great pride in his work.

After that, the warrior found a great café and was eating a giant slice of delicious apple pie when the telegrapher came in and sought him out. The Western Union man had garters on both sleeves and a visor band on his head. He was as skinny as a post, with a little tiny potbelly that hung over the waist of his homespun trousers. He wore spectacles and had a droopy gray mustache and bushy gray eyebrows.

Joshua grinned to himself when he looked at him. He would never grin openly at someone like that and make him feel uncomfortable or insecure. The only person he had ever made fun of was a heavyset boy in his class at school. The teacher mentioned it to Dan, and Josh got one of his hardest switchings ever, after having to cut the hickory stick himself.

He bade the man to sit down and looked at the telegraph while motioning for coffee for him.

It read: "STRONGHEART RETURN WESTCLIFFE AREA STOP NEW ASSIGNMENT STOP GOOD JOB STOP LUCKY."

Joshua tipped the man and wrote out a reply on a piece of paper from the café owner: "GOING THERE STOP HAVE A CHORE STOP NEED TIME TO HEAL BULLET WOUNDS STOP STRONGHEART."

The telegrapher read the message to insure he had it right and then departed. After a long, hot bath, Strongheart headed to bed and was just getting ready to turn in when there was a knock on his door. He drew his Colt.

"Who's there?"

"Western Union," came the meek reply.

Joshua knew the voice and holstered his pistol while opening the door.

The man came in, handing him the reply telegraph, and the tall warrior handed him a good tip. "Thank you. I sure have kept you busy today, sir."

The man waited while Joshua read the telegram: "I WILL STAY AT HOT SPRINGS HOTEL PAST THE PRISON IN CANON CITY STOP."

Joshua handed the man more money and said, "Thanks. Just acknowledge the wire."

"Yes, sir," the man said. "Sir, might I say you sure speak well for an Indian."

Joshua smiled, saying, "Maybe the white half of me speaks well. I bet the red half speaks well when I am in a Sioux village."

The little man looked perplexed for a second, then grinned with realization.

"Oh, you are half-white and half-Indian. I see," he said.

Joshua held the door for him and grinned. "Like a bowl of strawberries and cream. Thank you."

The man left and Joshua headed for the inviting feather bed.

After breakfast, the Pinkerton headed for the stable, feeling more rested than he had in days. His train would be boarding in less than an hour, and he was anxious to get going. On the trip to Canon City, he had to change trains several times, but he was appreciative of being able to ride the rails all the way there.

He worked on preparing a complete written report for Lucky while he rode and enjoyed the scenery. For miles he had vast expanses of prairie to the left side of the train and large forested mountains out the right side of the train. Joshua wished he was up in some of those mountains on his new horse. He thought about Gabriel and what a wonderful companion he had become already. It was strange that so many criminals had the very best horses around, but Joshua knew that was how outlaws were able to escape posses and ride the owlhoot trail, as Dan had always called it.

Grape Creek ran down from the Westcliffe area, a narrow rock-walled canyon, with cutthroat and brown trout filling the clear, bubbling waters, and much wildlife along the way. It was a wild, desolate channel and poured into the Arkansas River right where the 1,100-foot-tall vertical-walled

Grand Canyon of the Arkansas opened out at the west end
of Canon City. Just east of that junction were some hot
springs, and there was a hotel there. Many came to stay
there because they believed that the springs had healing
qualities.

Joshua rode the big spotted horse up to the front of
the hotel and ground reined him while he went inside.
He inquired about Lucky and learned he was shopping in
Canon City, so he went out, mounted up, and started east at
a slow trot. Joshua noticed that his horse loved to show off
and seemed to sense when people were watching him. He
flipped his white tail up over his rump, so the base of it was
arched and the long tail fell over one hip. He would toss
his mane from side to side and do more of a prance than a
slow trot, but in the saddle he provided the smoothest seat
Joshua had ever felt on any horse.

Strongheart spotted Lucky as he was entering a sad-
dlery and leather goods shop near Third and Main Streets.
He went in, and they spoke briefly, but it was a very hot
day, so they went outside. Both mounted up and rode a few
hundred yards downhill to the banks of the fast-flowing
Arkansas River, where they sat down in the shade of a number of towering cottonwoods and oak trees. It was shady all
along the Arkansas River.

Joshua handed Lucky his written reports. Lucky took
them and looked them over.

"You wrote zeese on zee train, *n'est ce pas*?"

Joshua said, "Yes. Why?"

Lucky grinned and held up one of the papers, saying,
"Two burn spots on zee paper from hot ash zat came in zee
window."

Joshua said, "One guy had his suit sleeve catch fire."

Lucky said, "I do not have to even read zeese, Joshua.
We have heard many stories about you and your courage.
You faced death, gunfighters, murderers, and all to keep
your pledge. Mr. Pinkerton is very happy with you now.
Your wounds?"

Joshua said, "They are healing."

The French-born detective said, "Well, we have a new assignment. We are making you an undercover agent for zees one. Eet ees a promotion. Congratulations."

"Thank you, Boss," Joshua replied with a smile and added, "I have to hunt down a wedding ring for the young widow on the stagecoach and return it, Lucky, before I do whatever my assignment is."

Lucky said, "Eet weel be to work in a mine near Westcliffe and learn about some crooked operation from zee inside out. Why must you get zee ring?"

"I gave my word," Joshua said with a shrug.

Lucky smiled. "You may think I do not understand, but I do. A man's word ees like hees shadow. Eet follows him everywhere he goes. Eet is easy to see when zee light is upon a man, and may disappear when things get dark, but weel come back when he sees the light."

Joshua's hand whipped for his gun, and Lucky jumped as a flash caught their eyes. Just like that, a magnificent bald eagle, with his white head and tail feathers flashing in the bright sun, swept down out of the sky, hit the water of the Arkansas, pulled out a large brown trout with both talons, and flew off out of sight. Joshua and Lucky gave each other a broad smile and shook their heads. With some shared events, words never have to be spoken.

They spoke for some time, and Lucky got the entire story of the holdup and the events that followed. His office already had numerous reports and eye-witness statements filed, plus everybody was talking about Joshua Strongheart and his exploits in saloons, mercantiles, and bawdy houses.

At Lucky's suggestion, Joshua rode with him and checked into the Hot Springs Hotel, and spent a lot of time in the hot springs during the next twenty-four hours, letting some of the soreness simply melt away.

After breakfast the next day, he rode off in search of a wedding ring. He learned from Lucky that Annabelle Ebert had purchased a home on Macon Avenue in Canon City, one block north of Main Street. The tall brave did not

want to see her until his promise was fulfilled. Little did he
know that while he had been riding up the long stage road
toward Cotopaxi and was now paralleling the Grand Canyon of the Arkansas, she was in her sitting room with a cup
of coffee staring up at Razorback Ridge, later called the
Hogback, which jutted up just west of Canon City, and was
again daydreaming about the tall, mysterious half-breed.

Joshua wondered what surprises awaited him on the
trail ahead.

7

A Pair of
Buzzards

Big Scars Cullen was nicknamed that for two reasons: one, he had big scars on his face and body, and two, he was just plain big. He was not just big. He was gargantuan. Some estimates had him at seven feet tall and more than 350 pounds. He had one scar that was jagged and very pronounced, causing puckering from the corner of his right eye, down past his mouth, and all the way to his neck.

Big Scars had grown up in the Seven Mountains area near Oil City, in Pennsylvania, in fact within just a few miles of the first oil well in the U.S., drilled by Colonel Edwin Drake in 1859; however, Big Scars grew up on a farm, in the broad valley between the Seven Mountains. Big Scars was full of wonder as a boy and loved the outdoors. He spent many days honing his stalking skills crawling up on woodchucks: groundhogs, which were plentiful throughout the valley. They covered the many farm fields, and he would spot them from the many patches of hardwoods between the plowed fields. His uncle, who was an exceptional hunter, taught him how to make a bow and arrows and told him that if he could sneak up on woodchucks and shoot them, especially with their telescopic eyesight, he would be able to sneak in close to any deer, elk, or moose.

As a boy, he was known as Butler Cullen, and the lad practiced stalking groundhogs all through the late winter, spring, summer, and early fall. Groundhogs fatten up in the months leading up to August and binge all through August, before going into hibernation in September. They then come out of hibernation usually the second week of February.

Butler could not wait until February each year, so he could pursue stalking them. They would come out of their burrows and sit on their hindquarters while surveying the large fields around them. He learned to find which way the wind was blowing, because they could smell him easily when upwind of him.

By the time he had gotten into his teens, his skills were being used on deer, which he found were easier to stalk than woodchucks. Butler was always challenging himself, and he started dreaming of living out in the Wild West.

When he was fifteen, he was taller than any of the men his family ever saw in the big valley. Walking through town one day, two toughs, both in their twenties, spotted him and chose him as a target, since he was so large but youthful and inexperienced.

When the fight started, Butler was very meek and tried talking them out of it, as he was so frightened. After all, smaller size or not, these were grown men. But as he tried to talk to them nicely, it seemed to fuel their desire to harass and dominate him. The fight was on, and as it continued, he kept getting more enraged. He learned that he was large enough and strong enough to toss these men around at will, even grabbing both at the same time. Many of their blows seemed to be merely a nuisance because he was so large and solid. As he gained the upper hand, Butler let years of taunting by older bullies affect his emotions, and his anger grew and grew. Soon, one of the men was down, and Butler sat astride his chest choking him for all he was worth. Even though the man's eyes rolled back in his head, it did not deter the fifteen-year-old. Butler kept choking him to death. The other man was scared and ran screaming down the street.

Butler's uncle helped him make his way all the way until they crossed the Clarion River, and the man told him how to work his way out west, going to blacksmiths, livery stables, and ranches or farms and doing what the uncle told him was "back work." He defined that as work that gave most men aching backs but that Butler could easily out-work them at because he was so strong and large. He gave him what money he had and a good pack, as well as a strict caution to never come back. Butler's family was older, a farming family, and his uncle was actually a good man, and his true mentor.

The problem was, as frightening as the fight was, Butler was thrilled by the damage he had been able to inflict. It was to him an awakening. He could not believe he had actually killed a man with his bare hands, while fighting another, too. Butler got into more fights over the next several years, and in Denver he killed another man, but this time he also used a piece of firewood to beat the unconscious man to a pulp. He fled north and west and ended up in the Wind River country. He fell in with some trappers and became a mountain man. By the time he was in his early twenties, he had filled out to enormous proportions and started his accumulation of scars.

The one on his face came from a large bull elk at the base of the majestic Grand Tetons in Wyoming Territory. Butler was so mad at himself that time because he committed an error that he had learned as a young boy never to do. He had shot a massive, sable-colored seven-by-seven bull and seen the bullet impact the beast's chest area right where the heart should be. The animal ran a short distance, not even forty yards, and went down unmoving in a large grove of aspens.

Instead of waiting to allow the animal a chance to die, and then tapping him on the eye with the tip of his rifle, Butler walked up to the bull, set his rifle down, and drew his skinning knife. As soon as the blade touched the bull near his genitalia, the bull exploded. The bullet had nicked a lung and both shoulders, lodging in one, but he was still full of adrenaline, and his right horn ripped upward, catching Cullen under the chin and tearing all the way up to his eye. Blood shot out everywhere as the big young mountain man screamed in pain. But he was so tough, he grabbed the rifle and put another round at the base of the fleeing animal's rib cage. It traveled through the lung and right into the heart. This time the bull went down for good.

Butler made it to a Cheyenne village, and even though he was a *wasicun*, they took him and nursed him back to health, even going back for his bull, which he shared. Because of their medical treatment for such wounds, however, he ended up with a hideous scar on his face.

Within the next couple of years, he gained a scar on his neck from an Assiniboine arrow after a little shooting scrap and a scar on his left hand from a Crow war club in another scrap. By the next mountain man rendezvous, everybody was calling him Big Scars Cullen.

Another fight with a much smaller young trapper, who was all enthusiasm with little muscle or size, made him sort of an outcast among his peers. The young trapper was small but popular because he had big courage and aspirations in his quest to be a man of the high lonesome. When Cullen beat the youngster half to death, other trappers started shunning him. When he got tired of being cold and sleeping on the ground, he ended up on the owlhoot trail.

Holding up stages and occasionally committing highwayman robberies seemed to assuage his need for the adrenaline to pump like it did when he got into fights. He noticed that he seemed to fight less when he kept busy robbing and intimidating people that way.

Now the big man was astride his seventeen-hands-tall chestnut Thoroughbred, riding toward a meeting with Harlance McMahon in Maverick Gulch, north of Cotopaxi. The gulch was narrow, and the intermittent stream that sprang up here and there in the sandy soil now made a serpentine rivulet running the length of it. Big Scars was riding toward the desolate Big Hole country, and he could see the distant bowl of high ridges that made up the large canyon, which was north of the Arkansas River, between Cotopaxi and Canon City, but much closer to the former. Small herds of mule deer moved ahead of him, where they would be sleeping under the low-hanging cedar and piñon branches along the steep, rocky, and sandy sides of the otherwise dry and very hot and unforgiving gulch.

He rounded a bend and came upon a large black bear eating the remains of a lightning-struck range cow. The bear stood on his hind legs, scenting him, and gave him a woof, then retreated off down the gulch at a lumbering gait. The green-dotted ridges along both sides of Maverick Gulch rose up steeply for about a five-hundred-foot rise in most places. From a large jumble of rocks near the top of the northern ridge came a bright flash of sunlight reflected from a mirror.

Big Scars looked up and saw Harlance, no small man himself, waving his arm. The ridges were steep but manageable, so he started a zigzag switchback course up the incline. Farther on he saw that the rocks flattened off and there was a natural fortress made of boulders. There was also a small, hidden spring-fed tank full of water and green grass growing around it. Harlance's horse was grazing there, and Big Scars stripped his saddle and gear off his horse and let him get reacquainted with Harlance's mouse-colored dun gelding.

He walked up and nodded, accepting a hot cup of coffee. "Nice perch ya got here, Harley."

Harlance grinned. "Thet ole half-blood son of a buck ain't put'n the sneaks on us heah. Look at the view."

Cullen looked up the gulch and could clearly see both sides and the entire gulch, and he had the same view in the other direction. They were only vulnerable from above. The jumble of rocks were positioned like a natural fortress, with some piñons above them to break up any possible smoke from their smokeless fire. The horses could graze and would stay in the area, and the group of boulders would not allow the light of a nighttime cooking fire, if kept small, to reach the ridgeline.

Harlance was proud of himself. He had found a great hiding place, the best.

He boasted, "Ah shot me thet steer comin' down the draw, 'cuz I figgered he'd smell and bring in critters to help cover our tracks. Never figgered on a bear. He covers 'em up purty good, Ah 'spect."

Harlance had a problem, though, covering all of his tracks. Joshua Strongheart had just ridden into Cotopaxi and was now drinking a cup of coffee with Zack Banta.

"Wal," Zachariah said, "reckon old Harlance McMahon's looking fer a place ta hibernate north a here."

"Really?" Joshua asked, knowing Zack liked to play mind games before letting all his news out.

"Reckon so. He bought a speck a fixin's, and he headed out Maverick Gulch," Zack said, as he pulled out a brown block of tobacco and bit off a chew.

He looked like a white-haired chipmunk to Joshua, who grinned to himself, seeing the large bulge in Zack's cheek, as he started chewing. He offered the plug to Joshua, who declined with a slight nod, still waiting patiently for more information to come out.

Zack poured Joshua another cup of hot coffee and went back to braiding some leather reins he had been working on. Joshua enjoyed the strong coffee and still waited.

"Cain't hardly believe how these ole boys on the owl-hoot trail stay alive," Zack mused.

Joshua decided to play Zack's game and finished his cup then responded, "Oh?"

Zack said, "Yep. Tell ya tomorrow over breakfast. 'Spect you'll wanna rest up next door in the hotel."

"If McMahon is around, I don't want him to get away."

Banta winked at him and grinned, "They'll keep."

"They?" Joshua said.

Zack said, "See ya at breakfast. I'll draw ya up a purty map tonight."

Joshua went out the door, laughing with a wave.

Zack waited until Joshua was halfway through with breakfast before he said, "Reason I said that was 'cause they don't cover their tracks good."

"How is that, Zack?" Joshua asked.

"Wal, he come in here fer supplies and tole me ta give a message to thet ole he-bear Big Scars Cullen," Zack replied. "I swear when he walks, he scratches the clouds with his hat, he is so durned tall."

Joshua grinned and waited. He had learned this game in the lodges of the Lakota.

Zack buttered a couple rolls and ate them, swallowed some coffee, then went on. "He was never smart enough ta ask me ta keep it quiet."

"What was the message?" Joshua queried, then had to wait through another cup of coffee.

Zack said, "The ole boy has him a hideout somewhere up Maverick Gulch. Reckon he tole me thet he wanted Big Scars ta jest ride up Maverick Gulch till Harlance give him sign."

Zack walked over to the table and sat down, pulling out a piece of paper. It was a very carefully handwritten map. Strongheart was impressed.

Pointing out the window, Zack said, "Now, ya cross the river and head right up thet trail. It ain't long fer ya get to Maverick Gulch. It'll be runnin' off to yer right, headin' east. It's gonna cut inta Long Gulch, right heah on the map. Long Gulch opens up and comes out on the river."

Joshua said, "I really appreciate this, Zack. You did a great job on this map."

"Reckon I figgered McMahon and Cullen are disposable. You ain't."

Joshua chuckled. "How is that, sir?"

Banta said, "Wal, yer gainfully employed. They don't like workin'. Yer a nice young feller. They ride the owlhoot trail. You might bring purty young gals around I kin look at. Them two attract vermin. Ain't no big reckonin' on my part."

The two spent the next half hour with Zachariah telling

Joshua all about the terrain, and Joshua especially wanted
to know what the two parallel gulches were like.

Strongheart set out for Maverick Gulch while it was still
early morning. He started out up the gulch to get a feel for
it, but Harlance's remark about spotting and signaling Big
Scars told him that he was up high and commanded a good
view. That remark also told Joshua that the outlaw was very
secure about his hiding place. Zack Banta had told him that
there were several rock outcroppings up high on the northern side of the ridge bordering the gulch, and Joshua felt
that it was more than likely Harlance's hiding place would
be closer to Long Gulch.

It was a simple trick, used by many tribes.

Harlance had paid a bottle of whiskey and ten dollars
to Charlie the Ute, a kind of worthless Ute Indian who had
emigrated all the way from the Towaoc area in what would
become the Four Corners and never fit in with his own people or whites. Charlie looked twenty years older than he
actually was and spent most of his time trying to earn free
drinks or drinking money.

Charlie the Ute made himself a camp atop the high red
cliff overlooking Cotopaxi and waited for two days. When
Joshua Strongheart rode down the road toward the new
settlement, Charlie set light to the piñon fire he had built
inside a box made of flat rocks. When the fire was going
well, he placed several branches of cedar greens on it and
smoke started pouring out. He placed a blanket over it and
let the smoke build up, then released a large cloud, then
did it again, and a third time. His directions were to do it
again in three segments of two puffs if and when Joshua
left Cotopaxi and headed north, in the direction of the head
of Maverick Gulch. If he rode any other direction, Charlie
the Ute was to send up single puffs.

It was morning when Harlance took a sip of coffee and
looked to the southwest, seeing three sets of two smokes
coming from Charlie's ridgeline.

He sat down on a log across from Cullen, saying, "Thet
Strongheart is on his way mebbe this direction."

"How do you know that?" Big Scars asked.

Harlance pointed at the smoke signals and chuckled.

Big Scars said, "You have your own tribe of redskins now?"

Harlance laughed. "Naw, jest need ya one blanket niggah to send ya a smoke. Done let me know thet breed showed up yesterday. He set out north from the store jest a little bit ago. He turns inta Maverick, we'll see a long column a smoke. He comes this way, we'll see 'im, and he cain't escape, no way. He's dead."

Joshua headed into Maverick Gulch with a long column of smoke reaching up into the morning sky far above and behind him. Charlie the Ute was amazed at how much this half-breed had stopped to fix his stirrups the past two days. He wondered if the man could even ride bareback like most red brothers. He was not sure of his tribe, but knew this warrior was not Ute. He thought he could be Cheyenne. Charlie did not realize that Strongheart, though half-white, had spent plenty of days in the villages of his father's people, and spotting Charlie's first signals had been nothing. Joshua would get off his horse, tighten the cinch strap, and try to figure out the simple message. When he saw the first smoke, he knew someone was signaling that he was arriving. He reasoned another would tell when he left and maybe more would indicate direction. So Joshua knew that Harlance was aware he was headed into Maverick Gulch. That was also part of Strongheart's plan. His eyes searched the left side of the gulch for the long crease and rocks he needed. The farther he went down the gulch, the greater his chance of being spotted by Harlance and Big Scars.

An hour passed and Harlance had his horse saddled.

Big Scars said, "What are you doing, Harley?"

Harlance said, "When he comes up the gulch, we're gonna fill 'im full of holes. Then I am gonna charge down and put six more in his durn haid. He's one tough hombre, an' we gotta be careful."

Big Scars said fairly calmly, "There he is."

Harlance looked and grabbed his carbine. Cullen grabbed

his Sharps buffalo gun, which probably was why he was so calm. With that, even shooting right then was a simple shot and could blow Joshua out of the saddle. Strongarm's eyes were on the ground, apparently sweeping the ground in front of him, his rifle across the swell behind the saddle horn and resting on his upper thighs, as Gabriel walked slowly down the trail at the bottom of the gulch.

Big Scars put his sights on the front brim of the hat, knowing his shot would take the back of Strongheart's head off. Harlance aimed at the center of his chest.

He whispered, "When his paint gets even with that dead tree, blow him outta thet saddle."

Cullen replied, "The side of the horse or the front of him?"

Harlance said, "The front. Soon as he's even, start the ball."

The horse kept approaching and was now just a few feet away. Two more steps. One more.

They both fired and hit Joshua simultaneously in the middle of the head and center mass. His lifeless body flew backwards out of the saddle and beyond the horse. Harlance ran for his own horse and leapt into the saddle.

"Stay here, whiles Ah finish him off!" he commanded, certain he would act heroic in this way, although he knew Strongheart was already very dead.

As he inched along the caprock above Big Scars Cullen, Joshua was upset that Harlance had taken off after Gabriel. Joshua wore moccasins, a Sioux breechcloth, and his gun rig and knife. His face and body were streaked in mud to better camouflage him.

Cullen turned around in time to see Joshua's body hurtling at him from the rock above, both heels striking him simultaneously, one in the jaw and the other in his massive chest. He flew backwards and landed hard on a flat rock, on his back and hitting the back of his head. The wind left him in a rush and the sky started swirling around. He shook his head and came to his feet with a roar.

Down below Gabriel trotted off up the gulch, and Harlance drew his pistol, approaching what he thought was the body of Joshua Strongheart. Then he saw that it was a dummy made of Joshua's clothes filled with leaves and cedar needles, and he cursed to himself.

It was then that he looked back up the ridge and saw the gargantuan Big Scars Cullen rush forward, arms outstretched. Strongheart grabbed Cullen's right sleeve with both hands, then stepped back, dropping to his left knee and pulling, and the big man's weight sent him flying past the warrior and face-first into a large boulder. He was clearly staggered, his face pulped and bleeding.

Harlance McMahon had never seen and had never dreamed he would see any man manhandle the monstrous Big Scars Cullen. He was too big, too strong, too grizzly bear mean.

He needed to see no more. Harlance put his spurs to his gelding and ran back up the gulch like his tail was on fire. The heck with his grub, his bedroll, slicker, and everything. This man had already killed his brother and others in his gang, after they thought they had shot him in the head. Harlance still wanted to pay him back for killing Jeeter, but he wanted to pick the battlefield. He wanted to pick the strategy for the fight, and he wanted to make sure he would win. For now, he would not even stop in Cotopaxi, but just ride on roads where his tracks would mix in with others, and he would not slow down for a long while.

In the meantime, Joshua Strongheart did indeed have a fight with a grizzly bear on his hands. Cullen was now growling and roaring with rage, and he beat his barrel chest with both hands. He swung a vicious right and Strongheart blocked it with both arms, yet it rammed his own arms into his face, bloodying his nose and swelling his left eye and sending him flying backwards about ten feet.

Cullen then came roaring in like a charging bull, and Strongheart reached out, grabbed both arms, and stuck his right foot in the giant's belly, then went backwards with the momentum and shoved as hard as he could, straightening the leg out. With a scream, Cullen sailed over Joshua's head, then over a small drop, landed on his back down below, and rolled twenty more feet down the ridge and up into a large cactus. Hundreds of needles penetrated his skin, and he screamed in pain, squirming to get away from the giant spiny monster.

As he came to his feet, weaving, and bleeding like a pig at a barbecue, his left hand grabbed his cross-draw holster, and his right hand closed on the handle of his .44. His eyes looked up to see flame shooting from Strongheart's gun, once, twice, and three times, as he felt the bullets slam into his chest. His knees failed him, and he saw the ground rushing at his face, then slamming into it. He rolled over on his back, moaning. Joshua walked forward, ejecting the three shells and thumbing three fresh bullets into his cylinder.

He saw the life slowly draining out of the behemoth and was shocked to see that tears filled the big man's eyes.

Cullen said, "Ya killed me, Strongheart, and one of your bullets broke my back. I can't feel anything. I deserve this. I have been a bully my whole life. You whupped me with your hands and plugged me with your shooter. Guess I deserve this. Wish I could do it all over."

"You chose the outlaw trail, Cullen. Nobody to blame but yourself," Joshua replied.

"Am I dying for sure?"

"Yes," Strongheart said honestly and bluntly. "You won't see tonight's sunset for sure."

Cullen said, "You are a good man. Can I ask a favor?"

"What?"

Big Scars said, "See that my horse gets a good home. You can sell him, but make sure he will get treated right. Also, please don't leave me for the bears and coyotes and buzzards. Please give me a grave and say some words over me."

Strongheart wanted to pursue Harlance, but he nodded and said, "I will. Want some water?"

"Yep."

Joshua said, "I am after an antique wedding ring that belonged to that pretty woman on the stage. I said I would get it back."

Big Scars started chuckling and coughed with a little blood coming up.

"That's why you've been chasing us and killing us? Over a ring?" Cullen asked.

Joshua said, "Reckon so."

Cullen tried to shake his head, but it would not move. He started to panic but stopped himself. He had been a miserable failure, he thought, but by God he would die a man.

"You know what, Injun?" he said.

"Strongheart, Joshua Strongheart is the name."

"Strongheart," Big Scars replied. "That suits you. Good name. At least I got killed over an important principle. That gives me some comfort. Harlance has the ring. He got it from Jeeter."

His gaze froze and his chest stopped rising up and down. Big Scars Cullen died just like that.

Joshua whistled, and Gabe soon appeared and came trotting up the hill, dodging rocks like a dancer negotiating a stage. His reins had been tied around the saddle horn, so neither would drop down and cause a stumble. He whinnied when he smelled death and blood, and Big Scars's giant horse whinnied back from the tank and little meadow.

Strongheart gave his horse some loving and removed his saddle and bridle, saying, "Go join your new sidekick and get some grass. I have a job ahead of me."

He dragged the body down the ridge, until he came to a cut-bank spot. Using a small flat rock, he tried to scrape away some of the rocky soil, and then dragged the body up against the cut bank. Next, he got above it and stomped dirt down on top of it. Then Joshua started rolling large rocks down and made a pile over the expedient grave. He laid the man's holster across the head of the grave and stood up, sides heaving with exertion, bowed his head, and said words over Big Scars, the man that two hours before was trying his best to kill him.

Joshua made his way down to the scarecrow and retrieved his clothes, then climbed back up to the camp of the outlaws. He walked over, stripped off his holster, moccasins, and breechcloth, and went straightaway into the tank. The water was cold and felt wonderful. He then sun-dried, dressed in his clothes, after examining the bullet hole in his wide hat brim, and made lunch. Joshua then lay down and took a nap.

When the warrior awakened a half hour later, his eye was almost completely swollen shut and very discolored. He felt very refreshed though.

When he walked into Zachariah Banta's store near sunset, the old man looked up, and seeing the swollen black eye, and the large bullet hole through Strongheart's hat brim and two more through his shirt, he just chuckled.

"Couldn't jest plug old Big Scars, could ya? He was too big and mean," the old man said between chuckles. "Ya jest had ta test yerself. Too much of a challenge."

Joshua just grinned and shook his head.

"Come on," Zack said, as he locked his store and walked out with the Pinkerton.

"What ya gonna do with thet big boy? Sell him ta Paul Bunyon?" Zack said, chuckling at his own joke.

"Who is that?" Joshua said as they walked into the hotel and restaurant and sat down at a table.

Zack said, "Aw, an old legend among timberjacks. Giant ole lumberjack an' he had a big blue ox named Babe."

"Is it in a book?" Joshua asked.

"Nope, not yet," Zack mused, "but someone'll write it up one a these years. Too big a legend. Been around a long time." He paused and took a sip of water, then said, "Harlance must a had an appointment. He shore moved through here earlier like someone had lit his horse's tail on fire."

Strongheart said, "Bet his banker wanted to talk to him about a mortgage."

Zack started chuckling even more.

With Zack's insistence, Strongheart tied a raw steak over his eye and wore it there while he ate. They both had a hearty dinner of wild turkey and vegetables, and followed it with fresh blueberry cobbler and coffee.

Joshua had eliminated six of the members of the holdup crew. Now he had three more outlaws to pursue if need be to recover the ring from Harlance. Meanwhile, miles to the south and still in the saddle, Harlance McMahon had other plans.

8

The Chase

In southern Colorado at the time there had been some upheaval about slavery. There were many Hispanic settlers and ranchers in the area, and many of them owned slaves, in full contradiction of the Civil Rights Act of 1866. Most of these slaves were either women or children and a great many of those slave-owners held captured Utes, Navajos, and even a few Apaches and southern Cheyenne. These captives were rounded up in raids, sometimes kidnapped, and given in exchange for money owed Spanish landholders. Some tribal elders or parents would actually allow these Spanish colonials to purchase captives, in order to keep the women and children from being killed if attack seemed inescapable.

Chief Ouray, the most famous of the Utes, was actually hired by the U.S. government as an official interpreter in 1864, and under his watch many deals were made for hapless Ute innocents.

Once enmeshed in these Hispanic ranching families, however, the slaves were often assimilated into the family, and in many cases, the wealthy ranchero fathered many children with Native American women or some captured

Mexican women. Although they were slaves, for many it actually turned out to be a very good situation.

Less than a decade before Joshua Strongheart showed up in the Wet Mountain Valley, several courts found Spanish- and Mexican-born landowners in southern Colorado guilty of violations of the Civil Rights Act of 1866. To that end, they lost slaves who had in effect become members of their household in many cases. A few of these cast-off American Indians, primarily from the Ute and Navajo nations, originally formed into little bands and caused some trouble for the population of southern Colorado. Most of them spoke Spanish, English, and their native languages.

Harlance had used a couple of these gangs previously on big holdup jobs and decided now he would hire one of the gangs to help him set up somewhere to bushwhack Joshua Strongheart when he came for him.

Jeeter was the real aggressor of the two brothers, but Harlance was the brains. It did not take a college professor to see that Joshua Strongheart had fought members of the gang that ambushed him and had eliminated six out of nine members so far, including one of the gang's two leaders. He also noted that the man did this with numerous wounds, as well. In short, Harlance was no dummy and Strongheart scared him. In fact, thinking about the half-blooded Pinkerton being on his trail sent chills down his spine.

Harlance thought Strongheart was simply executing the gang members one by one for revenge. He did not know that the man was seeking the ring, which really meant very little to McMahon, but a great deal to one of his many former victims. He had no clue that he might not have to worry about Strongheart again if he simply left the ring with Zachariah Banta at the Cotopaxi store or dropped it off in Westcliffe. He also had no idea that Strongheart was a Pinkerton agent. He had read the dispatch for General Davis, but it meant little to him, and nothing in that money belt really identified Joshua as a Pinkerton. Harlance only knew him as a powerful, wily fighter who seemed to be half-red and half-white and totally schooled in the warrior skills of both societies.

Harlance knew of a gang south of Westcliffe, down toward La Veta, and he would recruit them. As far as he remembered, there were six in the gang, so he would be recruiting as many as he had already lost. In the meantime, he would try to locate Gorilla and Percy Moss on the pretense of warning them. In reality, he wanted to recruit them for his ambush.

What he did not know, however, was that Joshua Strongheart already figured contacting them would be his next move. He and Zack had already talked over possibles as far as hideouts and whereabouts of the father-and-son hellions.

Joshua was now astride the saddle of Gabriel, but first he would take a quick side trip. As he left Cotopaxi, heading south toward Westcliffe, he was quickly climbing on an easy, winding road with high rocky ridges rising to his left and right, but more to his right. Before him he could see the top half of Spread Eagle Peak, Wulsten Baldy, and a couple more peaks in the more northern end of the Wet Mountain Valley. They loomed before him like giants rising up out of the land. Cloud banks on the western San Luis Valley side of the mountains pushed up against them, straining against the granite sentinels as if wanting to break over their fourteen-thousand-foot peaks and rush out east across the valley, over the shorter Greenhorns and across the great American prairies. However, the giant bodyguards of the plains and prairie stood unmoving, despite the large presence of the stratocumulus invaders.

Zack had heard that the Mosses were in the San Luis Valley, having crossed over the Big Range and passed through the Great Sand Dunes. He also told Joshua that he guessed they could possibly have said that to throw people off and might be hiding near Marble Mountain, which held the mysterious Caverna Del Oro, the "Cavern of Gold."

Joshua was fascinated when he heard the story about the mysterious place from the grizzled ole shopkeeper.

In 1541, long before any white men were around, three Spanish monks from the Coronado Expedition came to the area accompanied by some Utes. They found a large labyrinth of caves with an entrance at about eleven thousand feet of elevation and a higher entrance at twelve thousand feet of elevation on the thirteen-thousand-foot Marble Mountain. However, the Indians felt the caves were inhabited by demon spirits, so they killed two of the monks. Instead of arguing about the demons, the third monk, named De La Cruz, convinced the Indians that he was able to control the demons, and they would do no harm to the Indians unless they did not treat him right.

The expedition then started enthusiastically mining the gold out, using the Indians, who were actually slaves captured or purchased along the way by the armed Spaniards accompanying the monks. They built a fort near the lower entrance, and apparently because the upper entrance, at twelve thousand feet, was so frequently under snow, they painted a very bright crimson cross above the upper entrance. They also supposedly built in two large wooden doors within five hundred feet of the lower entrance and locked a lot of gold behind them, with plans to travel by pack train back to Mexico with their treasure, and then return. Upon making this decision, the monks killed the Indians who had done all the mining for them.

Just four years before Joshua Strongheart met Zack Banta, Captain Elisha P. Horn had explored the Sangre de Cristos, mapping one of the massive fourteeners, and it was named for him, Horn Peak. A little to the south of Horn Peak was Marble Mountain, so Horn explored there also, and after hundreds of years of its whereabouts only being rumored, the Caverna del Oro was rediscovered by Horn and his explorers. They climbed up through very thick woods on a very rocky, boulder-strewn trail, wondering if they would ever reach timberline. From the bottom, they had only gone six and a half miles, but it seemed more like fifty to the weary explorers because of the rugged trail, thick forest, and rocks everywhere. Then suddenly, at around twelve thousand feet, they hit timberline, and around August they could finally get into the big treeless bowl and Horn spotted the faded crimson cross. Traveling to it, he found a skeleton garbed in Spanish armor, and an old Ute arrow protruded right through the armor. He started the careful exploration of the labyrinth of caves that, to this day, are so filled with noxious gasses, straight drops, and winding passageways, they should only be explored by very experienced and knowledgeable spelunkers with the right equipment.

Later, looking down below in the treed area, Horn found the ruins of the old fort that the Spanish explorers had built, and his men found many arrowheads, both around the old fort and around the upper cave entrance as well. In later years, equipment from the 1600s would be found, including pottery, a windlass and rope, a two-hundred-foot ladder, a skeleton chained to a cave wall, shovels, picks, and many other items.

Upon inspecting the area and based on the few research materials he was able to discover, Horn came to believe that the lower entrance to the mine, which was located in the aspen forests near the ruins of the old Spanish fort, had been completely entombed by a giant rockslide of thousands of massive boulders jarred loose from the giant limestone cliff. Decades later, the lower entrance would still be hidden away, but many experts in later years agreed with Captain Horn's assessment that the entrance was probably buried under a slide, whereas the hidden gold was supposed to be locked away behind two, still undisclosed large wooden doors within five hundred feet of that entrance.

It was fascinating to Joshua to learn the many stories about the area. The Caverna del Oro was the talk of the entire territory right then because of its rediscovery by Elisha Horn.

Strongheart was not headed south yet, in the direction of Horn Peak and Marble Mountain just beyond, because he had some unfinished business to attend to. Charlie the Ute had no clue that Harlance had already come through and headed out of the area, because after sending up his smoke to alert McMahon of the approaching half-breed the day before, he had settled down with a bottle.

Joshua turned to his right and headed toward the ridge looming before him. He could clearly see a switchback mining trail going right up the side of the ridge, and he jumped a creek, spooking some bedded mule deer, and headed toward it. He zigzigged back and forth up the trail, which was farther south down the ridge and out of Charlie's sight.

When he saw him depart south from Westcliffe on the stage road, Charlie the Ute had sent up a smoke signal indicating that Strongheart was leaving the area, but he could not see him now climbing the mining trail he had used himself. He was wondering whether he should stay to send up more smokes or go back down.

Charlie thought about fixing breakfast, but instead he decided he should warm up by the fire and finish the bottle he had started on the day before. He grinned to himself as he raised it toward his lips.

Boom! The bottle exploded and liquid drenched his lap and legs with whiskey and broken pieces of glass. Charlie snapped his head and looked into the eyes of the half-breed he had been watching, holding a Colt .45 in his right hand, with smoke coming from the barrel. Joshua spun the gun back once into the holster. Charlie the Ute, eyes wide, raised his hands.

Strongheart said, "Put your hands down."

The drunkard complied.

Joshua said, "Relax, I'm not going to shoot you, unless you do something stupid."

He looked hard at Charlie's face and tried to figure out how old he might be. He wondered if he might end up like Charlie if he allowed himself to continue drinking. He decided he would and made an even stronger vow to remember he could never touch alcohol again.

Strongheart said, "Why do you sell out your own people, Uncle?"

Charlie got a sad look on his face and said, "I let the fire in the water think for me. The *wasicun* gives me money. I buy whiskey."

Strongheart said, "What are you called?"

"Charlie the Ute."

"Okay, that is what you are called, but what is your name?" Strongheart asked.

"Nuni Kawa Goo Cheeu," he responded. "But I have used the white man's name since I left my tribe."

Strongheart did not ask why he left the tribe, but he did admonish Charlie with "You make the white man look at us like women not warriors, when you drink like this."

Charlie said, "I know. I am not worthy to be a Ute."

Stiff-lipped, Joshua said, "Then become worthy again. Who paid you to send smokes about me? The one called Harlance?"

"Yes, it was he," Charlie said.

Strongheart said, "Did he tell you where he would go?"

"He told me if I did good as a watchman, he might give me more money later."

Joshua said, "How do you speak to him?"

Charlie said, "He said to go to the saloon in Westcliffe. It is—"

Joshua interrupted. "I know where it is."

Charlie went on. "He said to tell the white man there I was in Westcliffe, and he would find me."

Strongheart reached in his jeans and pulled out a twenty-dollar gold coin and tossed it to him. Charlie's eyes lit up.

Joshua said, "Since you are in the white man's world, you need money. Get a job. That will get you where you want to go. Maybe you could work in a mine or become a cowboy, but work. Do not drink again. If you spend this money on whiskey, I will shoot you and not the bottle."

Charlie stood and threw his shoulders back. "I will not drink. I will work. What tribe are you?"

Joshua said, "I have two hearts. One is white. The other is Lakota."

"Do you want to make a smoke, Two Hearts?" Charlie the Ute asked.

Joshua said, "Not two hearts. I am called Strongheart. I must go."

Charlie said, "You will kill this McMahon?"

Strongheart said, "Yes."

Charlie said, "Good. He has the badger in his heart. You have the eagle in yours. I see this."

Joshua touched his hat brim, saying, "The eagle must fly."

He wheeled Gabriel around and rode away. He did not realize it, but Charlie the Ute would never drink again, and he would get a job farther east on the Arkansas, working at a mine. And from there, he would go on to other mines and gain experience and a reputation as a hard worker and proud man.

Strongheart had an outlaw and killer to find, and the search would take him back to Westcliffe for now. He rode down from the ridge and returned to the road. The muscular warrior started off toward Westcliffe with Gabe floating along at a fast trot. Strongheart saw several harems of elk, herds of deer and of pronghorns along the way. He could not get enough of the sweeping view of the long valley with all the fourteeners rising up into the sky to his right.

It was a clear day, and far to the south he could see the rising volcanic-borne mounts called the Spanish Peaks, dozens of miles to the south, near the border of New Mexico Territory. These unusual and beautiful peaks stood alone, side by side, apart from the Sangre de Cristo range. Very unusual mountains, they had volcanic-made spines running down them in several places called the Dikes, which looked like dinosaur tails. They were made from molten magma weathered away and exposed by erosion, and they varied in size from one foot wide to, in some places, up to fourteen miles long. Visitors traveling from the east could see the Spanish Peaks from more than one hundred miles away. Joshua saw an angry thundering storm over the top of fourteen-thousand-foot Kit Carson Peak, and he could see lightning strikes high up in the snowy area. Some seconds later, he heard the low, rumbling sound of distant thunder.

That was one of the things that made the frontier of the Old West unique. Folks who had lived in the eastern United States their whole lives were always amazed at the vast expanses of space out west and how many miles you could see. From the top of the mountains the vast amount of land visible was incredible.

More than one "dude" traveling out west would see lightning and angry storm clouds in the distance and be ready to head for cover until hearing some old-timer saying, "Don't worry none, son. This is Monday. Yer lookin' at Thursday's weather."

Strongheart rode into Westcliffe, which was actually more like turning onto the one main street, which ran east and west, and he immediately headed toward the saloon where he had already educated the barkeep. The bartender was not there. Instead, there was a very large man with graying hair, a well-trimmed salt-and-pepper beard, and a leathery tanned face.

Joshua was waiting for a negative greeting when the graybeard said, "You the half-breed that roughed up my bartender?"

Strongheart was ready to draw quickly if need be, and he replied calmly, "He needed it."

The man stuck out his hand and grinned broadly. "I agree. I kicked his sorry tail out of here. Young man, my sister married a handsome young Comanche lad down Texas way, and a better brother-in-law or a more honorable one, I could never ask for. We are not all prejudiced like that polecat. My name is Jerome J. Guy, and I own this establishment. I apologize for your previous experience, but it shall not be repeated."

The Pinkerton grinned and stuck out his hand. "My name is Joshua Strongheart, sir."

Jerome said, "I live in Colorado Springs and have done well with investments. Mines are operating around here, and I think there will be some big strikes eventually. It's inevitable. I wanted to own real estate here when that occurs. Are you part Ute, Kiowa?"

Joshua said, "I am half Lakota. White men call us the Sioux. My father was a great warrior. My mother was white and married another great warrior, a lawman, who raised me as a father."

"Best of both worlds, young man," Jerome said. "I understand that you have been tracking down the members of the McMahon brothers gang one by one."

Joshua said, "They shot me up a little when they held up the stage on Copper Gulch Stage Road, and they stole an antique wedding ring that belonged to a widow from Canon City. It was all she had to remember her husband. I told her I would get her ring back."

"You, sir, are a man of substance," Jerome replied. "Do you need money to help your quest?"

Joshua laughed, "No, sir, thank you. I work. I have a job."

Jerome said, "May I inquire where you are employed?"

Joshua said, "Confidentially?"

Guy responded, "Of course."

Strongheart proudly said, "I am a Pinkerton agent."

"Oh, that is indeed fortuitous for the young lady that she met a man of your background," Jerome said.

He poured a beer, set it in front of Joshua, and went on. "If ever I have met a man who has impressed me as being able to keep his oath in such a manner, that man would be you, Mr. Strongheart."

"Joshua, please." Joshua pushed the beer back across the bar, saying, "Thank you, but you seem to be a man who lives in modern times. Don't drink, but I would love an iced tea if you have any iced tea."

"Sweet Mary!" exclaimed Jerome "I have found another iced tea lover. I enjoy it very much with sugar. I have tried to introduce it to others, especially on hot days, but everybody wants beer or whiskey."

He opened his icebox, produced two frosted beer mugs, and put chips of ice in each. He then pulled out a pitcher and poured iced tea into the mugs, adding sugar to his.

"Sugar?"

"No, thank you, sir," Strongheart said, lifting the mug in toast and then pouring the cold liquid down his throat.

All he could think about when he first came in was how good a cold beer would taste after a hot day of traveling, but he genuinely enjoyed iced tea and one swallow rid him of any beer temptation.

"I have seen Harlance McMahon, Big Scars Cullen, who looks more like a grizzly than a man, and I think I know what the Mosses look like. I heard they went to the San Luis Valley," Jerome added. "Do not let that Cullen get his hands on you. Biggest strongest man I ever saw."

Now on his second glass of tea, Joshua said, "I killed him yesterday."

"My word!" Jerome said. "He was deadly with a gun or a knife, too. How did you kill him?"

Strongheart said, "We had a difficulty. He did not like pain, so he grabbed iron and made me shoot him."

"I saw the marks on you and wondered, but you got into a scrap with Big Scars Cullen and survived, and then a shoot-out? Incredible!" Jerome said, genuinely impressed, "I shall always be on your side in any disagreement," and he ended that with a chuckle.

Strongheart promised to stop in when he was again in the Westcliffe area, and Jerome promised to try to get him information on any of the remaining three outlaws. After another mug of iced tea, and trail directions, Joshua decided to camp out near the trail leading to Music Pass. He would cross over into the Great Sand Dunes and try to locate the Moss outlaws, figuring that Harlance would want to enlist their aid.

He mounted up on Gabriel, and the spotted horse set out due west, toward the mountains looming a few miles before him.

What he did not know was that Harlance had ridden in the other direction, down the mountain due east from West-cliffe, on the winding wagon road that would take him all the way out into the prairie, to Pueblo on the Arkansas River.

But instead of heading into Pueblo, when Harlance got down off the winding road at the edge of the plains, he turned left, or north, toward Florence, a small community also on the Arkansas River, near Canon City. The second oil well in the United States had been discovered in Florence eleven years earlier, and many oil wells were producing at the time, making the berg start to come into its own as an oil refinery location. Harlance rode toward Florence, to the all-but-abandoned old trading community of Hardscrabble. At the base of the Greenhorn Mountains and looking out upon the prairie, Hardscrabble had been a trading post and fortress which was mainly visited by the many traders and trappers who ventured into the area from the mountains to the west, north, and south. Utes and Arapahos had many fights with each other over this area, as well. Hardscrabble was established in the 1830s originally as a trading post and later as a small settlement created by trader Maurice Leduc.

Now it was all but abandoned and off the beaten path. Backed up against the Greenhorns, it had numerous trails behind it, in the smaller range, that would head back uphill toward the Wet Mountain Valley, where Westcliffe was centered, or eventually get anybody fleeing to the road from Canon City to Westcliffe, called Oak Creek Grade.

Harlance had run into Mario Alkala, who had a gang of five other former slaves—three Utes, one Navajo, and two Arapahos—who were now banded together to make money any way they could but not become slaves ever again. They had one moral code and it was encompassed in one word—survival—and to its end they would be as ruthless as need be.

Hard Moccasins was a Jicarillo Apache who had scouted for the U.S. Army out of Fort Union, just south of the border, in New Mexico Territory, and was heading back after visiting the home of his now-retired commanding officer who lived near Denver. The retired officer had showered Hard Moccasins with gifts, as the scout had saved his life several times. These included a pack horse, panniers, and pack saddle to carry all the gifts on. He had resupplied in Florence, with plans to camp along the Front Range that night, and was riding near Hardscrabble, on the Hardscrabble Road running south out of Florence. The gang surrounded him, shot him out of the saddle, and divided up all his goods and food. They dragged his body to an arroyo and kicked the dirt of a cut bank over the body to get it out of sight until the next flash flood.

In Florence, they had also broken into the house of an oil man with money and stolen some jewelry, cash, and valuables. To that point in time, those two incidents were the extent of their criminal activities.

Right now, they were getting money from Harlance with promises of more later, and they were being briefed on Joshua Strongheart. They all had seen Big Scars Cullen and could not forget him, as he was so large and tall. Just looking at him, anybody could tell that he was tougher than a bull buffalo with a toothache. That Strongheart had killed him gave each young man pause for thought.

In the meantime, Joshua was heading at a rapid pace along the western edge of the Wet Mountain Valley, just below the foothills. It had been a long day and the sun was almost blocked out by the mountains that stuck up so high in the sky over his right shoulder. He went into the trees and rode until he found a small rushing stream and then rode around until he found a group of rocks that would hide his fire and reflect it as well, plus two overhanging slabs he and Gabe could get under in case a storm blew in during the night. If there was one lesson Strongheart had learned long before, it was that the Rocky Mountains were one of God's most majestic and beautiful creations, but they could also turn into one of His deadliest in minutes.

Many cowboys out in the mountains would find the first nice spot and curl up for the night without a thought. Strongheart had been taught too well to be a survivor, plus he knew he was after killers who knew he was coming for them. His campsite for the night was always picked out for its strategic significance, and he usually stopped early enough before sunset so he could set up a comfortable camp that was also hidden away from the elements and potential enemies. The cascading stream afforded not only fresh water for him and his horse, but sound as well to cover the clanging of a pan, a dropped piece of firewood, or the cracking of a branch. He'd also made sure there was good graze for Gabriel, as horses were grazing animals who needed that to feel normal.

The rocks, as mentioned, provided good shelter in case of storm, and his camp was situated a little above the stream on a bench to deter washing away in case of flash flood. His horse would let him know if anyone approached much better than any watchdog could. Horses' eyes, ears, and nose were much larger and more powerful than any dogs', so they could smell, hear, and see people or animals long before a dog could detect them. A simple whinny, with the nostrils flaring in and out and the neck strained forward and ears sticking toward whatever or whoever was approaching, would let Joshua know long before anyone or anything came into view.

Peering through the thick veil of trees, Joshua could see out into the valley below, and see anybody approaching, and he could also easily see Westcliffe and the activity in the rest of the valley. After placing a circle of dry rocks around a campfire hole he'd scooped out, he gathered firewood and kindling so he would have a fire and plenty of extra wood to use until his departure at first light. One of the most important things he made sure of was that there was a low, wide boulder between the campfire and the Wet Mountain Valley below, so nobody could see his fire.

Next, he broke evergreen branches and piled them on top of one another near the fire but not too close. He put on his small coffeepot and frying pan. Joshua had shot two rabbits while he was in the saddle and then gutted them after he had entered the trees. Now he walked over to the stream and knelt down to cut the head and paws off of each one with his knife. Next, he grabbed the skin on the belly next to where he had slit them open to gut them, stuck his fingers under the edges, and pulled hard, tearing the skin away from the flesh. Joshua tossed the bloody, furry hides into the stream and let them be carried downhill to where predators would smell them but not come near his camp. He then checked each carcass carefully for any signs of disease. He rinsed them and bushed away unwanted tissue with his fingers in the cold stream.

Next, after cutting a long green stick and two fairly thick green branches, he returned to his campfire. He set the cleaned carcasses on one of the evergreen boughs and, using his razor-sharp knife, quickly whittled into forked sticks the two thick green branches he'd brought from the stream. He then sharpened the other ends, and sharpened both ends of the long stick from the stream. Next, he quickly shaved all the bark off of each green branch and put his knife away. He stuck the pointed end of the forked sticks into the ground, then ran the long one through the body of each rabbit and set it on the forks. All he needed to do now was simply keep turning the long stick over the fire while the rabbits slowly cooked. While they smoked and sizzled over the fire, he walked out and found some sage, cleaned it in the brook, and brought it back. He'd also had found some mint, so he cleaned those leaves, too. He tore the sage into tiny pieces and sprinkled some on the rabbits. Joshua then cut off a slice of bacon and dropped it into the frying pan, where it started sizzling.

Two miles north, the wind coming from the south ruffled the silver-tipped hairs on the back of the large cinnamon-colored boar grizzly bear. He had fed on a lightning-struck heifer out beyond Westcliffe, but that was long gone and his hunger pangs were sharp. He had spent half the day tearing up a hillside to dig out a ground squirrel and had devoured it in minutes. As he walked up the long ridge-line, his nostrils grabbed the scents coming along the mountain breezes from the south. He smelled aspen, water, pine, the smell of a horse far off, and man. Instinctively, he almost left the area that carried that scent, but he was too hungry. There was the smell of bacon and cooking rabbit.

His large tongue came out and licked his lips. The mighty bruin stood on his hind legs and raised his head, over eight feet in the air now. His mouth hung open and his nostrils flared taking in the scents from Joshua's camp two miles distant.

Ursus horriblis, the mighty bear dropped to all fours and trotted forward along the face of the mountain, following the smell of cooking food on the wind. Although he hated and avoided man smells, since leaving his mother at the end of two years, this bear was motivated by two things: his stomach and the scent of sows in estrus.

Strongheart saw steam pouring out of his coffeepot and pulled the pot off the fire to set it on one of the flat-topped rocks. In the bacon grease he had dropped a couple biscuits he had packed in Westcliffe, and they were now heated up. He poured out a cup of coffee and started cutting chunks of meat off one of the rabbits. The warrior took a few bites and savored the flavor.

Gabe's head came up and his ears went forward, his eyes looking north along the side of the mountain. Joshua strained to glimpse anything through the trees but saw nothing. He crawled over to his saddle and withdrew his carbine from the scabbard, still eating rabbit and biscuits. Gabriel was now acting even more antsy, and Joshua knew the big horse was watching something with great interest.

Joshua spotted movement in the trees and within seconds saw the big bear coming down on him at a fast trot. He stood up and cocked the carbine. The bear's horrible eyesight had prevented him from recognizing the threat before. However, the sound of the gun being cocked did register with him, and he stopped abruptly. He stood on his hind legs and tested the wind. He smelled Joshua's soap, perspiration, and even the iced tea he had drunk, the coffee, rabbit, bacon, and biscuits. Joshua yelled at him, and the bear dropped to the ground, popping his teeth and growling.

Strongheart did not want to shoot this bear, especially with a carbine. His shots would have to be perfect, but he also had no need to take a bear right now. He was after even more dangerous predators.

He grabbed a biscuit, rubbed it in the grease, and tossed it at the bear. The bear ran forward, curious, and sniffed it, then grabbed the biscuit and swallowed it. He took two steps forward and sniffed the ground where the biscuit had hit.

Strongheart's shot hit the dirt just inches in front of the monster's highly sensitive nose. Dirt sprayed in the bear's eyes and went up his nostrils. The sound of the shot scared him, and with a roar, he swapped ends and took off at a race-horse-fast run away from the scents on the breeze.

Joshua and Gabe watched until long after the bear had disappeared into the forest. The hungry intruder did not slow down for miles, and his instincts as a survivor took priority over his hunger. He hated man scents, and bad things happened when he got near them.

Strongheart kept his rifle handy but went over to the big spotted gelding and petted him and gave him some loving. He went back to his coffee and unloaded the carbine and cleaned it. Next, he would sharpen his knife. These were lessons drummed into his head by Dan when he was a boy that had never left him.

While Strongheart slept lightly in his Sangre de Cristo camp, Harlance McMahon sat around in an old adobe building with his new gang of mixed-tribe American Indians who spoke more Spanish than English and had nowhere else to go in life. The little gang had become their family, and each, while plugging away on the bottle passed around, was pledging to lay his life down for the others.

Of course, they had not been in a real stand-up gunfight against someone like Joshua Strongheart. There were so many stories in the West of 1873 about gunfighters, and they were all glamorous. Many boys were growing up dreaming about becoming gunfighters. The end of the Civil War eight years earlier had spawned the beginning of the "Gunfighter era" in the Old West, and many kids thought that being one of them would make a man a somebody. Gunfighters often had been lawmen until a page turned in their lives and suddenly they were on the other side of the law. Men fought usually from just a few feet away, guns often misfired, and more often than not the shooters missed their targets. However, then as now, when the youngsters thought about gunfights, it was always quick draw, standing off at a distance, and most did not know what happened when your target fired back at you first. Harlance knew these things about his current young charges, and he had a short period of time to try to cram shooting, quick draw, aiming, reloading, and bonding into a cohesive unit for them to learn.

He did not really know Strongheart's background, but he had seen what the man could endure, what he could do in the face of danger, and he knew the man had single-handedly wiped out the rest of his gang of men, who had been to war, fought in gun battles, and wore battle scars on their bodies. He had even tackled the seven-foot-tall, thick-as-a-tree Big Scars Cullen in a bare-handed battle and bested him, then shot him down. So Harlance didn't really need to know Joshua's background.

The crook also had no mistaken impressions about this young gang. He knew they were just going to slow Strongheart down a little, but this man would keep coming. Harlance would plan an ambush, set a trap, and leave the gang to fight his battle. He would be hell-bent for leather to rejoin the two remaining gang members that he might have a chance with, Gorilla Moss and his son Percival. Harlance had no doubt that Strongheart would kill some of these inexperienced young men, but his hope was for them to get some bullets into the man, as well. He did not care if all of them were killed as long as they slowed Strongheart down, took away some of his power, weakened him in some way.

Another problem Harlance would have to tackle in the morning had cost him more money. All of these former slaves had pistols, but when young men in the Old West dreamed about becoming fast gunfighters, none of them ever had the money to spend on bullets to practice shooting for hour upon hour. They had all been practicing quick draw over and over, but he wanted them to have the experience with live shooting. Once they go that down, he planned to walk up and slam them unexpectedly in the chest or shoulder while they practiced, so they could handle shooting while getting hit by bullets and still keep fighting. So he had already gone into the mercantile and bought a good supply of bullets.

Harlance felt that he was really thinking this out. He had seen what Strongheart had accomplished when he set the ambush for him in a canyon. He had sniffed it out, even though someone miles away let Harlance know he was on his way. He had outsmarted him and outfought Big Scars Cullen, who he also put the sneak on. That in itself was no easy task, McMahon thought, as Cullen was certainly no pilgrim. The big man had been over the mountain and down the river a time or two. Outfighting Big Scars was something that McMahon had never dreamed anybody would ever be able to do.

He knew that he indeed had a fight on his hands, and he would do all he could to even the odds more or, better yet, make them all in his favor. Harlance wondered where Strongheart was this night.

The next morning, when the sun was just starting to climb up into the sky, Joshua climbed into the saddle and looked back at his camp. He had left plenty of firewood for the next hombre spending the night, the cooking fire pit, the bough bed, and other niceties. The fire was out, sprinkled with water and covered with dirt. Other than that, the whole area looked natural. Harlance and his new young gang would not be awake for another six hours.

The handsome young Pinkerton man set his horse at an easy trot down to the trail he could clearly see below, which wound along the base of the eastern side of the Sangre de Cristos. He was heading south to Music Pass. There were two passes that crossed over to the Great Sand Dunes,

Music Pass and Medano Pass, which was pronounced Madanow. Strongheart was taking Music Pass, which crossed over first. He did not know what awaited him on the western side of the Big Range. He had been in the San Luis Valley and had always seen the Great Sand Dunes as a far-off tancolored pile of sand. He was anxious to see what they were like up close. Medano Pass would bring him right out on the edge of the Great Sand Dunes, but Music Pass would actually bring him out slightly north of them.

Joshua rode down past Marble Mountain and Horn Peak and took the trail that would take him up to Music Pass and allow him to drop down into Sand Creek Lakes, both the upper and lower lakes. Music Pass got its name from the Ute Indians because of the musical sounds that could be heard from the various winds and rock formations. The panoramic ride did not begin right away, as Joshua went up through a very thick forest of aspens, hardwoods, and evergreens. It was also very rocky and steep at the beginning, but the scenery at the pass was invigorating, and the winds there gave him some comfort as it was an unreasonably hot day, even at that elevation. Towering above Strongheart and the whole valley were the thirteen-thousand-plus-foot Tijeras, Music, and Milwaukee Peaks. After a break for Gabe to catch his wind at a scenic overlook near the pass, Joshua started a pretty steep descent into the Sand Creek Valley.

The trail split into two different trails, and Joshua knew from talking to Jerome that they led to the Upper Sand Creek Lake and Lower Sand Creek Lake. Jerome had told him that if he was going to camp, the lower lake would be the place to do it. In the past, some had told him it was the most beautiful place they had seen ever. Joshua rode down the trail toward Lower Sand Creek Lake. The two lakes were about two miles apart, and the upper lake was a few hundred feet higher. Strongheart rode into a very large meadow and immediately spotted a large herd of bighorn sheep, and two magnificent rams were in a fight. He just sat his horse and watched. They would rear up on their hind legs and slam their heads into each other. Seconds later, the loud banging sound would reach Joshua's ears. At the other end of the meadow a large harem of elk grazed on the mountain gamma grasses. Gabriel snorted a little, and Joshua knew the horse wanted water from the creek. He rode him over and let him drink to his heart's content.

A short time later, Strongheart trotted up to the lake and was very much in awe of its majestic and pristine setting. Tijeras Peak towered dramatically over the lake, the shore of which came right up against the base of the mountain. The glacial lake itself was crystal clear and teeming with land-locked cutthroat and rainbow trout, which were popping bugs all over the smooth mirrored surface.

Across the lake, Joshua saw two men with a small canvas tent in the background, and both were fly-fishing near the base of the peak. They had long bamboo poles, and one started pulling in a small cutthroat. Strongheart gave them a wave, and they waved heartily in return. Men had been fly-fishing for years, centuries actually. In fact, as early as the second century, Claudius Aelianus had written about fishermen from Macedonia making lures out of feathers and red wool and catching many fish. Back east, Strongheart knew they had even started fly-fishing clubs in the Catskill Mountains of New York. Of course they also had not had any America Indian attacks back east for years, he thought.

Joshua thought about stopping here for late lunch, but then decided that since it was now later in the afternoon, he would camp by the lake and leave the next morning for the Great Sand Dunes. He trotted around the lake to the south shore, where he found a very secluded cove, which gave him total privacy. In fact, he found a campsite where someone had already camped, made a nice fire pit, and like Joshua, left a good supply of firewood. He had his coffee going when one of the fishermen rode over to him bareback on a mule. He introduced himself as a rancher near West-cliffe and gave Joshua three fish for lunch. Strongheart thanked him and offered coffee, but the man wanted to get back to his fishing. He spoke about having just the right kind of fly at the right time of year to catch fish after fish.

Joshua made lunch, ate, and decided to explore a bit on foot, while he left Gabe to share the grassy meadow with numerous deer, elk, and bighorn that appeared and disappeared.

Running behind his camp was a stream that led to an area full of cascading waterfalls. Joshua could not believe how many beautiful wildflowers grew all around here, and the place reminded him of home.

The next morning at daybreak, Joshua looked back at Tiejas Peak, Music Peak, and Milwaukee Peak and truly understood why these mountains were called the Sangre de Cristos, the "blood of Christ," when he saw the beautiful crimson hues on the snowfields.

The ride down the western slope of the Sangres was fairly uneventful except for rounding a bend in the trail and coming upon a large tom mountain lion feeding on a small doe he had apparently just killed right in the middle of the trail. The cat barely glanced at Joshua; he just disappeared into the trees without looking back. Most people living in lion country spent their entire lives without ever seeing one, but Joshua was in the wilds and in the saddle so much that he saw them from time to time.

Before noon, he rode into the Great Sand Dunes for the first time ever and was totally amazed. From a distance, in the San Luis Valley, he always thought the dunes were maybe fifty to one hundred feet in height, but that was because of the enormous size of the valley, the highest-altitude large valley in the world, with an average elevation about 7,500 feet, and it was large, 122 miles long and 74 miles wide.

So seeing the dunes at great distances, next to twelve-, thirteen-, and fourteen-thousand-foot peaks, it was not easy for Strongheart or anybody else to judge the immensity of the size, but now the warrior was riding into the sand dunes, which covered an area of more than thirty square miles, with sand dune after sand dune rising up into the sky. He was now looking up, not realizing that many of the sand dunes rose more than 750 feet into the sky. Joshua knew the Moss outlaws would not be here, but there was no way he would ride into this area without checking the dunes out.

Nobody was ever really sure exactly how or why these magnificent dunes had been formed and kept shifting shapes. But Joshua saw that Medano Creek ran around the dunes, going underground here and there and then reappearing in the sand as an easily waded shallow creek that meandered around the dunes, seeming to cut a new route each day. Many felt that the Rio Grande flowing through one end of the valley carried many sand deposits along its banks, which were carried as dust to the dunes. But in later years, contemporary geologists would conclude that much of the dust came from shallow lakes north of the dunes that would dry up and blow away, as well as Medano Creek and others, along with the accumulation of dust from a windy valley that was 122 by 74 miles in size, with a granite wall of large mountains blocking the dust's escape and downslope winds causing it to settle in the area of the Great Sand Dunes.

Joshua rode around the dunes, taking them all in. When spotted from the nearby Zebulon Pike in 1833, the dunes were said to look like a giant sea with ever-changing waves, except colored differently than ocean water.

Leaving the Great Sand Dunes behind him, the Pinkerton man now headed southwest, also leaving the Big Range to his rear and seeing the foothills of the San Juan Mountains across the massive valley ahead of him. He was headed toward Wolf Creek Pass, figuring that the Moss crooks had departed for the far-off bustling and busy mining area of Animas City or nearby Silverton.

Joshua had not even gone five miles when he came upon two cowboys. As they got closer, he saw that they were red, but they were obviously cowhands. Both put their hands up in greeting, and so did Strongheart.

"Howdy," one said.

Joshua smiled and said, "Ute?"

The other said, "Yes, we work for a cattle rancher east of La Veta. You are the half-Lakota who has been tracking the McMahon gang?"

Joshua was amazed at the cowboy-Indian gossip network in the West.

He said, "Yes. Name is Strongheart. Heard anything?"

The first Ute said, "Yes. Gorilla Moss and Percival Moss are north of here at Villa Grove. Do you know where it is?"

Joshua said, "Yep, I do. Thank you. You know what they are doing there?"

The second Ute laughed, saying, "Trying to hide from you. Good hunting, brother."

The two chuckled and rode on, giving him a wave. He nodded and smiled as they departed, then turned his horse toward the right front and now had the Big Range off to his right as he rode along the big valley, headed toward the distant whistle-stop turnaround Villa Grove.

The town of Villa Grove had only had that name for just over one year, having officially become Villa Grove on January 19, 1872. Prior to that, the town had been organized and named two years earlier, on June 13, 1870. At that time it had been given a very unusual name for a Western town, Garibaldi, after an Italian revolutionary named Giuseppe Garibaldi. It really was not much of a town, but it was built and established by the Denver & Rio Grande Railroad as the southernmost terminal of the tiny Rio Grande's narrow-gauge Poncha Pass line, which would only exist for seventeen more years. Ironically, the town's name would be changed to Villagrove on October 12, 1894, and then back to Villa Grove on July 1, 1950, long after Strongheart's time.

The burg possessed one of the most beautiful mountain views in the world, set in the northern bottleneck end of the San Luis Valley, fourteen miles south of Poncha Pass. Out in the valley but only two miles from the steep-sided Big Range to the east, the Sangre de Cristos stretched across the horizon from as far as one could see in the north to as far as one could see in the south. Shortly to the west of the town were the beginnings of the foothills for both the Collegiate range to the north and the San Juan Mountain range to the west. Many prospectors were coming into the area now and digging glory holes all over the treed foothills.

Strongheart rode until he was just a few miles out, and saw a couple small herds of buffalo and large herds of antelope along the way. Villa Grove was well within sight when he decided to ride off into the trees on the side of the Sangres and make camp for the night. He would enter the town in the morning after a night's sleep and food, and rest for his horse, as well.

It was shortly after daybreak when Strongheart rode forward with no plan. He would look for Gorilla, Percival, or Harlance and deal with whatever situation confronted him.

Gorilla and Percival had been keeping watch and staying in the one small hotel in the tiny little town that had only two restaurants, along with a smattering of houses and businesses. They slept in shifts and worked part-time by day doing odd jobs at the terminal for the Rio Grande's Poncha Pass line. They did not really like working the way most men did, but they wanted to keep an eye on the comings and goings into and out of the valley. Very few entered the San Luis Valley by crossing the Big Range. They almost always came in through Poncha Pass or a long distance to the south, over La Veta Pass.

Gorilla Moss had decided to take about the same attitude about Joshua that Joshua had taken about him and his son, and that was to play it by ear. He would see if Strongheart even came, from what direction, how, when, and figure out a strategy then. In the meantime, he had feelers out on the owlhoot trail. Honor among thieves. All the bushwhackers, highwaymen, and scoundrels around were keeping an eye peeled for the big, tough half Indian called Strongheart and trying to pass the information along. The idea was to get the intelligence reports about him, gossip, or rumors, into the hands of Harlance, Gorilla, or Percival. After all, this crazy man might come after them someday. The word was already out that he was pursuing the McMahon gang members, not for revenge, but to keep his word to somebody. These unprincipled, ne'er-do-wells just could not comprehend a man standing on a moral code he set for himself, as they had none.

When he looked out his hotel room window, however, in the early morning and spotted the magnificent red and white Overo pinto horse coming toward him in that unmistakable stiff-legged trot, Gorilla became a nervous wreck.

He banged on the wall with the heel of his hand and yelled, "Percival! He's coming!"

Seconds later, Percival burst through Gorilla's door, his prostitute behind him clutching a gaudy green dress around her. Gorilla nodded at the window, while putting his six-shooters on, a pair of .44s in cross-draw holsters.

He said to his own prostitute, "Git yer dress and fixin's on, little lady."

Gorilla had a bald head and no neck. Both of the Mosses were tall, but Gorilla's son had a more slender build, though he still had Gorilla's features. He wore a Russian .44 also, with another tucked into his waist as a belly gun.

Gorilla's whore said, "I'm gonna stay here in bed, sweetheart."

"The hell you say!" he growled and tossed her the bustle sitting by him. "Git yer clothes on now! Both of you!"

The angry glare in his eyes made them both move extremely fast, more so than the bellowing voice. They quickly got dressed, even donning feathered hats to match their dresses. Both men took them by the arms and escorted them down the hotel steps, then looked out the back door. Now they could clearly see that the rider was Strongheart and he was fast-approaching.

He spotted them as they walked out through the hotel door and toward him.

Well, here it is, he thought.

He had wondered if they would try to ambush him, but

to their credit, it appeared that they were going to face him straight on. Then Strongheart saw each man wrap an arm around the neck of one of the women and move forward in a gunfighter's crouch. He could not believe this. *What a gang,* he thought.

First, Long Legs wanted to assault Annabelle, and now these two were using two women for shields in a gunfight. There were so few women in the West, there had been actual cases of outlaws turning on other outlaws and hanging them for molesting women. It was not that these highwaymen were noble or moral. It was preservation of the species, in fact. There were so few women, and even fewer hardy ones, that men actually strove to conserve females.

It had been a move of self-preservation on Gorilla's part, as he knew what this man had done to the rest of his gang single-handed. His brazen frontal approach on the town was also unnerving. Gorilla did not realize how savvy Strongheart actually was. He had not camped due east of town and ridden in during the early morning for no reason. The sun had peeked over the Big Range and was shining directly in the eyes of Percival and Gorilla. It made them a more illuminated target while making it difficult for them to see what Joshua's hands were doing or his overall movement in general.

He knew he had to think quickly. He reached back into the scabbard under his right leg, pulled out his carbine, and cocked a round into the chamber.

The women were screaming now, even after Gorilla growled, "Shut up!"

They squirmed, but the two crooks were too strong. Now Strongheart was sizing the men up, and he understood them, or at least Gorilla. By his mannerisms, he could tell the dad was scared but also tough, and he was going down shooting if need be. Percival was acting too confident, and with his youth, Joshua knew it was false bravado. The father would be more dangerous. Percival had sweat pouring down his face and there was a twitch in his right cheek. He wanted to impress his dad, so he would back Gorilla's play. Gorilla was the one who would have to take the first bullet. He had been in shoot-outs before.

Percival now stuck his gun barrel up to his prostitute's head and laughed a loud, nervous chuckle.

In the meantime, Strongheart did a sliding stop on Gabe and stepped out of the stirrups without taking his eyes off the two. He moved his horse to the left, so he would not get hit by any stray bullets, and dropped the reins. Joshua then walked rapidly toward the two and had closed the distance to within yards before Percival stopped him with a scream.

"I'll kill her, you red nigger! I'll do it! Drop yer iron now!"

That is what Strongheart wanted. He tossed the carbine barrel-up to Percival, who subconsciously knew that it was cocked, could go off if it hit the ground, and a bullet could hit him. This was simply instant recognition of the danger. He moved the barrel away from the woman's head to grab the rifle launched toward him, and Strongheart's right hand whipped down, the Colt .45 slid up and out of the holster, and flame shot from the barrel, just as Gorilla glanced to see if Percival would catch the carbine. Strongheart's bullet caught Gorilla directly between the eyes and he died on his feet just like that.

Percival caught the rifle and felt something slam into his stomach and then another. He saw smoke coming out of Strongheart's gun, and he tried to draw, but then realized that his arm holding the stock of the carbine had been struck. The bullet had passed through it into his stomach, and then a second bullet had hit him close to the first hole. The two women ran screaming as people poured out of buildings. Strongheart walked up to the dazed Percival, who was losing color and staring at the growing crimson stain on his stomach. Still in shock, he looked at his father, whose eyes had disappeared into his head, toward the gaping hole where the bridge of his nose used to be. His body was unmoving.

Joshua said, "Do you or your pa have the antique wedding ring taken from the widow on the stage?"

Percival said, "Harlance has it. It's true, ain't it? You kilt us all over a pledge?"

Strongheart said, "Yes."

Percival fell to his knees and was now weaving.

He said weakly, "Will ya gimme your word, you'll see we get a good funeral?"

Strongheart said, "No. You don't deserve it after what you tried with those two women. Buzzards have to eat, too."

Percival's eyes opened wide, like a deer's at night when a light is suddenly shined in his eyes. Then the eyes went lifeless, and Percival fell forward on his face like a limp rag doll. His left leg twitched spasmodically for a half a minute, then all was still. Strongheart could smell gunpowder.

Citizens came running up, some carrying assorted weapons. They did not know him or the others.

Strongheart said, "These two were bandits and held up the stage on Copper Gulch Coach Road a few months ago. They just tried to use two women as shields in a gunfight."

A man in the crowd said, "I saw it, Injun. That was a righteous shooting and quick thinking on your part."

People seemed to relax then, and they set their guns down at their sides.

Strongheart said, "I am emptying their pockets. They held up the stage and robbed everyone, including me."

An important-looking man in a business suit came forward. When he spoke, everyone seemed riveted on each word.

He said, "You are named, Steel, no, Strongheart. Heard about you. Half-white, half-Sioux. Those men in the holdup shot you to a rag doll, but you survived, and have hunted them all down, save one. Is it true you gave your word to a girl that you would get her music box back and that is why you hunted them down?"

Joshua was feeling weak in the knees and shaky from adrenaline letdown, but he would not show it.

He smiled. "No, sir, somebody got the facts a little twisted. I *am* half-Sioux. But it was a widow on the stage, she had lost her husband in a fire, and all that she had left was an antique wedding ring. I said I would get it back for her."

Another man said, "Yeah, but you have killed a whole gang to get that ring."

Strongheart chuckled. "Well, mister, all those boys seemed to be pretty attached to it. None of them have wanted to talk. Just fight."

Another said, "Seems like you have awful short conversations if people disagree with you, Mr. Strongheart."

Everybody including Joshua laughed heartily.

Still another shouted out, "I see what them jaspers done to save their sorry hides when ya rode up. I ain't gonna bury 'em or waste wood on a casket after what they done. I'll fork my horse and toss a rope on them carcasses and haul 'em out somewhar so the coyotes and buzzards kin eat."

Another said, "Good idea, Slim."

A woman with a British accent said, "I would say so. Be gone with them, I say."

The rest of the crowd nodded and mumbled in agreement. Joshua thought to himself, "Civilized white society, and they call my father's people savages."

He checked the fallen men's pockets and retrieved money and a gold watch. He also removed their gun belts and guns and handed them to a volunteer. The man nodded and bit off a big plug of tobacco.

Joshua then asked for directions for the shortest way to Cotopaxi and was directed to cross over the Big Range at Hayden Creek Pass. This was easy. The telegrapher pointed at Hayden Baldy Mountain and Nipple Mountain, which was named for its appearance, and showed him the short drop between peaks.

He said, "Ride that way, Mr. Strongheart. You'll find the crossover trail and follow it. Several nice harems of elk in the dark timber near the top of the pass. You will come out west of Cotopaxi by maybe five to eight miles, I'll guess. Follow the river down to it."

Strongheart spoke with folks for a few minutes and then headed northeast from the tiny town, ready for another adventure in his quest to fulfill a pledge to a sad, beautiful young widow. The ride back over the Big Range was much, much longer than it seemed looking at it from out in the valley. It gave Joshua a long time to plan, to think, to deal with the fact that he had killed two more men. He saw a lot of wildlife heading up the trail that crossed over the pass, and hardly any on the other side. He camped at the bottom of the trail, along Hayden Creek, and took off the next morning for Cotopaxi, which was becoming his stomping ground now.

Strongheart really had no grandparents growing up, and he thoroughly enjoyed parlaying with the old white-haired Zachariah Banta. Joshua felt that the thing he liked most was the ever-present twinkle in the elder's eye. He also had a lot of common-sense wisdom, which was blanketed and camouflaged under several layers of dry humor.

It was still early morning when Joshua walked in through the door of Banta's store and waited to see what kind of reception he would get that day. Each time it was different. Zack did not even acknowledge him.

He walked over and stacked a pile of seven blankets on Strongheart's arms and said, "Here, take these over ta the hotel yonder."

Joshua just laughed and walked out the door carrying the blankets. He delivered the blankets and went back to the store. Banta was now sitting down drinking coffee, with a second cup poured for Joshua.

Strongheart grabbed the steaming cup and lifted it in Zack's direction as a thank-you before he sat down.

Zack said, "You always goin' around and shootin' gents fer jest wantin' to dance with some ladies?"

Strongheart had coffee come out his nose he burst out laughing so hard, and it burned like the dickens. He could not stop laughing, though, despite the pain.

"Now, Zack, I left there after the shooting, crossed over the Sangres at Hayden Creek Pass, camped, and lit out of there this morning at first light," Strongheart exclaimed.

"How in the world did you find out about the shooting so fast?"

Zack replied, "Wal, I reckon it was acause a old Robin."

"Robin?" Joshua said, "Robin who?"

Zack said, "Robin, my friend. Tells me a lot a things afore others find out. Robin Redbreast."

He walked outside while Joshua just shook his head. A few minutes later, Zack walked back into the store. The old man hooked his finger at Strongheart and summoned him out the door. Joshua was puzzled.

He walked outside and spotted Zack standing by the barn and corral, where Gabe was eating hay and enjoying the morning sun. Joshua was once again puzzled by the old man. He walked over to him.

Zack pointed toward Joshua's knife and said, "Don't reckon ya ever learnt how ta use thet thing, did ya?"

Joshua chuckled, saying, "Yes, sir. Why?"

Zack pointed at a target he had just nailed to a pole about twenty feet away, near the front of the barn.

"Kin ya throw from here and stick the target?"

Zachariah was very amazed, but would never let on, as the warrior's arm extended and the knife suddenly seemed to fly from his side and sail quickly through the air, spinning twice and sticking right into the bull's-eye.

Zack said, "Wal, reckon ya kin. I'm gittin' me some more coffee. You kin stand out here whittling if ya want."

He walked quickly back to the store. Joshua again shook his head, laughing, and walked over to pull the knife out of the target. He looked up at the pole above him and noticed the telegraph wire. This was a telegraph pole. Then it hit him. He had asked Zack how he had learned so quickly about his gunfight in Villa Grove. Strongheart was embarrassed and thought about how much he had to learn as a detective. He laughed heartily at himself and at Banta's antics.

Returning to the store, Joshua poured himself a fresh cup and sat down. "Who knows how to use a key here, Zack?"

Zack took a spoon and tapped two slower hits and one fast one, then said, "Dah, dah. Dit."

"What's that spell?" Strongheart said.

"Me."

They both chuckled and finished their coffee.

Banta got serious, saying, "Heared twicet now thet McMahon put hisself together a ganga young Injun bucks what was slaves with Mexican rancher families down south near New Mexico Territory. These boys banded together and started stealin', robbin', and sech as thet. Think they are holed up in Hardscrabble, down southa Florence a few miles, up against the range."

"You think he put them together to fight me?"

Banta laughed.

Zack said, "Sonny Boy, ole Harlance shore don't bring no Gatlin' gun when he comes ta visit mah store, 'cause a fearin' me. Ya have kilt every one a his gang, which does include his brother. I guarantee ya, they're aimin' ta dry-gulch ya."

"Well, sir," Joshua said, heading toward the door, "thanks for the coffee, but if they want to dance, I better go and open up the ball."

Zack's shouting stopped him. "Son!"

Joshua turned and Zack said, "Reckon ya better keep a good eye ta yer back trail."

Strongheart winked and went out the door. He brushed Gabriel, saddled up, and headed toward Westcliffe.

A few hours later, Strongheart was having coffee and a sandwich with his new friend Jerome Guy.

"Zachariah Banta is probably the best and most accurate source of information in this whole area, and he was correct," Jerome said. "Harlance was in here buying drinks for his young gunfighters. I speak Spanish and could overhear what they were saying, yet they had no idea I could understand them. I also heard him say things which I combined with their words. He definitely was taking them to Hardscrabble to train them and prepare them for a big fight with you. I know he bought a lot of ammunition, so they were going to be doing a lot of shooting, presumably to practice. You need to get with the Fremont County sheriff, Frank Bengley, and maybe form a posse. He is a good man."

Strongheart said, "The sheriff has to have evidence to justify forming a posse. Although you and a few others are credible, he is not going to do anything."

Guy replied, "Good point. Nonetheless, he needs to know what is going on anyway. That covers you if there is a shooting. My wife Jan is good friends with the sheriff's wife. She is going to Canon City today, and I will have her carry him a message."

"Thanks," Joshua said. "Now I need to know all you can tell me about Hardscrabble, Florence, and the whole area."

From Jerome Guy, Strongheart learned that when Hardscrabble was originally settled as a trading post by traders from Pueblo in 1844, it was not called Hardscabble. It was originally named San Buenaventura de los Tres Arrollos, which meant "St. Bonaventure of the three windings." Jerome figured that was because of the winding rocky canyon that Joshua would be riding down toward Hardscrabble, which the locals referred to as Hardscrabble Canyon. The whole area had been inhabited by Kiowa, Cheyenne, and Utes, as well as many French traders, Americans trappers, mountain men, settlers, and Mexican farmers and their families. The local farmers said they changed the name because of all the "hard scrabbling to get in a crop" in the very rocky soil.

Later, after oil was discovered in Florence, and it was such a big find, many oil people came to the town and the surrounding area, including prospectors who figured there might be yellow gold there, too, and not just liquid "black gold." Since the oil field turned into the second largest and most productive in the United States, the word quickly spread, which brought more people into the area. But Hardscrabble remained pretty much of a shambles of a ghost town.

Joshua wondered if Florence was named for Florence, Italy, as several residents had told him. He found out from

Jerome, though, that the little berg, just downstream on the
Arkansas River from Canon City, was actually named for
the daughter of a local pioneer, James McCandless.

With the information Jerome Guy had given him, Joshua
set off east toward distant Pueblo and traveled down the
high-cliffed, winding Hardscabble Canyon. Armed with
his new facts about the Hardscrabble area, first he would
go onto the high ground protected by trees and locate
and reconnoiter the gang's hideout area. Then, he would
formulate a plan. He was thinking that maybe, with the
sheriff having read the letter Jerome sent with his wife, he
might be able to present the lawman with some evidence
that would at least get him to thoroughly investigate Harlance and his gang. Joshua was a warrior, and mighty in a
stand-up brawl, with a knife, bow, pistol, and long gun, but
the last thing he wanted to do was tangle with a gang of
seven in a gunfight.

As he rode through the beautiful foothill country east
of Westcliffe, the Sangre de Cristos falling away behind
him, Joshua wondered what lay before him and what was
happening with the beautiful young widow he had made
his promise to.

9

The Widow

Annabelle Ebert had been keeping herself busy. Every single day she was hearing about the latest exploits of the tall, handsome half-Sioux, half-white hero who had been championing the cause of finding and returning her ring. When she visualized him riding up and handing her the ring, she would picture being swept into his powerful arms and them kissing. It took her breath away, but she wondered if she was wrong thinking about such a thing.

When she had first arrived in Canon City, she had gotten a room in a small mansion on Macon Avenue, surrounded by high oaks and maples. Needing money, Annabelle went to work in the mansion as a live-in housekeeper and nanny for a very wealthy family who owned oil in Florence and several businesses in downtown Canon City. That became her goal, to eventually open her own business in Canon City, but first she would remember the constant admonition of her father, "Crawl before you walk," when she would get overly enthused about any new idea or project she was ready to undertake.

For right now, she was working hard and taking other jobs as well to earn as much as she could.

Annabelle had grown up in the Finger Lakes region

of New York. Her father had been an industrialist in New York City, made a fortune, and moved to Canandaigua, New York. It was a beautiful area, with tough winters and magnificent woods and waters. The town actually had been the primary residence of the Seneca when the white men came and started settling the East. The Finger Lakes were several very large wooded lakes in upper west-central New York State, the home of hardy people. In fact, at the same time Annabelle was cleaning the mansion in Canon City, suffragist Susan B. Anthony was in the Ontario County courthouse in Canandaigua being ordered to pay a $100 fine, which the women's rights advocate refused to pay and never would.

Annabelle was a very tough-minded person herself. When Joshua Strongheart saw the tear in her eye on the stage, it was very unusual, but she had been at the end of her rope. After moving, her father had made several large investments in the area and lost heavily. Then he started making more risky investments, trying to recoup or make up for his previous losses, which only made matters worse.

The long and the short of it was that Annabelle's family had gone from being wealthy to struggling for every penny by the time she fell in love and got married. Then, when her husband died, she was left with nothing but a very small amount of money.

Annabelle, however, viewed all this as in part good fortune, as she had developed a real toughness emotionally and physically, as well as an incredible work ethic growing up. She knew she would be successful someday, another husband or not, and she had now made her mind up that with God's help, she would do it on her own. In short, she was a survivor. On the other hand, she did not like being alone, and a part of her hoped she would fall in love again and marry someone whom she could spend out her days with.

A good example of her survivor skills came shortly after she moved to Canon City and started working at the mansion. She had gone into town for supplies, and her long black hair and piercing blue eyes made many men take notice, but one day she caught the eye of a beast who had come to town to trade some furs and buy supplies.

Bear Borgadine was quite simply a man of enormous dimension. He could move any rock that was not larger than himself, and reach tree branches that others could not even touch, and break off most of those with his cantaloupe-sized hands. Garbed in a massive suit of animal armor, the fur-clad mountain man spent all his time in the Sangre de Cristo, Collegiate, and San Juan Mountains, always out of sight from man. Each fall, though, he would end his trapping and start looking for winter quarters, and every fall he would find some prospector high up in the mountains and kill the man for his cabin. In the springtime, Bear was on his way.

It was such a fall day, after dispatching a longtime hermit, that he went down below to prepare for a long winter and spotted Trish Garman, a beautiful blond young woman who was the youngest offspring of the Garman clan, with nine older brothers, each a cold-blooded hard-core outlaw. If not a killer yet, each of the brothers was galloping in that direction.

Bear had made his once-in-a-year trip for supplies to the small town of Poncha Springs and was returning to the Big Range, when he happened on the beautiful Trish. He decided he wanted her as a prize to have during his long winter stay, knowing he would get rid of her once the snows were gone and he was ready to start traveling and trapping again.

He laid a trap for her on the river road, along the churning Arkansas River, west of Cotopaxi, as she returned home from a shopping trip at Colorado City. Having captured the beauty, Bear took her with him to his cabin high up in the Collegiate range, where she became his virtual slave.

This man was half-animal in his thinking and instincts anyway and did not care that she was the sister of outlaws, or that she was innocent herself. She was simply a new object he wanted, and he had gotten everything he wanted by sheer force and intimidation his whole life. Much as Big Scars Cullen had, except Cullen needed to be led. Bear Borgadine was a loner and did whatever he wanted.

The outlaw family searched high and low for Trish, but because of their high-profile status, they did not want to enlist the aid of others, especially the law. They figured they were so dominant in numbers and toughness that they would be able to find their sister and string up the hombre that took her. But they finally had to give up their search.

Bear did not get his nickname for no reason. Every winter he almost went into hibernation. He spent a good deal of time in the summer and late fall preparing his alpine cabin for this winter seclusion. He jerked meat, shot game, cut firewood, took in supplies, set up his winter trapline, and usually kidnapped one or two tribal women to spend the winter with him. Then in the spring he would kill them and get rid of the body, usually just stuffing it under rocks. That is what he did with Trish Garman. He liked having a white woman so he could have some conversations over the winter.

When he spotted the ravishing, raven-haired, blue-eyed Annabelle, he knew he had his target for the upcoming winter.

Annabelle went to several different stores that day, thinking often about Strongheart, who was at that time on his way to Oregon. She, as mentioned, was indeed a survivor, so she was very aware of her surroundings, especially people. Annabelle was used to men staring at her and took that in stride, never taking herself too seriously, but the giant of a man following her around downtown Canon City was very obvious. Her mind started working on how to handle the situation.

Walking quickly down toward Old Max, the territorial prison that could be found at the west end of Main Street, Annabelle checked behind her occasionally. She saw that the big fur-covered man was still following her. She concluded that if he did not have evil plans, he would simply have approached her. So, she reasoned, he must be up to no good.

Going into the livery stable and blacksmith shop, she wanted to try to solve this on her own if she could, without enlisting the aid of any men. It was not defensiveness or an overinflated ego on the part of the young lady. She was actually being thoughtful and considerate. Annabelle knew the farrier, also a large and muscular man, but very kind and a true gentleman, seemingly very devoted to his wife, who ran a laundry down the street. She figured if she talked to him, then the beast following her would maybe stay back when he saw the size of the blacksmith. The other possibility would be the blacksmith or another man getting into a fight on her behalf. She did not want that.

Annabelle greeted the blacksmith and started asking him questions about shoeing her horse, which she already knew the answers to. She was killing time, so she could think.

She had already decided that she was not going back to the mansion that day, which was a quarter mile away anyway, with several alleyways and empty lots in between. She did not want the behemoth to know where she lived. Further, Annabelle did not want to needlessly expose any innocent man to danger, such as the blacksmith, who would surely go confront the large mountain man on her behalf. Annabelle could sense that the stranger following her was pure evil.

She asked the blacksmith if he would rent her a horse, and he said absolutely. He saddled it while they spoke, and she noticed that the big bear of a man remained across the street lounging in a rocking chair a business owner had set out for his own comfort. The merchant certainly saw the big man through his shop window, but he was not going to approach such a rough-looking monster of a man. This intimidation factor had allowed Bear to function for decades in any manner he chose, but it was not going to work with Annabelle, especially after what had happened on the stage.

When the horse was saddled, she asked if the blacksmith could let her borrow some saddlebags as well. He did so, and she put her shopping items inside them, letting him think she was tired, had more errands to run, and did not want to walk her legs into the ground. In actuality, she normally loved walking into and around town. There was a lot of traffic, especially horse traffic, in Canon City, and there was a bridge not too far away, called simply the Fourth Street Bridge.

She had also noticed earlier that the big bear man had a large draft horse, a Percheron, that he rode, and it was tied at a hitching rail in front of a tavern. Further she knew that he would be able to see her from many spots on Main Street riding across the Fourth Street Bridge, which she wanted to do.

She mounted up and almost trotted out of the livery stable, turning and heading toward Fourth Street, where she turned toward the river. She carefully looked back and saw her husky pursuer scrambling down the street toward his own horse. As she crossed the bridge, one glance back told her that the man was almost to his horse. When she got to the other side of the bridge and was now out of sight of downtown, she put the horse into a fast trot. She knew that if she galloped, her horse would leave obvious tracks mixed with all the other horses that had passed that way. But if she trotted, the tracks her horse left would not be as obvious. There was a lot more vegetation closer to the river, and at one point where there were a lot of bushes and trees, she carefully picked a spot, put her arm across her face, and turned her horse into the foliage. Once out of sight, she dismounted, walked him a short distance in the woods, and tied him to a tree. She then made her way back to Fourth Street and crawled forward to where she was well hidden but could see the hard-packed road heading south of town.

Annabelle waited anxious minutes until she heard the big horse approaching. She almost held her breath, as the big man and his draft horse rode by. After he passed, she crawled forward and watched until he rode to the hill a quarter mile south and the road then turned to the left and up onto a hill above town called Prospect Heights. Once he was out of sight, she returned to her horse, led him out of the undergrowth, and galloped back to town, constantly checking behind her. She galloped and trotted the horse all the way to the mansion, which was north and east of where she'd been at Fourth Street. Once there, she walked the horse around outside the stable, letting him cool down and constantly watching to the south to insure that the hairy giant did not reappear. Bear did not. He was already well south of town, trying to pick up her trail.

What she did not know that day was that one month later, he would be well west of Canon City, near Poncha Springs, heading up toward his cabin in the Collegiate range with a captured young Ute woman in tow. The woman was the betrothed of a very courageous young Ute warrior named Old Moccasins, who followed the giant. When the mountain man rounded a bend in a switchback trail heading up the mountain, he came face-to-face with the warrior, who launched an arrow that took Bear right in the side of the neck, slicing his carotid artery and windpipe both. He panicked and tried to whirl his horse, and both went off the side of the trail, rolling down the rocky cliff and hardly recognizable as man and horse when they landed at the bottom of the cliff, a bloody pile.

Old Moccasins retrieved his very happy fiancée as well as Bear's pack mule and supplies. The two returned to his home area several days' riding away, on past Pagosa Springs and south near New Mexico Territory.

Buzzards, several coyotes, two different actual bears, and other predators would make Bear Borgadine and his large horse disappear within a few days' time. He would simply become one more of many who roamed the West and disappeared in avalanches, rock slides, and flash floods, with a few people wondering whatever happened to them but never really finding out.

Annabelle kept the livery horse in the mansion's stable

and returned it the next day, enjoying her leisurely stroll
back to the big stone house on Macon Avenue.

One of Canon City's founding families, the Anson
Rudds took notice of her, after hearing about her personality and her work ethic at the mansion. She had not even
been there a full month when they asked her what kind of
business she wanted to start, and she said she loved to cook
and wanted a small café. They owned a small, empty building just off Main Street and a small house on Greenwood
with a nice yard and nice mountain views, and they offered
to set her up in both and gave her a modest payment plan,
so she could have them paid back within ten years.

Annabelle was deeply grateful to them and immediately
started cleaning and decorating both the small cabin and
the new café. The blacksmith let her have credit and helped
by installing a good cooking stove.

Within weeks, she had water in both the café and the
cabin. That was very unusual, as most homes had wells
outside, but the café building had an indoor pump, and the
Rudds had one installed in the cabin, too, as the water table
was high in the lowland area along the Arkansas River
basin, and water from wells in the area was good. Plus they
had wanted to update the cabin previously and had already
planned to do so by putting a well inside with a pump.

Annabelle learned from other merchants that Canon
City, unlike a lot of Colorado, had very mild winters and
got less than a foot of snow per year. The climate was semi-
arid and the town was surrounded by mountains on three
sides, with the prairie opening up out to the east, so it was
protected. Plus, in the drier atmosphere, she would learn
that she could go outside without a shawl or coat in the winter as long as the sun was out. Unlike during her upbringing back east, the winters here generally would not bring
the humid freezing cold that would chill her to the bone.
Also, the summers were hot, but because of the nearby
mountains, there was often a cooling breeze blowing. On
top of that, there were more than 330 days of sunshine each

year, so she immediately started putting in a garden behind
the café and at her little house. Within a week or so, she
also started learning which local farmers provided the best
fruits and vegetables, and that most of the best crops came
from the south side of the river and from around Florence,
as the soil seemed to be a little more alkaline on the north
side. This was especially true the farther you got away
from the river. Just a few miles north of her, she learned
there were patches of white alkali in the soil. As far she
could learn, there were no areas of alkali south of the river
around Canon City.

Annabelle was able to get some used tables from a hotel
down the street, and she sanded and finished them herself.
Within a few weeks, she was ready to open her new café,
and she gave thought to the operating oil wells and mines
in the area, as well as the hungry travelers who frequented
the town. She decided to start with large portions and low
prices. It did not take long for her small restaurant to be
packed at each meal. The men in the area especially loved
being waited on by the beautiful widow, and the food was
delicious and plentiful.

Plenty of wives from around town were brought to the
café by their husbands to eat, with admonishments to "Get
the recipe."

By the time Strongheart was in his fight in Villa Grove
with Gorilla and Percival Moss, "The Café" as it was being
called, had become the most popular eatery in the Canon
City or Florence area. The place was packed with diners at
breakfast, lunch, and dinner, and despite working her fingers to the bone, Annabelle always seemed to look fresh
and to wear an ever-present smile.

One day at lunch, she waited on a man who gave her
the chills. He was large, gruff, bearded, and had a strong
Southern accent. Then it hit her: He was one of the holdup
men. He had simply grown a long, unkempt beard. It was
Harlance McMahon.

It was almost as if an alarm bell went off with the

outlaw, because she could tell he realized that she had recognized him, or at least he had sensed it. Fremont County sheriff Frank Begley had become a regular customer in her café, and she wished he was there right then. She could tell that Harlance was nervous now, and she kept glancing at the door to see if the sheriff or a deputy might walk in.

Harlance had to get out of there as quickly as he could and decided to forgo a lot of the supplies he was planning on buying. He could have bought them in Florence, but the tree broke in half on his saddle. The tree was the hardwood frame inside the leather of the saddle, and a broken tree made the saddle almost useless. His horse and saddle were two of the most important tools of an outlaw, second only to his guns.

It was imperative that he have good ones, and he had bought a new saddle down the street and just happened to go into the café to eat. He was totally shocked to see Annabelle and recognized her immediately, as her beauty would be difficult to hide or forget. He made his way toward the front door, having left money on the table, as he did not want any men chasing him down the street.

Annabelle did not know what to do, but she set her jaw as she headed toward him. There were so many customers around, though, that she could not get there in time and could only watch helplessly as he rode out of town, turning south on Fourth Street, perhaps using her own escape technique.

Seeing Harlance had unnerved her and sent chills up and down her spine. What if he came back, she wondered, and why had he come in? It hit an emotional nerve with her as well, causing her to relive the fear, anger, and feelings of intrusion and violation she had felt during the holdup.

Actually, Annabelle had to go out her back door, stand outside, and just sob for a minute. Then she got angry. She looked up at the evergreen-covered mountains in the near distance south and west of town.

And she got angrier. She got shaking angry and set her jaw.

Looking at the clear blue sky, jaw firmly jutting out, Annabelle said, "That scoundrel—no scoundrel is going to have that kind of control over my emotions. Only I shall. Oh, Joshua, where are you?"

10

The Gunfight

Joshua Strongheart went back to town. He decided to buy some more ammunition, sensing he was in for a fight. Maybe it was apprehension, but on a whim, he turned Gabriel around and rode back to the little smattering of buildings. Before him, directly across the valley beyond Westcliffe, he saw lightning flashes and angry clouds up smothering the top of Hermit Peak. Shortly after, he heard the distant sound of thunder. This was common along this long range of fourteeners, seeing blizzards way above timberline, or thunderstorms, even hearing thunder, but the storms were only above those mountains and seldom came overhead. It was strange to have such raging storms seemingly so near, yet also have beautiful sunny weather.

He bought ammunition and then stopped at the saloon again.

As soon as he entered, Jerome Guy raised a finger and smiled, saying, "Strongheart, so glad you returned. I forgot. Hold on please."

He walked into his back room and emerged with a hatbox. Opening it, he produced a black hat with round crown and flat, wide brim, identical to the one Joshua was wearing, minus the wide beaded headband. And also minus the large bullet hole produced by Big Scars Cullen during the shoot-out in Maverick Gulch.

Joshua was shocked, and even more so when Jerome said, "I forgot to give this to you. Zachariah Banta from up north rode in here yesterday and told me you would be riding through. He said to tell you simply that your new hat had come in. He had to order it from Texas from John B. Stetson, best hatmaker around, he said."

Strongheart shook his head and took the hat, then removed his own and switched the hatband to the new hat.

He handed the one with the bullet hole to Jerome. "I swear. That Zack Banta is one strange hombre. I never ordered a hat."

Guy chuckled. "That sounds just like Banta."

The Pinkerton put the new hat on, and it fit perfectly.

Jerome asked, "Why did you come back anyway?"

Joshua said, "I decided you can never have enough ammunition."

"In fact," Jerome Guy said, placing his index finger alongside his nose, "I would like to contribute to your continued survival, too. I just got a brand-new Winchester's newest model, the 1873. Instead of the straight .44 you shoot in your old Henry, it shoots a .44-40 center-fire cartridge and shoots much better than that Henry rimfire Yellowboy you have been carrying. I had mine specially tooled and am giving it and several boxes of ammunition to you as a gift. I will be totally insulted if you refuse it or say anything other than thanks."

Strongheart was touched, deeply, and he humbly said, "Thanks."

"Yellowboy" was the nickname for the Model 1866 Winchester repeater, so named for the bronze-alloy receiver, which was actually made from a metal called "gunmetal."

Joshua gulped when the wealthy businessman produced the weapon from the back. The lever-action rifle was engraved along the entire barrel, and there was a gold inlaid grizzly bear on one side of the receiver and a bald eagle on the other. The stock was engraved as well. There was just no telling how many hours of labor had been put into the engraving. Strongheart knew that this brand-new rifle was a very expensive weapon.

They went out behind the saloon and Joshua test-fired it, loving the action and the handling. Having shot for only a few minutes, they went back inside, where he quickly cleaned the rifle, thanked Jerome profusely, and left for a destination uncertain and a fate even more so.

Within an hour, he was riding down through Hardscrabble Canyon, knowing a very ruthless killer and a gang of wannabe shootists were probably practicing and plotting his impending death.

If nothing else, Strongheart's mother had made him study and read constantly. One of his favorites was a poem written nineteen years earlier, in his youth, by Alfred, Lord Tennyson, called the "The Charge of the Light Brigade," after the famous action during the Crimean War the same year.

As he rode, looking up at the sheer cliffs on his left and the tall evergreen-enshrouded peaks rising above them, he recited the poem, maybe hoping to alleviate some of the fear and apprehension he was feeling.

With a deep voice, Joshua recited the first several stanzas:

Half a league, half a league,
Half a league onward,
All in the valley of Death
Rode the six hundred.
"Forward, the Light Brigade!
Charge for the guns!" he said:
Into the valley of Death
Rode the six hundred.
"Forward, the Light Brigade!"
Was there a man dismay'd?
Not tho' the soldier knew
Some one had blunder'd:
Theirs was not to make reply,

Theirs was not to reason why,
Theirs was but to do and die:
Into the valley of Death
Rode the six hundred.
Cannon to the right of them,
Cannon to the left of them,
Cannon in front of them
Volley'd and thunder'd;
Storm'd at with shot and shell,
Boldly they rode and well,
Into the jaws of Death,
Into the mouth of Hell,
Rode the six hundred.

Then, following that, Strongheart chuckled, saying aloud, "What in the hell am I doing? All of this over a promise? I have to be insane."

He patted Gabe's neck and laughed, and Gabriel nickered in response. He seemed to raise his head a little higher, collecting himself even more regally, and went into his floating stiff-legged trot, as Strongheart called it. Joshua felt the long tail slap him in the small of the back, so he knew the horse was doing his peacock strutting, with his tail curled up over his rump and hanging off to one side. The horse tossed his long mane from the left side of his neck, and it quickly fell back over the right side of his neck, where it usually lay.

The miles dropped away beneath the long legs and the easy riding fast trot. Joshua thought about other horses he had ridden, and he compared riding them with riding an old buckboard, while riding atop Gabriel was like riding in a Concord stage it was so smooth.

At the bottom of the grade, he turned north and now had the mountains to his immediate left and a wide valley opening out to his right with prairie to the east. He stayed at the edge of the range and kept close to the trees. Strongheart was close enough now that he decided to go into the trees at the first gulch and make camp for the night.

He did, not totally realizing that the gang of Harlance's was already in camp in their hideout at Hardscrabble, less than five miles north of him. At that time, there was actually the Hardscabble Mining District several miles south and west of him, which contained the nearby Pocahontas-Humboldt and Bassick Mines.

Joshua found a good site and made camp with a smokeless fire. What little smoke it made was totally filtered by the trees so it was not visible by anybody traveling between Hardscrabble Junction, also known as Wetmore, and Florence eleven miles to the north. He heard a few shots well before dark, echoing off the ridges, which he correctly guessed were the young Indians practicing quick draw.

At first light the next morning, Joshua Strongheart dismounted, leaving Gabriel grazing in a small meadow among the trees on a ridge running from the peak directly overlooking the ruins of Hardscrabble and the sleeping outlaws down below. The Pinkerton considered just raining fire down on them from the safety of the rocks above with his new Winchester 1873. The Lakota half of him saw that as practical, but the white half of him, raised by a lawman, knew that he would have no solid argument in any court. He knew these men were training to kill him, plotting to kill him, practicing to kill him, but they had not attacked him, yet.

He slowly made his way down the ridge overlooking their hideout and simply watched. They had one man as a lookout in the rocks above their camp, but he was out of sight hundreds of feet below Joshua right now. Strongheart lay down with a telescope he carried in his saddlebags and simply watched the morning activities.

He was surprised at how lazy criminals actually were. These men slept until well past dawn, then he could tell they argued over who would stir up the morning fire. The outlaws had the remains of adobe buildings to stay in, which could have been made into very efficient shelters with a little effort. Strongheart had made camp during the night, eaten a nice dinner, breakfast, had hot coffee, good cover, water, and had struck camp, ridden several miles, climbed the mountain he was on, and down to his perch, all while these young men and Harlance were still in bed burning daylight. Their hideout was inefficient and trashy. They finally got a fire going and put a large coffeepot on it. Each man seemed to be responsible for his own breakfast, and two of them were drinking from whiskey bottles. A couple more had only coffee. The others seemed to just eat hardtack and maybe jerky. He saw one man make himself breakfast with a skillet and that was Harlance. Finally, two of them went to the makeshift stable to take care of the horses. Joshua's horse always ate and drank before he did. That was his rule.

Four of them got into a card game with a lot of arguing, and two practiced quick draw a short distance from the camp. Strongheart watched and started mentally making notes on each man. In a gunfight, if forced, he would probably concentrate on eliminating these two first, as they were practicing. None of these young men impressed him, but there were seven of them altogether. He knew they would not come after him individually, but probably by ambush or by confronting him all at one time.

Fortunately Strongheart had his canteen with him, as they did not really do anything until noon. Then they all saddled up and rode toward Florence. He watched until they were several miles away, and then he sneaked down into their hideout to snoop around.

Joshua found several boxes of Colt .45 rounds, and even a box of .44-40s. He took them, figuring it was more important for him to possess them, than those who would kill him. He also figured that they would accuse one another and that would help his cause even further. He found items that he felt certain had been stolen, probably from Florence, such as women's jewelry, and he made a mental note of each so he could tell the sheriff and provide descriptions. He figured maybe he could get these men arrested and avoid having to fight them, or at the least avoid having to fight all of them.

Joshua poked around their camp for another hour and decided he'd better get out of there. He carefully covered all tracks and signs of his presence and made his way back to the ridge. Just as he got to the base of the ridge, he heard them riding back toward camp, and he scrambled up the slope, trying not to leave obvious tracks and using every available piece of cover to conceal his movements.

He was slowly moving up when one of the outlaws came toward him. Strongheart rolled slightly to his left and lay still under some piñon branches. Half his body was exposed. His hand closed around the handle of his Colt, as the footsteps crunched menacingly upward. Then, he slowly moved the hand to his knife, thinking it would be better to be silent if he had to kill this man. Closer and closer the steps came, and now the man's shadow fell across him, but he climbed right by Joshua. Strongheart looked, and the man went another fifteen feet, then crawled into the lookout position over the hideout, rifle in hand. The back of his left side was toward Joshua, who remained motionless.

Now he would need to use the stealth of his red forefathers to get himself out of danger. He was surprised the man had come so quickly to the lookout perch; he must have had another unsaddle his horse. Joshua slowly reached down with one hand and pulled each leg up, one at a time. Strongheart slowly, carefully removed his large-roweled Mexican spurs. There was a little metal bell on each that tinkled against the rowel as it spun. He carefully held the spurs still, put them together, and tucked them in his shirt. Next, he removed his boots and socks. Then he replaced his boots with no socks on under them. Now, knowing he still had many rocks to climb over, he placed a sock on each boot and pulled it up tight. This would help cover his footsteps, although much of his movement upward would be on hands and knees.

Now low-crawling on his belly, arms, and knees, he inched his way up the ridge past the lookout, being careful to move only when nobody below was looking his way. He was amazed that this lookout did not spot him, but the man apparently just was not very aware. It took Joshua two hours to crawl about one hundred yards up the ridge, where he could start moving crouched over from rock pile to tree to bush or cactus. An hour later, he was back up on top and his arms and legs were visibly shaking from overexertion.

He rejoined Gabe, who nuzzled him as if he sensed that Joshua had been through an ordeal. He saddled up and moved deeper back up the ridge, looking for a night location to operate from. The next day he would ride into Florence and then Canon City and try to give the information he had on the stolen property to the sheriff, and maybe see Annabelle briefly. If Joshua could get some of these men arrested for having that property, his job might be easier getting the ring back from Harlance. His pledge would be fulfilled.

Joshua rode until he found a jumble of boulders that would provide all he wanted in a camp, except water. Then he decided he would go ahead and move farther along the ridgeline and get closer to Florence, where he was headed the next day, plus he needed water for his horse. That could prove to be a fatal mistake, but he had no way of knowing it beforehand.

He headed along the ridge and finally decided to drop down into a deep wooded gulch that had a fast-flowing small stream in it. He would simply stay well upstream, where he was sure the outlaws would not venture, and make a good camp. There were many large rock piles in the gulch, and it was surrounded by high, rocky cliffs on both sides. He would simply have to be careful to make his camp a little higher than the stream, in case of flash flood. Strongheart knew how often dudes died in the mountains simply because they had no idea about the suddenness and extreme power of flash floods.

A man might make camp in a gulch or canyon in the mountains, unaware that a major rainstorm was occurring thousands of feet higher, at the head of the gulch. Suddenly, a wall of water, boulders, logs, and debris, sometimes twenty or thirty feet in height, would come roaring down the gulch with no warning and drop at close to the speed of gravitational pulls because of the gulch's steepness. Like a giant avalanche of water instead of snow, such flash floods sometimes washed away whole parties of travelers, who were unaware until the wall of water was upon them, striking with such force it often killed them instantly.

Strongheart found a good spot among many large boulders, well up above the stream, but with water easily accessible for his horse to drink. There were many thick trees around to filter smoke and plenty of lush grass for Gabriel. The problem was he was now out of earshot and eyesight of the outlaws, assuming they would bed down in camp for the night.

They started to, until someone noticed that his box of .45s was missing. He accused another one of the Indian lads, and soon the knife fight was raging. Harlance intervened with a bullet in the air and a stern lecture about needing to cooperate or perish. He made the two shake hands, and he figured they had all been practicing hard and getting stir crazy in the hideout. They would go into Florence, visit the saloon, and find a brothel. His men, he decided, needed to let their hair down this night, so they rode toward Florence right after sunset.

The men certainly were starved for wild times, and they all drank heavily well into the night, and three of them spent the night in a bawdy house just off the main street.

The next day found Joshua Strongheart feeling well rested and ready to go. His main reason for heading into town was to take the information to the sheriff, but he could not get Annabelle out of his mind.

After a hearty and leisurely breakfast, he broke camp a little later than usual and started out for Florence well after sunrise. It was a sunny day and the white on distant Pikes Peak glistened as he rode toward it southern slopes. As with many mountain sites in the West, riding there actually took a couple of days, but it looked not that far away.

At the same time, Harlance, knowing daylight was the enemy of the outlaw, was trudging around Florence on his horse trying to locate and round up his young charges. Having finally gathered up his gang, he took them to a small café on the main street to buy them breakfast. He figured that after the previous night, and his treating them to breakfast, they might not fight among themselves again. He knew he needed this force to keep him alive. He had no idea whether or not he was buying any last meals. The men were young and cocky and sure of their abilities, never doubting for a moment that they could all take Joshua Strongheart, even in a stand-up gunfight.

The seven ordered a large breakfast and Harlance told the cafe owner to keep the hot coffee coming. They were all halfway through the meal and starting to feel almost awake when the door opened up and a tall man walked in, wearing a new black round-topped, wide-brimmed hat. He had long, shiny black hair and was obviously half-white and half-red. It was Joshua Strongheart.

Harlance's eyes opened wide, and his hand flashed down for his six-shooter, but he heard a click and saw the cocked Colt Peacemaker in Strongheart's hand, while a second cocking sound came from the fancy Winchester he held in his other hand. That gun Joshua slowly moved back and forth, covering the gang of men, who foolishly all bunched up too close together.

He said, "All of you, both hands, palms down, on the table."

He heard two translating to others in Spanish, and they all complied.

Even though he held the guns in his hands, Strongheart was facing seven armed men, and he knew he had to be extremely careful about how he handled this. Bold would be best and most intimidating, he figured.

Joshua said, "On the stage, you boys stole an antique wedding ring from the pretty widow. You have it, McMahon?"

Harlance did not want to take water in front of his young gang, and he tried his normal approach, talking tough and not backing down.

"Ya kin go ta hell, Strongheart!" he snarled.

Boom!

The explosion split the air, and simultaneously Harlance's left hand flew backwards and immediately started burning like there was a branding iron being held to it. The café owner screamed and ran out the back door along with the one other patron, a gray-haired old oil engineer. Harlance looked at his hand, and the little finger and ring finger of his left hand were missing. He quickly yanked off his scarf and wrapped it tightly around his hand. Tough as horseshoe nails, he would not let on how much pain he was in.

Strongheart had meant to shoot him in the hand, but he considered it fortuitous that he'd shot off two fingers. He now could use that as leverage.

Joshua said, "Harlance, I have followed everybody in your gang and killed them all, keeping my word to that widow, so now I will just start removing your fingers one or two at a time, until you hand that ring over."

Harlance pulled his stolen watch fob out and removed the ring from it as quickly as he could.

"Bring it over," Joshua said, "and stick it into my pocket of my Levi's."

"What's a Levi?" Harlance snarled.

"These trousers I am wearing," Joshua said, realizing that most people had never even heard about the rugged new trousers, much less seen them.

Joshua moved the end of his Peacemaker as Harlance gingerly placed the ring into the front pocket of the pants. The outlaw then backed up slowly, just waiting for a chance to draw, a diversion. Then it hit him.

"Ya have got ta be jesting, half-breed!" Harlance said. "You don't mean ta tell me ya have been chasing me and hunting mah boys down one-by-one ta keep a promise ta some woman?"

Strongheart said, "Man gives his word, he keeps it."

Harlance shook his head and just could not believe this.

Joshua said, "Okay, one at a time starting with you,

McMahon. Use your left hand only and drop your gun belts.

They removed their gun belts, except for two who carried belly guns and had no holsters. Then Joshua backed out the door. That was all he could think of at the moment, and by the time he got down the main street a short distance, he knew it was a bad idea—when he felt a bullet clip his left calf, heard a series of gunshots, and saw wood splinter on walls nearby.

He spun around and the six gang members were outside the café shooting with their newly acquired skills. Joshua tucked his .45 into the holster and brought the Winchester up. There was one thing that Dan had taught him, and that was that a man who kept his head in a gunfight would fare far better than anybody who simply tried fast draw. That kind of action was for pulp books. Joshua brought the rifle up and shot one young man through the heart. He simply folded up like an accordion.

Joshua also felt something rising up in him, maybe anger, or maybe righteous indignation: Here were six men firing six-shooters wildly at him. That was also when he noticed that Harlance had dashed back into the café. Joshua walked forward slowly, shooting a second man through the shoulder. He cocked the rifle and felt something slam into his stomach. He fired again at the man and caught him full in the chest. These two men down were the two he'd identified as the most careful shooters. He had not even realized he was operating in the way he had already programmed his mind to work. Another bullet slammed into his thigh just as he shot again, missing horribly as he was spun halfway around. His leg did not feel like it would hold him up.

The warrior quickly cocked and fired at another outlaw; he caught him in the middle of the forehead and half the man's head disappeared. His body remained upright for a split second, then he fell forward on what used to be his face.

The outlaws were still firing wildly and reloading as fast as they could. Dogs were barking, and Joshua could hear women screaming and a child crying somewhere. Another bullet slammed into the left side of his abdomen, and Strongheart knew he was dying, but these men were all going with him, and in the aftermath, they would find Annabelle's ring in his pocket. He felt weak and dizzy now, but he started laughing thinking about the look on Harlance's face when he realized why Strongheart had been pursuing him.

He fired once more with the rifle and saw another hopeful young gunfighter fall. Joshua's leg was broken, but he was still moving forward, intoxicated now by battle lust. He dropped his Winchester and drew his six-shooter and fanned shots at the remaining two men. He saw one get hit twice in the chest, and the other as flame spat from the young man's gun.

Strongheart literally saw a red flash coming at his right eye and felt something slam into his right temple, and suddenly the world went black. The sounds and echoes of gunfire quickly faded, and he heard that same dog barking, and he heard his own laughter, then nothing. He fell into a deep, dark pool of blackness.

The outlaw and highwayman, the cold killer Harlance McMahon heard the shots of the gun battle die down a half mile behind him as he galloped his horse toward his hideout to grab his gear and get the heck out of there. He could not believe that crazy fool had gone through all that Strongheart had done simply to keep a promise. Harlance just could not conceive of that kind of honor or principle in anybody. When the fight started, and he saw Strongheart turn and start firing instead of rushing for a building, he remembered what had happened at the stage holdup when they thought this same man was dead. He had no clue the warrior was lying motionless on the main street of Florence right now, filled with bullet holes. He just knew that the shooting had stopped, and he was certain he had no gang left. He was right. They were all dead. Killed in a gunfight by the one man they had trained and practiced to kill.

Harlance rode his horse hard, although he knew better. He wondered if Strongheart knew where his hideout was. He wondered if Joshua was wounded and maybe slowed down. He would put plenty of miles between himself and Florence before he would even stop to eat or rest.

McMahon thought about heading south toward Hardscrabble Junction, or Wetmore, then east and maybe make it to Bent's Fort or Pueblo and try to get lost easier by heading toward more civilization.

An hour later, he could not help himself. Harlance and Jeeter had been raised in the mountains and the mountains were what they knew. He turned right, or west, and headed back toward Westcliffe. Twice he rode up on ridges to glass the country back toward Florence and see if Strongheart was in pursuit.

The outlaw just could not get it out of his mind that the crazy half-breed had traveled all those miles and fought so many men only to keep a promise. He just could not understand that kind of thinking. He had never been so frightened in his life, and he did not understand why. He'd known plenty of tough men.

The problem was, though, Harlance had never in all his years, with all the toughs he'd known, met a man with the heart and emotional toughness of Joshua Strongheart. Harlance hated the man, maybe because he could never be like him, not in a day. Not in a million years.

The outlaw started being more sensible with his horse. He had been riding the owlhoot trail too long to ride such a good mount into the ground. He decided he would take it easy, at a brisk but careful pace, in the climb back up to the Wet Mountain Valley. He would stop at the saloon in Westcliffe and have a whiskey. Heck, he thought, he would have a bottle of whiskey. Then he would either head over Music Pass into the San Luis Valley or maybe he would have to go Cotopaxi and go west from there.

After McMahon had heard the shooting stop and wondered if Strongheart was saddling up to pursue him, the tall warrior had lain on his back as people emerged from buildings. Blood dripped out of several gun holes in his body. The right side of his head was misshapen, and his right eye was swollen completely shut. He continued to lie on his back as wide-eyed citizens walked up slowly, and all that moved was his long, shiny hair blowing across his rugged face.

One merchant said, "I saw. The bloke killed six of them, by himself. What a shootist! What a man!"

Another looked at Strongheart and said, "What a fool. He's dead, ain't he? What's amazing 'bout that, partner?"

11

The Haven

Joshua Strongheart saw a bright light that was so brilliant it might have been blinding. However, it was not. Instead, it attracted him the way a gasoline lamp attracted moths. It kept drawing him closer, and he felt a peace that he had never felt. He also felt a very deep happiness that he could not explain. Unexplainable to him was the sense of knowing and the sense of understanding he was feeling. It was like he had the answers to many questions that would normally nag him from time to time. He felt confidently wise and discerning. It was a wonderful feeling, a true euphoria he had never felt before. Suddenly, he remembered the gunfight, and he remembered how he started laughing in it. That made him feel happy, too. It was a feeling that the gunfight itself was not important at all, but his laughter was.

Then the light beckoned him again. He looked at it and smiled softly, feeling that he would find even more contentment and love inside that light. He moved toward it, and his feelings of wonderment magnified sevenfold. The closer he got, the better he felt. Then he suddenly stopped, still looking at the light. The euphoric feelings subsided momentarily, as he felt unsettled. He wanted that tranquility in the light, but a sense of duty pulled him back away from it. He had to give Annabelle her ring, and he had to protect her, but from what? Joshua became restless. He started feeling very restless. And then he heard it. The voice. Her voice. Annabelle was calling him.

"Joshua, please come back! Joshua do not leave me now before our love is realized," came the tearful pleas.

It was hard, but he had to open his eyes. The right one hurt badly. He felt her presence and smelled her.

"Doctor!" Annabelle yelled close by. "Doctor, he smiled!"

He tried again to open his eyes and the left one opened. He saw Annabelle's back and the back of her head, but only with his left eye. He could not open his right eye. He smiled again, and suddenly he felt himself falling, swirling back down into that murky abyss of darkness and comfort.

The doctor came into the room and held Annabelle by the shoulders as she sobbed. She threw herself against the kindly gray-haired man. He looked at the Pinkerton agent, then Lucky came into the room behind him. Annabelle had dark circles under her beautiful blue eyes, now flooding over with tears of relief.

She pulled back, saying, "Doctor, Lucky, he smiled. I told you both he would live."

The doctor said gently, "Miss Ebert, I didn't say he wouldn't live. I said it would be a miracle if he did. Look at him."

Lucky hated doing so himself.

They all looked at Strongheart lying on Annabelle's bed, where he had been for days now. His right eye was still swollen almost shut, and the ugly bruise from the bullet that had torn across his temple, hairline, and eye was no longer black and blue but was now yellow and brown. The swelling had gone down considerably though. His torso and legs were bandaged, and the young warrior was a magnificent specimen of muscles and sinew, but now covered with scars and new ones forming.

His legend was spreading everywhere and grew with each telling. It was the story of a man who refused to be

a mongrel, but was a mighty warrior of two races. His tale
was being told in the lodges of his people, the Lakota, but
also in the lodges of their allies, the Cheyenne and the
Arapaho, and even in the lodges of their enemies, such as
the Crow. At the same time, the story was being carried
from one saloon to the next, to church meetings, and other
rendezvous. Everywhere, the tale of Strongheart, a man
of two hearts, a will of iron, and principle of pure gold,
was being told. A story of how he hunted down a simple
wedding ring, a keepsake, because of one reason, a pledge
to the widow of a hero, a cavalry officer who lost his life
in the line of duty. Strongheart had bested many men in
search of that ring, and then, attacked by six armed thugs,
he did not run. He did not hide. He shot it out with six men
at once, killing them all, and getting filled with bullet holes
himself.

The widow now had her ring back because of his incredible courage and unquestionable integrity and tenacity.
And the great young man lay lingering near death, while
she tirelessly cared for him. People far and wide prayed for
him. Neighbors in Canon City, like the Rudd women, took
over her café and kept her recipes and good service going,
while she stayed by Joshua's bed. The Pinkertons, through
Lucky, gave her money, which she tried to refuse, to care
for him. A saloon owner in Westcliffe and a storekeeper in
Cotopaxi had come to see the young man in near funeral-
parlor repose, and before leaving, they had each placed
large sums of money on the widow's table just to help with
expenses. There was no hospital around Canon City.

Joshua rode atop Gabriel, and his hair streamed out
behind him, a bald eagle tail feather attached to it, with a
beaded base. He wore his Levi's and moccasins, his father's
knife and his stepfather's pistol, and in his hand was his
beautiful Winchester '73, but he now had it decorated
with horsehair, dyed porcupine quills, and an eagle feather
attached to the front stock and two red-tailed hawk feathers attached to the rear stock, near the receiver. Instead of
his saddle, he sat atop a Hudson's Bay blanket, while Gabe

galloped across a high mountain meadow and Joshua's father, Claw Marks, and his mother rode before him, each on matching Golden palominos. He was trying to catch up, but far behind him, he heard Annabelle's voice again, pleading. He looked wistfully at his parents and reined the mighty pinto back and looked behind him. Somewhere in the thickness of the trees was the woman he loved calling for him.

"Joshua, please come back!" came her distant cries, and they grew louder as he rode closer to the woods. "I love you Joshua. I cannot lose you, too! Come back please."

He felt a presence. He was in a room and opened his eyes. In the firelight he saw the beautiful features of Annabelle Ebert, looking away, tears running down both perfectly formed cheekbones. He smiled again and his eyes closed.

Joshua felt warm, and the smells of the cooking fire were wonderful. He smelled bacon, egg, potatoes, apple pie, coffee. It made him so hungry he thought his throat had been slit.

He opened his eyes, and it was a sunny morning. Joshua could see from both eyes now and suddenly realized that. His eyes looked around the room. There was a table with clean sheets and towels and bandages on it. There was a washbasin and a pitcher next to it, and a bar of soap. Everything sat on lace doilies, and the room was very clean and smelled nice. He could see into another room where there was a fireplace, and he saw the edge of a table. He was in a comfortable feather bed and was covered by a down comforter. He moved it and looked down. Joshua saw several obvious bullet wounds, now unbandaged and scabbing over.

Then he heard Annabelle's voice in the other room, saying, "Oh, Joshua, will today be the day you wake up and join me?"

He said as loud as he could manage it, "Yes!"

It did not come out too strong, but he clearly heard her stop. Footsteps, and there she was as beautiful as ever in the doorway, wearing a bright dress and apron, with a smile a mile wide and the prettiest blue eyes he had ever seen set off by her jet black hair. The eyes glistened with the brand-new tears he was watching form.

"Oh, Joshua!" she exclaimed and ran forward, unable to contain herself. "I knew this day would come."

He smiled and said softly, "Did you get the ring?"

She said, "Oh yes. God bless you. Thank you so very, very much. How are you feeling?"

"I am starved! My stomach is rubbing a blister on my backbone," he mused.

She laughed and walked over to prop him up on several pillows from the bedside.

Bidding him to be patient, she returned with a small table with shortened legs, which she placed across his lap. Then she brought in a plate heaping with bacon, three eggs sunny side up, sliced potatoes, and biscuits. She then brought him a large cup of coffee. Strongheart ate two helpings that first meal, while she just watched him eat and smiled nonstop.

"How long have I been here?" he asked.

"Weeks!" she said enthusiastically.

"Dr. Barry Greenfield was in a store in Florence the day of the fight and was one of the first to find you. He got your bleeding stopped right away, and several told me that was what saved you," she replied.

"How did I end up here?" he asked.

She said, "I told them to bring you here and I would take care of you."

She looked down now, having embarrassed herself.

Strongheart said softly, "Thank you."

Annabelle said, "You are welcome. I have been speaking to you for weeks, trying to get you to awaken. They all said you would die."

Joshua said, "I tried to, but I think I heard you. It made me want to stay."

"You think you heard me?"

"Yes, several times. Did you yell one time that I was smiling?"

"Yes, weeks ago. The doctor was here and your boss, Lucky. I saw a smile on your face and knew you would live," she answered.

He said, "Your back was turned, but I opened my eyes, well one of them, and saw you."

She said, "You did? Oh, I wish I would have turned around. Yes, you would not have seen from your right eye then. It was terribly swollen for a long time. A bullet hit you in the temple right next to your eye and tore the skin along your temple and into your hair. It is healed now, but there is a scar. It was horribly swollen on that side of your head and around your eye. Even your other eye was black and blue from it."

Joshua said, "What about those owlhoots I had the disagreement with?"

"You killed them all! You were magnificent, folks said who saw it," she replied. "They said you were shot to doll rags and were walking towards them shooting, and they all said you were laughing."

He chuckled and accepted a third cup of coffee. She brought him a generous slice of apple pie.

Strongheart said, "Annabelle, you make the best food I have ever tasted. This pie is the best I have ever eaten."

She blushed and played with her apron. She replied, "That is just because you were so hungry."

"No," he replied immediately. "It is because you are such a great cook."

There was a long, awkward pause.

Finally he said, "How have I lived without food? How did I get so clean? I have so many questions."

She said, "I have had to force-feed you mashed up food and water. I have kept you bathed."

Joshua said, "You have seen me naked?"

She really blushed now, but then chuckled and said, "Joshua, I did not give you baths with your clothes on. It defeats the purpose."

He laughed, and it was his turn to blush. Then he got very serious.

"Thank you for saving my life. I must have cost you a ton of money. I will pay you when I am up and about."

She started laughing, and he wondered why. She told him about Lucky, Jerome Guy, and Zack Banta, about receiving money from all three men. She told about the women who ran her café for her, and Joshua was simply amazed that people who did not even know him had helped so much and cared so. He really felt humbled.

Joshua suddenly felt a strong urge to void his bladder and bowels. He tried to get up and his head started swimming.

Embarrassed again, he said, "I guess eating all that after so long of not eating."

She did not say a word, but brought a bedpan over to him and a washrag. She left the room and closed a large curtain behind her in the doorway. He heard her go outside and was grateful.

Joshua slept most of the rest of that day, but the next day, with Annabelle holding his upper arm, he walked into the other room and sat in front of the fireplace in a rocking chair, wrapped in a quilted blanket. She made him hot chocolate. He ate liver for lunch and steak for dinner, and within two more days, he was feeling more alive and healthier. Strongheart wanted to try walking outside, but he saw snow on the ground.

Annabelle came in with an armload of firewood, and he said, "It is wintertime?"

She smiled and it hit her again that he had missed so much.

She said, "Yes. You know in this area the snow never stays, so it should be gone tomorrow."

"I know," he said. "I like the climate around here better than any place in Colorado Territory. What month is it?"

"December. You just missed Christmas," she said. "A new year starts in just two days."

Annabelle got dressed and then came up to Joshua, saying, "I have to go to my café and check on things, collect my receipts, and deposit money in the bank. Will you be okay?"

"Yes, ma'am," he said.

Annabelle returned two hours later and saw that Strongheart was in bed sleeping soundly.

She went to the table and saw something lying there. It was a small package, wrapped in old newspaper, and there was red yarn tied around it and into a bow. A small folded piece of paper was attached to the bow and she looked at it.

It read, "Merry Christmas. Thanks for all you do and for being you. Joshua."

She opened the package and inside was a rolled-up piece of her good paper with some script written on it. Attached was an eagle feather with the base wrapped in colored beads.

The note read, "My dearest Annabelle, I have had no way to shop for you for Christmas, so all I have to offer is my undying gratitude and affection and some words from William Shakespeare. Your most humble servant, Joshua

> *Doubt thou the stars are fire;*
> *Doubt that the sun doth move;*
> *Doubt truth to be a liar;*
> *But never doubt I love.*

William Shakespeare, *Hamlet*, Act II, Scene II"

She sat there with tears once again tumbling from her eyes, staring into the bedroom yet seeing only his legs and feet.

She shook her head, whispering to herself, "What an amazing man!"

Strongheart asked if he could try sitting at the table for dinner, and afterward, when they both were drinking coffee, Annabelle excused herself. She returned from the fruit cellar and carried a wrapped package herself.

Smiling, she handed it to Joshua, saying softly, "Merry Christmas."

He said, "Annabelle, you have done enough already."

He opened the package slowly, and she bit her lower lip in nervousness and anticipation. Joshua looked down into the wrapping paper and smiled broadly.

She said, "I have been working out Gabriel a couple of times each week and noticed you do not have one."

Joshua said, "Thank you very much. I have needed one. That is really thoughtful."

He lifted up a braided thirty-foot leather lariat.

She said, "I hope you like it. I was going to get a rope one, but I thought you might like this better."

"Better?" Strongheart said. "Annabelle, do you know how many men would love a braided leather lasso? This is much stronger and lasts longer than rope. Thank you very much."

He was very impressed. A lasso was one thing Strongheart had been lacking, and he'd known he needed one, but he'd always been so busy he never remembered to buy one.

The riata, lariat, or lasso was one of the cowboy's most important tools. Besides being used for the obvious, lassoing cows or horses, it had a whole myriad of other uses. It could become a clothesline, the main ridgepole for a tent, an aid to climbing, the tie to lash items on a travois or to make a travois, an emergency bridle and reins, a frame for a hammock, a repair tool for harness or wagons, a snare for large predators, a pull for large items that needed to be moved, a splint for broken legs or arms, the binding to tie up outlaws, and many other things.

"I can't wait to see Gabe. Thanks for riding him," Joshua said.

"He is a wonderful horse," she replied, "the best I have ever ridden on. His gaits are so comfortable. I curry him and brush him down all the time."

"Oh no," Joshua said. "He's going to hate me when he sees me."

She giggled, as this really tickled her fancy.

Strongheart said, "Annabelle, I have seen that you have that old army cot in the corner you have been sleeping on, and I sleep in your feather bed. I am doing better. Why don't I sleep on the cot?"

She started laughing, "Because your legs and arms and shoulders would hang out all over the place. Besides, you have not even been able to go outside yet, Joshua. You are doing better and getting stronger, but we have a ways to go."

"Annabelle," he said, "why are you doing this for me? Nobody deserves this kind of treatment."

"You do," she said without hesitation, embarrassing herself again. "Joshua Strongheart, how can you say that? You spent months and almost died keeping a promise to me, over a ring, a simple little ring."

"It is not the ring," Strongheart said, getting serious. "I want all men and women to always know that my words are iron. If a man says he will stand in the rain, he should get wet. If a man says he can fly, he should jump from a cliff and fly to his death keeping his word. I did nothing. I only kept my word. That is what all men should do."

"You did nothing? Ha ha." She laughed. "Joshua, you are indeed a real man and there are none any more. We have politicians in Washington who tell people lies about the men from the other party and make hollow promises just to get elected. These are our leaders. Men do not really risk their lives to keep their word, except you."

The next day, she made sure he had been fed and checked his wounds, which were now healing very well, and with his reassurance all would be well, she went to the restaurant. That is what Joshua had been waiting for. He made his way to the door and went outside. The snow was gone and the sun was out, so the day in the semi-arid climate was nice, especially in the direct sunshine. He made his way to the woodpile and grabbed a piece of firewood, then another, and another. He still had his muscles, so it did not seem that he would overburden himself with any amount of logs. He carried them inside and stacked them near the fireplace. So far, so good. Strongheart headed back out the door. He carried four loads of firewood inside, then had to sit down in the rocker and rest. He fell asleep and had a nice nap for an hour.

Annabelle came home before dark, carrying a meal for him from the restaurant, but he was asleep in the bed. Annabelle walked into the other room and saw all the firewood he had stacked, and she smiled, shaking her head.

She went into the bedroom and decided to check his wounds to make sure he had not torn anything open. As she pulled back the sheet and started to touch his rippled abdomen, his right hand shot down and grabbed her wrist like a vise. As his eyes opened, he let loose immediately, saying, "Sorry. I guess I am getting my reflexes back."

Their faces were inches apart, and she did not speak. She wanted him to kiss her so badly and sweep her into his arms.

He had never wanted a woman so much in his life, but this was no dance hall chippy. This was the woman he had fallen in love with. Joshua felt so conflicted. Her husband had now been dead just over a year. That was not a long time. He wanted to taste those soft lips. He wanted to hold her.

They stared for awkward moments, and he finally smiled backed, lifted his head up a little, and said, "Do I smell some delicious food?"

She said, "I brought you dinner from the restaurant. It's still hot. Do you want to eat?"

"Yes, ma'am," he said, getting out of bed.

They went into the other room and sat at the table. As she had already gotten used to, he held her chair as she sat down. They talked well into the night, and he really slept well.

The next day he was sore from the previous day's exertion, but he was not as sore as he'd expected to be. He would add some more exercise this day.

Two days later, Dr. Greenfield showed up. Jewish, he had graying black hair, a pleasant smile, and was short, with a bit of a paunch. Joshua liked him.

After introductions, Strongheart said, "Dr. Greenfield, I just do not know how I can possibly thank you. You saved my life. If it were not for you, I would be in Greenwood Cemetery right now."

Dr. Greenfield nodded at Annabelle, saying, "She is who you should thank. This young lady would not give up on you, and everybody else did. She stayed with you day in and day out, watching over you like a meadowlark watching her nest. She would speak to you and act like you were awake. Best nurse I have ever seen."

Joshua smiled at Annabelle, and she blushed and turned her back to find busywork.

Greenfield examined Joshua and said, "So you have started doing things, huh?"

Joshua said, "Yes, Doc, a little each day."

The doctor said, "Well, several months ago, I would not have believed it, but your wounds seem to have healed. You lost lots of blood, but I do not think you will hurt yourself with exercise. You need that, sunshine, and food."

He turned to Annabelle, saying, "Young lady, I would get lynched by the good people of Canon City if I tried to get you to give up your café, but if you ever want to be a full-time nurse, I have got plenty of work for you."

He smiled and left.

In the days ahead, Annabelle kept the food pouring into Joshua, and he kept adding more vigorous exercise. By the following week, he was able to saddle Gabriel and Annabelle's horse, and they took a short ride together. He had been practicing his quick draw each day behind her house, too, including bringing the Winchester to bear fast. They started going to the hot springs, and he would soak there each day.

Once Strongheart started gaining his strength back, it came back quickly, though he still would get winded and sometimes a little light-headed.

Spring was coming on, and there was a real dry and warm spell, which was very common to Canon City. Annabelle and Joshua had eaten dinner and were outside working in her garden, when he suddenly stopped and said, "Can we go in and talk?"

They went inside, washed up, and sat down.

Joshua said, "When you spoke to me all the time, you said many things, didn't you?"

She said, "Yes. Why?"

Strongheart said, "Even though I was in a deep sleep, I am sure I heard you several times."

She said, "I am so glad."

Joshua said, "I have always wondered, and it has bothered me since. Did you say to me not to leave, that you loved me?"

Annabelle said, "I uh, I am embarrassed."

"I'm sorry," he said. "I should not have asked."

"No," she answered. "I always want us to be honest with each other. I loved my husband, Joshua, and I tried not to fall in love with you, but I did. I could not help myself at all. You are too wonderful."

He swept her into his arms and kissed her softly but passionately. She pushed against him, and then he held her at arm's length and took several deep breaths.

Strongheart said, "Annabelle, I have been in love with you since the very first time I saw you on the stage."

"Oh, Joshua," she cooed.

He put his hand up.

"Hear me out," he said. "Tomorrow, I am moving maybe into a hotel. You are a widow, and I have healed a great deal and am much stronger. I do not want your neighbors to gossip about you."

She started to argue, but what he said made sense. She did have a business, but she also wanted him so much. She had dreamed so many nights of lying against him, her head on that massive chest.

"Joshua," she said, "sometimes I could hardly contain myself. I want you so badly. I want to be held by you, not for a moment but for all time."

He said, "You have no idea how difficult it has been for me to be around you. Each day, I have grown more deeply in love with you. But your husband has been gone less than two years. I want you to make sure it is love and not an end to loneliness. I also have to feel right inside. Even though I never knew your husband, I do not want to feel like I have betrayed him. I cannot explain that."

She said, "I understand."

12

The Evil That Men Do

At the west end of Canon City the road to the river began with a large curve called Soda Point. It was near the hot springs and just past the territorial prison. That point rose up to become an eight-hundred-foot-high rocky ridgeline, very steep on both sides, referred to as Razor Ridge. It consisted of Precambrian rock formations as well as Dakota sandstone, and it ran parallel to much of the west side of Canon City. It was *the* vantage point to reconnoiter anyone and anything in Canon City, and that was exactly where Harlance McMahon had made his hideout and lookout for several days.

After the shoot-out in Florence, the word about Joshua Strongheart's incredible skills, tenacity, and raw courage had spread far and wide. At the same time, the word had also been spread that Harlance McMahon ran in the beginning of the fight and abandoned his own gang.

He could not go anywhere without hearing whispers and snickers behind his back. His own cowardice had totally backfired on him.

One thing that Joshua had learned long ago was a simple principle: The one problem with being one of the Joshua Stronghearts in the world was that some of those who just cannot measure up, or who refuse to try, end up hating you.

To aggravate that, Harlance was totally ashamed of himself. Even though he was afraid to live as an honest citizen giving a hard day's work for a full day's wages, he had never taken water before in a fight. He had even had a couple stand-up gunfights. Now he had completely turned tail, run out on his own men. It made him crazy. . . . literally.

So, thinking in the manner of an outlaw, which is to say ignorantly and outside the norms of logical behavior, Harlance had come up with a plan. He would get back at Strongheart by attacking what he saw as the man's Achilles' heel. And that would be Annabelle Ebert. He would kidnap her, knowing Strongheart would pursue them to the ends of the earth. In Harlance's mind it was quite simple. He would set a trap for Strongheart and bushwhack him. He knew it was risky, because this was the West, not back east. Good women were scarce, so even outlaws protected them. Harlance did not care if what he planned to do was right or not. His only concern was whether or not he could get away with it. He would have to be rough to abduct the woman, but he decided he would be very careful about how he touched her and treated her, just in case he got caught. Although, again with the convoluted thinking of an outlaw, he decided that after he killed Strongheart, he would have to kill the woman, too, as a witness. And if he got that far with her, he would first have all the fun he wanted and then kill her.

He made camp among rocks on the far side of Razor Ridge, and during the day he hid among rocks on the town side, the eastern side, and watched Annabelle's house and café with his spyglass as much as he could. There were plenty of hardwoods near the river, but spring buds had not come out yet—too early—so Harlance was able to see some of the comings and goings.

Harlance might have been crazy, and he might have possessed the naïveté of the criminal mind, but he was not stupid. As he watched Annabelle, he was looking for a pattern or a weakness. He also wanted to see how long Joshua would stay away from her when he left her house. Maybe if there was some kind of pattern he could figure out, he could set up a proper ambush to kidnap her.

He would see her go to the café at different times and return at different times during the day. Joshua seemed to be healing and was splitting firewood all the time, doing work in the yard and in her garden. The two would occasionally ride together.

Harlance wanted to be patient, as he did not want to try to tangle with Joshua straight-up. The man had already proven too dangerous, although what Harlance did not realize was that Strongheart didn't really care about him now. He had gotten the ring back.

But Joshua also knew human nature, and he knew that Harlance would be recognized often now and referred to as a coward, as he had organized a gunfight and run out on it in the beginning. Especially on the owlhoot trail, McMahon would be spoken about behind his back in hushed tones. He would be regarded as a joke by his own peers, criminals. And if that didn't drive him over the cliff mentally, Harlance was also still desperately fearing for his life, that Strongheart was still going to hunt him down and kill him. He just could not conceive that Strongheart was no longer a threat to him.

Although Harlance wanted to be careful, on the other hand he wanted to strike before Strongheart was fully recovered.

Now he got an unexpected surprise. He saw Strongheart with his horse saddled up and full saddlebags. Judging from the body language of the pair as she walked outside and handed him his rifle and a bag of something, it seemed he might be moving out of her house.

Annabelle had spent most of the day at the café, and Joshua had ridden Gabe to the Hot Springs Hotel and rented a room. When she arrived home, he waited until she freshened up, and then he swept her into his arms. Faces inches apart, they stared into each other's eyes for a long time. Their lips parted and came together and kissed slowly, as if both wanted to savor every second of their kiss, of their embrace. When they finally stepped back, she had tears running down her cheeks, as she knew what he was going to say.

She smiled bravely, joking, "I thought Indians did not know much about kissing."

He grinned and replied, "My stepfather taught me to be a gentleman, and my mother told me over and over that real women want a real man, and they want romance."

She smiled, "They taught you well."

He smiled.

Joshua said, "I rented a room at the Hot Springs Hotel. I have to move."

"Why?" she asked.

"You know why," he said softly.

She looked down and then lifted her chin, saying, "Yes, I know why."

He had made coffee, and she poured each of them a cup. She handed his to him and gave him a soft kiss at the same time.

They drank, and she said, "Joshua, I want you to understand something. I have thought about this a lot. I loved my husband very much, Joshua, and I was true to him. However, he is gone now and I was raised to always survive. And I have already wrestled with my thoughts and emotions. I know that there is part of you, half of you actually, that is Sioux, which I may not always understand, but I am willing to. I also have thought about this without my emotions. I mean analyzing our situation. I truly and deeply love you, and Joshua, I can honestly say I love you even more than I loved my husband. He was a wonderful man and he was all man, but you are even more so."

He sighed.

She went on, "I know that life with you would sometimes be difficult because you are half-red and I am white. Only because some people are ignorant. But it is important to me that you understand, I know for certain I love you with all my heart. I also respect you and am willing to wait until you feel totally good about this."

He set both of their cups on the table and pulled her into his arms, and they kissed long and hard.

"I have to leave, or I never will," he said. "May I take you to dinner tomorrow?"

"Oh yes, I would love that," she said.

He said, "I will be here with my horse to pick you up at six o'clock."

He walked to the door and turned, smiling. Using his right hand, he brought his thumb toward his chest and touched himself with it. He then crossed his arms at the wrists, with the left wrist on top of the right and the backs of his hands toward her, fists closed. With the right hand actually touching his breast over his heart on the left side, he struck himself with some power in the chest, and then pointed at her with the index finger of his right hand.

Before she could ask, he said, "That is Indian sign language. Since most nations have totally different languages, for many years we have spoken to each other in sign language. All the tribes and nations use the same sign language. I just told you, 'I love you.' With the power that I struck my heart with I told you how strong that love is. If I would have just touched my chest with my fists, that would have meant that I am fond of you."

He pulled his shirt out of his jeans and said, "How deeply do I love you, Annabelle?"

He raised his shirt, and there was a big, angry red spot on his heart where he had struck his chest. He tucked his shirt back in.

Smiling and opening the door, Strongheart said, "You make my chest red."

He walked to his horse.

She followed him out, smiling broadly, eyes glistening, feeling giddy like a schoolgirl. She handed him his Winchester and the oilskin bag that contained the rest of his belongings.

This was the action watched by Harlance through his spyglass from Razor Ridge.

He was safe in his hideout, but little did he or anybody else know that in just over thirty years' time, a little after the turn of the century, prison labor would build a single lane road that would run the length of the ridge, and it would become a major tourist attraction for decades, named Skyline Drive.

Now Harlance watched Strongheart as he rode to the hotel, and he could even see him unsaddling his horse and putting him in a stall at the hotel stable. He knew that the time to strike would be now.

With the woman as a hostage, he would be at a considerable advantage over Strongheart because of the harm he could do to her. He also had been an outlaw in this area for years, and he knew the Big Hole country, the Little Hole country, the Nesterville and Cotopaxi area, North Park, Red Canyon, Grape Creek Canyon, Lookout Mountain, the Grand Canyon of the Arkansas, the entire Arkansas drainage, Phantom Canyon, Beaver Creek Canyon, Garden Park, and everything in between and all around. Basically, as a somewhat successful outlaw, Harlance McMahon knew every nook and cranny in the very large county, which was part prairie and mainly mountain.

He figured that he had not been able to ambush Strongheart successfully with Big Scars Cullen because he did not have an edge like he would with the beautiful woman. But he began to worry now, because Strongheart had been living with Annabelle and now had moved out. Again, he saw things like a criminal and did not understand the kind of principled thinking that came from people such as Strongheart. He saw ulterior motives in every situation, because that was his own mind-set always. He assumed that Strongheart had been sleeping with Annabelle all along, and he wondered if they had now had a falling out. If so, would Strongheart come to save her? he wondered. Again, with his thinking, Harlance would not even consider that Strongheart had moved out to protect her reputation, that they had not been intimate and that he was doing this out of love and common sense as opposed to any selfish reasons.

Joshua enjoyed soaking in the hot springs, and like others he felt that the mineral spring–fed hot water had medicinal advantages for those soaking there. Whether it did or did not, it felt good on his now healing body. There was still soreness, especially from the hard work that he had been doing. He would work hard again the next day and get his clothes washed and make preparations for a romantic dinner. His mind was already working on that.

From the time he was a young boy, Joshua had heard stories about his biological father and how much he and Joshua's mother had loved each other. The other thing that stuck in his mind was his father's total unselfishness in not marrying her. Those days were well over two decades earlier, even well before the War Between the States. Joshua knew his father was correct in assuming that many people would treat him and Joshua's ma horribly because of racism, not just in the white community but among the Lakota as well. He still ran into many problems in the white man's world. Trouble was brewing with the Lakota and their allies, such as the Cheyenne and the Arapaho. In just less than three years' time, Civil War hero and presidential hopeful Lieutenant Colonel George Armstrong Custer and his entire battalion would be killed at the Battle of the Little Bighorn, which would be known by many whites as Custer's Last Stand, but by the Lakota as the Battle of the Greasy Grass.

Joshua had always wanted that great love like his father had with his mother, but he also would remember his father's selfless act, which he respected and admired so much. He knew that there was always a chance for a good life anyway, even with love lost. The Pinkerton was reminded that Dan had maybe been more distant and a stern taskmaster, but he'd done every action out of love and concern for Joshua and a desire to make the young half-breed tough for a tough, ofttimes unforgiving world.

Joshua had sent Lucky a telegraph earlier and let him

know he was well on the mend and had rented a room at the hotel where they had both stayed.

Zack Banta knew he was fine simply because Banta knew everything that was going on in southern Colorado almost before it happened.

Harlance made his way down the switchback trail on the east side of Razor Ridge. At the bottom were smaller hog-backs and dirt mounds, and he would use these for cover as he worked his way closer to the house. He would wait until dark to actually get close enough to carry out his kidnapping plan. He moved as near as he dared go to the territorial prison, which was at the far south end of the ridge on the eastern side. Harlance waited with his horse behind the last large dirt mound.

The sun had been well hidden by the mountains as he came down, and the sky was now dark. He mounted his horse and, avoiding houses, rode toward hers a half mile distant. Arriving, Harlance tied his horse to a corner post of the corral behind her barn and grabbed his Henry repeater. He then went into the corral, caught her horse, and slipped on its bridle and saddled it. When he was finished, he left his horse and led hers to the front of the house. He tied the horse to a tree in the front yard and went up next to the small porch.

Harlance figured that if she saw her horse was saddled, she might think it a surprise by Joshua or a friend and would be curious enough to come out of the house. He correctly assumed she would not dream that anyone would saddle her horse and tie it there if they were up to no good. It just would not make sense.

On the other hand, the outlaw figured that she would remain in the house or bring a gun if he knocked or did anything else more obvious to try to get her to come outside.

Unfortunately for Annabelle, he assumed correctly. He used a long stick to tap on her window and backed away into the shadows, gun at the ready. Annabelle was stitching on a dress, getting ready for her date tomorrow. She was so excited just thinking about it. She could not believe she had actually kissed Joshua, and she loved his words about his mother teaching him that women want romance. She wondered what he would do for their date, but she was certain it would be romantic.

It was right at that wonderful fantasy moment that there was a tap on the window. She looked out and saw her horse tied out front, saddled, and ready to ride. Annabelle smiled, thinking Joshua had planned an evening ride for them. She put on her boots and a warm coat in preparation for the late winter night air. She grabbed her gloves and walked out the door and up to her horse, looking left and right for the man she loved. There was a click as Harlance cocked his Henry and stepped from the shadows.

"Ya say one word above a whisper," he said quietly, "and I'll shoot ya where ya stand, git back on mah horse, and ride off inta the darkness. Ya understand, little lady?"

Her heart sank. Annabelle wanted to scream, but she believed him that he would shoot. Her mind flashed from one scenario to the next. She wished Joshua would appear, but she knew better. It was night. They had a date tomorrow night. He would not appear now.

Harlance said, "Climb inta the saddle."

Then she got a plan. She stepped toward her horse and pretended to stumble, falling to her knees. She set her two leather gloves down side by side and pulled several fingers toward each other, forming the letter H on her pathway. She got up and brushed her dress at the knees. Using her body as a shield, she kept Harlance from seeing the H in the dark. She climbed into her saddle, placing her dress over both sides of it. She decided then that she would tear strips from her petticoat and drop them along their trail.

But Harlance walked up to her and tied her hands to the saddle horn with a cotton piggin string, normally used to tie calves' legs together for branding. He grabbed her reins and led her to the corral. Once there, he secured a long lead line and attached it under her horse's bridle and mounted up himself. He led her off into the night, avoiding houses as best as he could. He led her up over the hogbacks and

Razor Ridge, to the road to Eight Mile Hill, which would parallel the Grand Canyon of the Arkansas and bring him back to the river at Parkdale. This was the same road the stage had taken when Joshua first met Annabelle. She and Harlance now rode well into the night, crossed the bridge over the whitewater at Parkdale, and headed out Copper Gulch Stage Road. He took her to the first gulch off the stage road and made camp for the night, tying her to a tree.

What Harlance did not know about was Annabelle's little ruse. Although her wrists had been bound to the saddle horn, she would bring one leg at a time up as he led her, and would still tear strips off her petticoat to drop along their trail. When he tied her to the tree, she figured she could wait until he was asleep, and by again lifting her leg up she could tear many off with the bark of the tree. The challenge then would be to hide them to drop off the horse the next day. She also figured she would be able to tear a number of pieces off her petticoat when he allowed her to go behind bushes when nature called. She would then hide the strips in one hand and drop them one at a time along the trail.

The next day, he gave her hardtack and coffee and nothing else. She was glad she tore strips, because instead of leading her back to the stagecoach road, he started that way then turned north on a flat rock outcropping, heading back toward the river. At the trail along the river, he headed west, and within a quarter mile he entered the big rocky Arkansas River canyon, which ran for miles.

Harlance had been to the headwaters of the Arkansas and actually stepped across them near Oro City, which was a gold town located at 10,123 feet elevation that in a few short years, after silver discoveries in the lead deposits there, it would be replaced by Leadville, which would continue to grow and become the highest incorporated city in North America and to have the highest airport on the continent, too. For now, it was attracting many miners and would for several decades to come.

Through the river canyon where they now rode, the river often roared on their right, but during this time of year it was at its lowest, so those spots were less frequent. During June, after the beginning of the snowmelt in the Sangre de Cristo range and the Collegiate range, the Arkansas through that canyon would host the nastiest, most dangerous rapids in North America. Fortunately, Annabelle was able to drop her cloth strips at several critical spots, so Joshua or anybody else following should be able to find them easily.

She knew that he would come, and she knew that he would save her. On the other hand, she knew this Harlance McMahon was ruthless and had to be insane. Women were just not kidnapped or molested very often in the West. Back east, yes, where there were plenty of women, but not on what was called "the frontier."

In that very regard, she feared much for Strongheart: Her kidnapper was clever, but he was also mentally unstable, and she had no idea what type of trap he was planning. She made her mind up then that if he was luring Joshua into a trap and Joshua was approaching and would certainly be bushwhacked, she would cry out and warn him. She decided firmly this would be her action, even if it was obvious it would cost her her life.

Strongheart was soaking in the mineral hot springs when the blacksmith came in. He walked up to him, introduced himself, and told Joshua he was sent by the two women working at the café. They said that Annabelle was supposed to be there for breakfast, but never showed up. He had gone in to eat, and they asked him to go check at her house. He told Joshua about the pair of gloves and said that he had left them there for him to see for himself. Joshua climbed out of the springs and dried off, asking the blacksmith to find the sheriff immediately and warn him.

When the blacksmith explained the specific positioning of the gloves, Joshua said immediately, "Harlance McMahon! Tell the sheriff it was Harlance, and I am going after him. I will leave the sheriff an obvious trail to follow."

He ran to his room to throw on clothes, pack some food, and get on the trail.

In less than a half hour, Strongheart was at Annabelle's house checking inside and inspecting the gloves. He left them for the sheriff to see. He then followed the tracks to the barn and now had in his mind the whole scenario of what had happened. At the tree in the front yard he found where the bark had been scraped off by a horse's reins making a little ring around the trunk, and numerous tracks where the horse had pranced when tied there, and droppings from the animal as well. He found where Harlance had hidden by the porch and the broken off and stripped branch he'd used to tap on the window.

Joshua inspected the inside of the house to see if it had been burglarized and to check for other clues. There had been a pot of coffee on the stove, which had boiled away, leaving a dark brown layer of crud within. He returned to the stable and saw where Annabelle's horse had been saddled and where Harlance had tied his own horse.

Strongheart was ready to move on their trail as fast as he could, but first he took a pair of underwear he had gotten from her laundry basket and had Gabriel smell it. The big horse snorted. Tossing the undies into the stable, he mounted up and headed after a date with destiny.

The tracks headed northwest toward the hogbacks, and entering there, he found the first strip of white cloth. Gabriel climbed the long ridgeline easily and seemed to be eager to be on this new adventure.

The warrior had had the horse sniff her used pantaloons on a hunch. He knew that the territorial prison used bloodhounds to track prisoners when they escaped. Joshua knew how many times he had been riding and Gabriel would smell a deer, bear, human, or anything else out of the ordinary and warn him with a whinny or shiver. Joshua need simply to watch the big ears on the horse, and they would turn toward whatever would end up coming into view later. There were other times Gabe would spot an animal and his eyes would clearly be focused on it, and Joshua could feel his body tighten up until the horse identified the animal.

He had thought about it before. A horse's nostrils were

much, much larger than any dogs, his eyes were much larger, and his ears much larger, plus a horse's ears could turn in any direction to capture a sound, unlike a dog's ears. A horse could not howl like a dog to alert his master, but he could whinny, nicker, blow, or shiver to let the man know something or someone was coming. Joshua knew that he was not the only one: Many Indians and frontiersmen watched their horse's ears to spot enemies or animals before a man would actually see them.

Joshua figured maybe from inhaling her scent the big horse would instinctively be able to tell he was searching for Annabelle. Maybe he could pick up the smell and bail Joshua out if he lost the trail. Once on the stagecoach road, he alternated between a fast trot and a canter, climbing several miles and a thousand feet higher up, to the top of Eight Mile Hill, which was a plateau of maybe six square miles that gave view to mountains on every side except the eastern and, on Joshua's left a few miles away, to the north rim of the Grand Canyon of the Arkansas. Far off in the distance, he could see the snowcaps of the Sangre de Cristo range. This was the first he had seen them in months, and they certainly had much more snow on them now. They were more than thirty miles away but clearly visible.

Harlance looked above him on both sides. This canyon was almost all rocks and steep cliffs. It was noted for its many herds of bighorn sheep, as well as mule deer and the highest concentration of mountain lions in the United States. It also contained a good share of grizzlies and black bear, which was an actual species, not just a color description. In fact, seldom were black bear in Colorado actually black. Most ranged in color from cinnamon to blond to brown. The grizzlies were many shades, as well, but invariably had silver-tipped hairs on their prominent shoulder hump. They also had a dish face, as opposed to the much smaller black bears, and very, very long claws.

Additionally, there were several herds of pure white Rocky Mountain goats with small black horns. The river was teeming with brown trout, rainbows, and cutthroat.

At several points as he and Annabelle rode along they saw large birds of prey riding along the tall steep canyon walls searching for food. These included golden eagles, bald eagles, red-tailed hawks, and buzzards.

Harlance had a plan. They would ride for several miles, to Five Points, a spot halfway to Texas Creek along the river, and they would then turn south and go up Five Points Gulch, one of the most rugged gulches in the area. It was frequently used by knowledgeable outlaws, as there was even one spot, called the "Narrows," where the rocky walls of the gulch came so close together that you had to dismount and tie your stirrups up over the top of the saddle and lead your horse.

The gulch climbed more than two thousand feet for the next six miles and oddly enough ended at the southern base of Lookout Mountain, where Harlance's brother Jeeter McMahon had kept his horse picketed when Joshua shot it out with him at his hideout.

Thanks to the pieces of cloth along the way, which he had now identified as strips of petticoat, Joshua made very good time tracking the outlaw and Annabelle. Before noon, he was at their night location, and he got off of Gabe and crawled around on his hands and knees looking for clues. By this time, the sheriff and his posse were on the early part of the trail.

Strongheart remembered all the days he had been taken out by uncles and older cousins in his father's village and taught how to track, how to look for and work out sign.

He was very glad that he'd decided to check thoroughly on his hands and knees. He found where Annabelle had been tied to a tree and slept. He was also very happy to see by the sign that she had not been accosted. On a hunch, he carefully turned over leaves and branches close to the tree where she slept. He uncovered where she had used her toes to write in the ground and then used her feet together to pick up leaves and branches and drop them over the scratchings.

"Good girl," Strongheart said aloud.

In one spot she wrote simply "HM," meaning of course Harlance McMahon. She also wrote "bush U." Then in a third spot she had traced a Valentine-type heart.

On hands and knees, Strongheart followed all of her tracks, and he found where she had gone behind bushes to relieve her bladder and bowels. In the ground next to that place, she had written with her hand, "I M waiting. Luv U. Careful!"

Strongheart smiled and got on his feet. He was so proud that this woman he loved had had the presence of mind to leave him messages and that she had trusted he would find them. She was even smart enough, he noticed, to drop her strips of petticoat on bushes and limbs where they would not get covered by snow if an early spring or late winter storm came in.

He saw where Harlance had made a flimsy attempt to make it look like they were heading back to the stagecoach road, but he only used his horse. When Joshua saw that the two horses together had turned north and headed toward the river, he knew Harlance was actually going along the river, west toward Cotopaxi. Joshua would need to watch only for where Harlance turned off, and he assumed that Annabelle would clearly mark that spot with one or two strips from her petticoat. Gabriel had already crunched about fifteen miles under his hooves since the day started, but most horses could easily handle twenty miles in a day, and in an emergency, a horse in good shape could handle as much as one hundred miles in a twenty-four-hour period without getting seriously hurt.

Joshua had had reasonably easy road travel most of the time so far, and he hoped that continued. There was no road along the river, but there was a wide, well-worn trail. He put Gabriel at a slow-comfortable mile-eating trot along the Arkansas. He made sure he stopped several times and went to the river's edge to let Gabe drink if he wanted. Gabe drank once and refused water the second time, but he tried to grab in his mouth as many weeds along the river's edge as he could.

As Joshua was entering the narrow canyon, Harlance had Annabelle, hands-bound, walking in front, while he led both horses, one behind the other, through the Narrows. Their stirrups were tied up over the tops of their saddles. Their passage through the Narrows was fairly short-lived or it would have become a bit claustrophobic. In fact, Annabelle's horse did balk, and it took an additional hour almost to get the gelding through. All horses are claustrophobic, no matter how good the horse, but normally if the horse is following another horse, he will not balk. This horse, however, had not read any of the books on horse behavior. Instead of pulling him, Harlance actually untied his lead line, which was tied to his own horse's tail. What the outlaw did not know was that Annabelle's horse had been kicked under the jaw by another horse a few years earlier when the same thing had been done, tying the horse's lead to another horse's tail. He might have followed Gabriel, because they had become pasture mates, and he'd learned Gabe was not a kicker. Being a herd animal, a horse does not want to be left alone, so once Harlance had removed the threat of the tied lead line, Annabelle's horse readily followed the owlhoot's mount through the Narrows.

The delay, though, helped Strongheart, as his big horse was chewing up the miles, and though he was protecting his horse, he had no desire to stop for food or anything. He rode along the winding river, and on the other side, the high ridgeline leaned away from the river, as if looking down its marble nose at the serpentine, living waterway. However, the ledges went almost straight up on Joshua's immediate left. Across the river a point came out and a large herd of bighorns were bedded down on the grassy park there. At the same place, suddenly the ledges dropped away from the trail a little on the left and Joshua could see the convergence of three narrow, rocky gulches. This was Five Points. And "God bless her" was in his thoughts as he saw a big white strip of cloth hanging on a branch along the trail. He saw the tracks end in the river trail, then saw sweeping arches in the dirt heading into Five Points Gulch, where Harlance had foolishly tried to use a branch to wipe out their tracks. That left a better trail than hoofprints.

Strongheart went up into the rocks and immediately saw another strip of cloth sitting on a rock next to the trail letting him know this was the direction they'd headed. He left his horse standing there so he could rest, and he walked back to the main trail along the river. He grabbed three large rocks and placed them in a stack on the left side of the trail, then two more rocks toward Five Points Gulch, so the sheriff and posse would be able to follow. He walked back to his horse and mounted up, having never ridden this route before. He would have to move more slowly now, as this narrow canyon would provide many ideal ambush spots. They moved forward, and the big horse, having smelled Annabelle at Harlance's camp, instinctively knew that they were after this woman, and her scent was in the air now. It had been several hours, but such was the horse's amazing olfactory memory. The thrill of the chase made Gabriel's adrenaline flow, and even though the trail went uphill slowly, he did not want to walk. Strongheart let him have his head. They went up through the high, narrow canyon at a slow trot, seeing many animals, mule deer, bighorn sheep, elk, three coyotes, and a few Rocky Mountain goats on a high peak. These were not the snowcapped peaks of the Sangre de Cristos, but a more intimate and imposing herd of vicious-looking rocky ridges, covered with few trees and many ledges. Riding through the narrow canyon, and looking up and all around, waiting for several fast rounds from McMahon's Henry repeater carbine, Joshua, if he had a vivid imagination, could have easily pictured this silent granite and sandstone herd swooping down on him from the heights.

He saw the Narrows ahead of him and read the ground where Annabelle's horse had pranced and danced, balked, was prodded, and finally went through. He hoped his own horse would not have a tantrum also, but to his chagrin, he tied his stirrups, too, and walked right through with the anxious animal close at hand. Gabriel was now single-minded in his total purpose, and that was to take his pasture mate, partner, master, or however Joshua would be seen from a horse's eyes, to Annabelle. By her smell, Gabe also knew she was a mare and not a male.

The canyon opened up and a few more gulches came in from the sides, as the rocky sentinel of Lookout Mountain suddenly loomed before Harlance. He knew his brother had been killed there by Strongheart. He had ridden out and recovered and buried what was left of the body. The problem, though, was that Lookout Mountain had long been a hideout area for highwaymen, robbers, and other hooligans. And men like Harlance had an arrogance. He saw himself as tougher and smarter than his brother. He knew that they could hide high on Lookout and have a camp with a fire during the night. He would leave their saddles, tack, and horses near the same water tank and good grass, and he and the woman would climb up, with Harlance carrying his saddlebags and both of them carrying their bedrolls.

The horses were already at the water tank when Joshua Strongheart came to the point where the gulch opened up and he could see Lookout Mountain. He started laughing and shook his head. Already he was formulating a plan in his mind. The first part of that would be to seek the tank and see if the two horses were there.

It took another hour of careful riding, trying not to expose himself to Lookout Mountain, so he wouldn't be spotted, before Strongheart got to a spot on the western side of Five Points Gulch where he could see the watering hole with binoculars. Sure enough, within one minute he spotted her horse and then Harlance's, both grazing in the late afternoon sun.

Joshua looked up above the horses on the rocky peak and focused on Jeeter's old hideout. Sure enough, in minutes, he saw small puffs of smoke rising up from the rocky enclave. Strongheart smiled. He would save his love, but he wanted to insure he could do it safely. He had to wait several hours until well after dark, so he set off up a side gulch protected by two east-west running ridges, so he could build his own fire safely, eat, let his horse rest, take a nap, and then get back to work maybe around midnight.

Strongheart had an oilskin bag in his saddlebags in which was some corn and oats mixed. The corn would give Gabriel warmth during the chilly mountain night, as there were still patches of snow in the tree and ledge shadows on the north slopes of the ridges. The oats would give him nourishment along with the corn. When Strongheart finished his food, he shoved the frying pan into some snow and melted and boiled it on the fire. After cleaning the pan, he put it back in the snow to cool it off, dried it, and poured the grain into it for Gabriel. It was a good treat for the horse, who had worked so hard during the day and would need to work maybe harder the next morning and yet again that night.

The night would be cold, and Strongheart always made sure he had large rocks near the fire as heat reflectors, but he also surrounded this small fire pit with smaller round rocks. He then dug in the ground near the fire, where the ground was, and buried the warmed stones under the dirt, to make a good spot for his bedding area. Having made sure he had some nice logs crossed in the pit, he lay down and went right to sleep. When he awakened several hours later, he could tell from the sky that it was around midnight. It was hard to crawl out from under that blanket, but he built the fire up and put his coffeepot on it.

Fifteen minutes or so after finishing his coffee, Joshua had covered his fire with snow, then dirt, and headed out on Gabriel. The big horse was alert and ready to pursue the smell of his master's mare, Annabelle. His thinking was not really that precise, but instinctively that is how Gabe viewed it. He could smell her horse, her, the other human, smoke, and the man's horse. When Joshua had ridden close to the two horses, he dismounted and walked up. Catching each, he saddled the horse, put the horse's bridle on, and led him off to the left, the east. The two horses disappeared into the trees, with Joshua looking back and seeing some smoke coming from the camp and a red glare on the

overhanging rocks. He was glad Annabelle would at least
be warm during the night, since he was taking her horse
away as well as Harlance's. He rode for several miles and
then turned south toward Road Gulch Stage Road. He came
to the spring and good grass on the other side of Lookout
Mountain, where he had camped before sneaking up on
Jeeter McMahon's hideout. He unsaddled both horses and
left them to enjoy the lush graze and good water, and he
rode back to cover their trail, which was another task of
several hours.

There would be only one way Harlance and Annabelle
could go after losing their horses. They would have to cross
over Lookout or go around and come down this side and go
to Road Gulch Stage Road. There, they would meet a stage,
a wagon, or riders on horses. It was a reasonably busy road.
Strongheart took the time and care to actually cover the
horses' hoofprints with rocks and sticks, carefully brush
away tracks, and cover the ground with faux deer or elk
tracks by making V's with his fingers. After covering their
backtrail, he returned to the two horses, left Gabe saddled
but removed his reins from his hackamore, and let him
graze, too.

He broke off several pine branches and lay on them
under a tree, wrapped himself in his bedroll, and went
to sleep again. When he awakened, it was past dawn. He
had slept in. He did not make a fire, not wishing to take a
chance on Harlance seeing it. After some jerky and hardtack with canteen water, he mounted Gabriel and headed
again toward Lookout Mountain, which was just over the
low rise. It had snowed in the past few hours, and now the
sun was out and glaring. Joshua had wisely put a small coal
stick in his saddlebag, and he drew a line under each of his
eyes with charcoal. This black line under each eye would
keep him from being bothered by snow glare, and he would
thus avoid snow blindness.

Ready for more chase, the horse pranced uphill as Strongheart searched for a good vantage point from which to watch
this side of the mountain. He found a little promontory on a

wooded ridge coming from a much smaller peak. It extended like a long, narrow finger pointing at the frequent hideaway for road agents and other miscreants.

On the other side of the mountain, Harlance had a rope tied around Annabelle's neck and was cursing a blue streak. They had tramped all over the area the horses had been grazing, and he could not find any sign of where they could have wandered to. It made no sense that they wandered. His was an outlaw horse. It was too well trained. Besides, the graze and water was there. It dawned on him that Strongheart had found them already, that quickly. And it frightened him to no end.

Although she was frightened by his red-faced. vein-bulging outburst, Annabelle could hardly contain herself. She knew her man had come to save her, and he would somehow.

The night before had been miserable for her because of the way she kept catching Harlance looking at her when she was lying there in the flickering firelight. He might have followed that much of the code of the West about women so far, but he would not much longer. She could tell. When he put the rope around her neck, he had pretended like he accidentally let his hands fall down on her breasts after tying it. She knew it was not accidental touching. and she knew she had guessed right about him the night before.

They eventually returned to the hideout, and he made her make them breakfast.

Strongheart did not see any of this, but a couple times he heard the shouted curses, and he chuckled. Joshua waited and watched.

13

Showdown

An hour later, they both emerged from the western rimrock of the canyon. Joshua had to ride closer to get a better look. They were heading down the mountain, as he had predicted. But he did not like what he was seeing at a distance.

Harlance was totally frightened, and as Joshua snuck in behind them and off to the side, he looked with his telescope and saw that the outlaw had tied a small rope around Annabelle's neck many times and then tied it around the barrel of his Henry carbine. The end of the barrel was up against her neck and Harlance was holding the trigger, with the rifle cocked. He looked all around him with certain paranoia while they rushed down the mountain.

This was not what Joshua had wanted to happen, but what he'd feared might. He had decided against sneaking in and sneaking Annabelle out, because he did not want to start a gunfight in which any stray bullet could kill her. But now Harlance McMahon was apparently in total panic, and Joshua knew he had to defuse the situation somewhat for Annabelle's sake.

He rode closer and yelled, "Harlance! I am over here!"

Harlance yelled, "Ya come near me, she is going under! Ya hear me, ya red blanket nigger son of a bitch!"

Joshua put his hand up and said, "Harlance, I believe you! I am backing off. You need to uncock that gun. If either of you stumbles, she will die. If she dies, or gets hurt, I will take four or five days to kill you, Lakota style! But, McMahon, I do not want her hurt. I am backing off. Take your time! I will not rush you while you are walking! Just relax!'

Annabelle said quietly, "Mr. McMahon, Joshua Strongheart never breaks his word. Please listen. Just let the hammer down. You can always cock it and shoot me if he rushes you."

Harlance said, "Good point, okay, but walk faster once I do."

He uncocked the rifle and Annabelle felt her legs almost give way, but she steeled herself to her task ahead. That was to stay alive and trust Joshua. Harlance looked back and saw that Joshua had dismounted and was sitting on a rock drinking from his canteen. Annabelle could not turn her head, but she now walked faster down the mountain.

Harlance settled down a little and even bragged to her.

"Ya see how tough yer blanket nigger boyfriend is?" he said. "He knows I'm smarter'n him. He shore didn't know how ta get around thet one, did he?"

"No, he didn't," she said, humoring him. "I have to admit, you certainly outsmarted him that time. Where are we going?"

He looked at his stolen pocket watch and wondered why he had not gone on to Animas City like he'd told Jeeter he was going to.

He said, "Walk faster. The morning stage comes by down below anytime now. They stay up on Copper Gulch Stage Road 'bout a mile past the turnoff and rest their horses overnight. I'm outsmartin' him again. We are takin' over thet stage, and if he follows us, I'm a-gonna ear back thet hammer again and let er rip, right through thet purty little haid of yourn."

They arrived soon on the dirty stage road, and Joshua was nowhere to be seen, but he was watching. He had gone over every possible scenario to rescue her before, and he felt the safest way would be to take away Harlance's tools, one by one. Now he was stuck with this decision, wishing he had sneaked in during the night with his moccasins on and stolen her away. Now, though, he had to deal with the hand that was dealt.

Joshua heard the distant creaking and rattling of the traces and wooden workings of the big red Concord stage-coach. He moved from his hiding spot beneath the branches of a stunted cedar and climbed into Gabe's saddle. Looking through the trees with his telescope, he saw Harlance finally untie the thong from the carbine barrel and remove it from Annabelle's head. Holding her with his left hand, he stepped into the road and held the cocked carbine with his other hand.

Again, he appeared to be in wide-eyed panic mode. The stage came into view, and the driver slowed the horses to a stop then held his hands high in the air.

Harlance yelled, "Toss the express gun down!"

The driver carefully grabbed the double-barreled sawed-off shotgun at his side and tossed it into the road, then raised his hands again.

He yelled, "I ain't carryin' no strongbox, mister!"

Harlance ran to the side of the stage and yelled inside, "Everybody out, now!"

Five passengers, three women and two men, got out, hands raised.

Harlance had started to shove Annabelle up into the coach, when the driver decided to grab for his Russian .44 in a cross-draw holster. Harlance shot and the women screamed. The driver, dead, fell off the boot and released the brake. The movement made the coach lurch and knocked Harlance forward into the stage, to land on top of the rifle, which was now grasped in both of his hands. The stage horses bolted and started running, driverless, in a panic down the winding Road Gulch Stage Road. Seated in the coach, Annabelle slammed both feet down on the rifle barrel, pinning Harlance's hands underneath it, with his legs hanging out the door of the stage as it raced down the dangerous road. Harlance started cursing and threatening her, but she kept her weight on the rifle.

She looked up and saw Gabriel racing along parallel to the stagecoach, dashing through and around trees and boulders. Just as she feared that the mighty horse would trip over a branch, log, or rock, and both he and his rider would go tumbling down, Joshua would look over at her, smile, and wink. It took her breath away. Gabe came off the ridge and ran right alongside the stage in the road, coming up next to the lead horses. Strongheart tried to reach over and grab their reins but could not. Annabelle continued to put her weight on the rifle as Harlance screamed, kicked, and struggled. She screamed as Joshua suddenly leapt from his saddle over the back of the right lead horse and landed on the wooden shaft running along under the inside traces between the six-horse team. He started to rein the horses in, but just then Harlance broke free and scrambled up, leaving the rifle there and leaning out to fire his pistol, hitting Strongheart in the back of his left shoulder.

Joshua fell beneath the horses and Harlance grinned, holstering his pistol and crawling out the door, up onto the roof, and into the box.

In the meantime, Joshua was underneath the center shaft walking his hands down one by one as he slid underneath the stage, his heels dragging in the dirt, his butt held off the ground. He walked his hands down the undercarriage of the stage, grabbed the leather thoroughbraces, and swung his legs up from the underside of the luggage boot in the back. He pulled down with his knees, grabbing the boot, and pulled himself up onto the back of the it.

Harlance saw him and slammed on the brake lever, while he pulled hard on the reins, yelling, "Whoa! Whoa! Settle down!"

He got the stage stopped and then he spun around with his pistol firing wildly at Strongheart. Inside the coach, Annabelle stopped crying. Joshua was alive! Now she could feel him moving behind her.

Strongheart reached for his gun, but it was gone.

Harlance sensed the big man's hesitation and jumped up on the roof.

"Lost yer gun, dint ya, ya damned blanket nigger! Go haid and pop that little red face up again."

Joshua popped up and back down as a bullet flashed right over his head. He leapt back up while Harlance cocked the pistol. Strongheart's upraised right arm whipped forward and his father's big knife flipped over once in the air before it buried itself in Harlance's hip. He screamed in pain, and Joshua knew this was his chance. He pulled himself up quickly onto the roof, and Harlance raised the pistol up, grinning evilly.

"Whoopsy daisy, huh, buck?" he said to taunt him. "Now yer gonna find out ya ain't so tough. Where ya want it, halfbreed, in yer haid or yer gut?"

Joshua said, "How about in you?"

At that point he felt as if he were just trying to joke in the face of certain death, but suddenly something exploded through the roof of the stage and both men heard Harlance's rifle fire below them in the coach. A bright spot of crimson appeared on Harlance's stomach, and he looked down at it in horror. Then Annabelle could be heard cocking the repeater and firing again, and a second bullet exploded through the coach roof, smashing into Harlance's chest. He dropped his pistol and in sheer panic tore his shirt open, sticking his fingers in both bullet holes.

Strongheart said calmly, "The fingers won't help, McMahon. You are going to be dead shortly. Killed by a tiny, pretty woman who bested you. Take that to Hell with you." Joshua laughed.

This realization hit Harlance, and his face turned from white to bright red in anger. He started to speak, but when he did, blood spewed from his mouth, and he only gurgled. His face again turned white, ghostly white, and his eyes rolled back in his head. His body went limp, and he folded like an accordion, and fell off the roof, headfirst onto the dirt stage road. He did not feel it. He was already dead.

The door of the stagecoach flew open, and tears streaming,

Annabelle leapt out, smiling broadly. She looked under the stage and saw McMahon's lifeless body and dropped his rifle.

Joshua said, "You sure saved my bacon."

She said, "Get down here, redskin!"

They both laughed, and he climbed down, and she threw herself into his arms. They kissed long and passionately and were in that embrace when the stage passengers came running around the corner. One was carrying Joshua's pistol, and another the shotgun, and they were all cheering. The couple stepped back and looked at them and then at each other, smiling.

One of the passengers boasted that he had been a barber and done some dentistry and was not without some healing skills. He poured whiskey on the bullet hole in Joshua's shoulder and bandaged it. The bullet had passed cleanly through the top of the trapezius muscle, but compared to the wounds Strongheart had recently survived, it was like a bee sting to him.

Within an hour, Joshua had retrieved the two horses, and the bodies of Harlance and the stage driver were loaded into the boot and covered by the leather cover. The luggage had all been transferred to the top of the coach and strapped down. Gabriel and Annabelle's gelding were tied to the back of the stage, and Strongheart sat in the front, grabbing the coach team's reins, with Annabelle next to him grabbing his massive right bicep.

Five hours later, the sheriff of Fremont County, Frank Bengley, found a note nailed to a tree next to Road Gulch Coach Road. It read, "Sheriff, McMahon dead, Annabelle safe, driver dead, took passengers, bodies, and stage to Cotopaxi. Wait for you there."

That night, Bengley, Zachariah Banta, Annabelle Ebert, and Joshua Stongheart sat in the Cotopaxi hotel enjoying a nice brown trout dinner.

Banta said, "So what's on the horizon fer you two now?"

Before Joshua could answer and not wanting to pressure him, Annabelle answered, smiling broadly, "Right now,

Joshua has another assignment, Mr. Banta. He has to get back to work. We can talk about the horizon later."

Pointing to the bandage on Strongheart's shoulder, Zack said, "Reckon he oughta git back to work. Look what the heck happens ta you two when yer jest relaxin."

Everybody in the place laughed heartily, then Strongheart looked into the eyes of the woman he loved, saying, "Zack, I suppose if somebody painted a picture of that horizon you mentioned, there would be lots and lots of children in the painting."

Smiling softly, they looked deep into each other's eyes; the secrets hidden therein held the key to their future.

EPILOGUE

The descendants of Zachariah Banta all had a quick wit and a dry humor, and ran cattle all around the Cotopaxi area for many decades, finally moving the ranching operation to southwestern Texas in the early twenty-first century.

Frank Begley was in fact the sheriff of Fremont County, Colorado, in 1873, one of many in a long line of fine lawmen in southern Colorado.

Except for the fictional town name, Flower Valley, all the locations and local histories mentioned herein were actual places, and many still exist today. I have ridden my horse over almost every piece of land mentioned in this book and in my other westerns, so you will know it is real and not a Hollywood movie set. For example, the old settlement of Hardscrabble is visible by binoculars from the back porch of my ranch outside Florence, Colorado, and the spot of the night camp of Joshua Strongheart at the top of Five Points Gulch is exactly where I killed a large cinnamon- and blond-colored bear in 1985.

Please come along and join in sharing with me the rest of the tale about Pinkerton Agent Joshua Strongheart in his next adventure, *Half-Breed*, also from Berkley.

Until then, partner, keep your powder dry and an eye on

the horizon, take an occasional glance at your backtrail, and sit tall in the saddle. It does not matter if your saddle is a computer desk chair, La-Z-Boy, porch swing, or deck chair on a cruise ship. Many of us grew up with the spirit of the American cowboy or the pioneer woman. It is good to keep a door to our past open, so we know where our strength, courage, and tenacity came from. It is the legacy of honor forged from the steel characters blessed by God who created some of his mightiest warriors in the American West. It is indeed the backbone of America.

If you need me, I will be on my horse up in the high lonesome coming up with more stories for you. That is where I get my tales. They are up there above the timberline, written on the clouds, and I swear that handwriting looks *perfect*.

ABOUT THE AUTHOR

Don Bendell is the author of well over two dozen books with more than 2,000,000 copies in print worldwide, as well as a successful feature film. An action/adventure man, he is a disabled U.S. Army Special Forces (Green Beret) officer, Vietnam veteran, a grandmaster instructor in four martial arts, and he and his wife were the first couple in history to both be inducted into the International Karate and Kickboxing Hall of Fame.

Don describes himself as "a real cowboy with a real horse and a real ranch." He and his wife own a beautiful ranch outside of Florence, Colorado, and he tries to ride his pinto National Show Horse, Eagle, over all the ground that he writes about.

Don and Shirley Bendell enjoy bow hunting, fishing, and camping with their horses in the Rocky Mountains. Don is the father of six grown children and has eight grandchildren.

BERKLEY WESTERNS TAKE OFF LIKE A SHOT

LYLE BRANDT
PETER BRANDVOLD
JACK BALLAS
J. LEE BUTTS
JORY SHERMAN
ED GORMAN
MIKE JAMESON

Don't miss the best Westerns from Berkley.